BEER, BAIT, AND AMMO

Chap Harper

Smoking Gun Publishing, LLC
St. Louis, MO

ISBN: 978-1-940586-28-1

Library of Congress Control Number: 2016938776

Visit us on the web at www.smokinggunpublishing.com

Published by Smoking Gun Publishing, LLC
Printed in the United States of America

Acknowledgements

I am sure that Chalmette, Louisiana is a wonderful town with beautiful people, but I had to pick a place for the Louisiana Sportsman's Super Store. And, a home for the bad guys. The area has a waterway and is close to New Orleans, so I used it as a location. My apologies if I demeaned your community in anyway. It's just a story, just a book, and devoid of most anything truthful. I do hope the people of St. Bernard Parish enjoy reading the novel solely for entertainment.

Chap Harper
May, 2016

To Jessica & Bart Schroder,
Everyone needs to believe
in something.
I believe I'll have another beer!

Chap Harper

8/29/2016

Dedication

This book is dedicated to my adoptive city of Hot Springs, Arkansas. The city's history is rich and matched only by the lives of the great people that live there now. There is always something going on.

Chapter One

Royal, Arkansas - August 2014

The singing of sexually-frustrated tree frogs and crickets stopped instantly as the blast of a shotgun shredded the night air. Only seconds before, Vikki Jackson, a pretty, flaxen-haired young woman, had answered a knock on the screen door of her raggedy-ass mobile home. Without hesitation, she swung open the old torn screen door to confront the man she now hated. Quince, her estranged husband, raised the twelve-gauge weapon he held hidden next to his leg. Vikki didn't have time to react. Buckshot exploded in her chest, leaving a gaping hole. The small child she had been holding on her hip slid from her grasp and landed on a frayed Razorback floor mat, screaming and holding his arm where an errant double-aught buckshot pellet had grazed him.

The shooter wasn't finished. He stepped over the child and burst through the ripped screen door propped open by his wife's body and fired a round at a man running to the back of the trailer.

"Goddamn it! Missed the fucker!" he mumbled.

In case the fleeing man was going for a gun, the shooter placed his back flat against the hallway wall to make less of a target. He slid along the wall until he came to a bathroom and noticed a plunger sticking out of a toilet. The smell of shitty diapers and a backed-up commode stung his nostrils. He pushed two more shells into the Remington Wingmaster and listened for the man, but heard only Pat Sajak: "Oh, no! You've hit bankrupt. I'll need that half-a-car back," from a sixty-inch flat screen TV which covered half the living room. It was set on loud.

Using the entrance of the bathroom as cover, he looked in the direction of what he knew to be the master bedroom. He moved his head out of the doorway and glanced to the rear. Shots exploded from a pistol. One bullet struck him in the jaw, ripping out teeth and exiting through his cheek.

"Fuck—fuck—fuck!" he said, spitting out blood and broken teeth.

Something told him to fall to the floor in the hallway to return fire from a lower level. It was not one of his better decisions. The .40 caliber Glock slammed rounds into his body from the back of the trailer before he hit the floor. He could feel his body shutting down.

"Die, ya mother fucker!" yelled the man in the back room.

Still conscious, the dying man lifted his gun and pumped out two blasts. One caught the other shooter in the face. A couple of big lead pellets lodged in his brain. The man yelped and fell backward onto the bed. The second blast destroyed a framed Elvis painting on the back wall above the bed. The King, decked out in a matador outfit, red cape and sword, stood erect, facing the attacking bull. Several large holes sadly marred the black velvet background and the ass end of the bull.

Both men and the woman lay dead. The baby stopped screaming and crawled around the porch trying to pet a small yellow dog that sniffed at the corpse and licked the puddle of blood oozing from the woman.

An hour later, two Garland County Sheriff's patrol cars and an Arkansas State Trooper vehicle skidded to a stop in front of the trailer. The yellow dog scrambled under the mobile home, his tail tucked under him. A neighbor had rescued the baby and placed him with the dead woman's sister. She lived a few miles away, in a classy doublewide—it might give the kid a better chance in life.

* * *

Corporal Lester McFarlin opened the door of his cruiser and grabbed a notepad attached to a metal cover. Lester looked more like a senator or CEO of a large company than a lowly corporal in the Garland County Sheriff's office. Standing over six feet tall, with blond hair and piercing blue eyes, he easily could have been a movie star filming on a set that day. Lester looked at the old mobile home and saw the siding was marred with algae growth, plywood covered a busted window, and rotted-out tires hung below the sad structure. He walked up to the porch, stepped over the dead woman and walked into the trailer. The neighbors who picked up the baby said they had found two more bodies. After checking out the other two corpses, he left the trailer just as a crime scene photographer entered. *How badly had a person screwed up in their photography class to get this gig?* Lester thought.

Outside, the superior officers and the state policeman were interviewing one of the relatives. The officers couldn't be bothered stepping over dead bodies when they could question people and boss around the rest of the law enforcement staff. According to the relative, the dead were Vikki Jackson, her almost ex-husband Quince Jackson, and Vikki's live-in boyfriend Marvin Burt. No one was sure who the baby daddy was, and no one much cared. Meth was found in the ex-husband's pants pocket and baggies in his truck.

Lester held up the baggies and a jar half-filled with a white crystalline substance.

"Don't dey know dis shit'll rot out jer teeth?" Lester said, in his best redneck voice.

The officers smiled and continued to talk among themselves. Three people bailed out of a Garland County Coroner's vehicle that pulled up, with a stretcher and body bags. At the same time, a young sheriff's officer, carrying a pistol in one gloved hand and a shotgun in the other, exited the trailer. Lester stopped him.

"Check those guns. See who owned 'em. Quince was a felon… clearly wasn't following the rules," he said.

In writing his report, Lester followed a five-step process: interview, examine, photograph, sketch, and process. He never deviated from this protocol, and although his reports were impossible to read by anyone else, they were the most accurate of all the officers'. However, the senior level had little respect for his supervisory skills. He could not evaluate the reports of fellow officers because he couldn't read. Lester had taken the test for advancement to sergeant for five consecutive years, failing every time. They refused to give him the test orally, since the point was to measure reading comprehension. The leadership believed he had reached his capacity for advancement in rank, yet they loved the way he solved crimes. In this area, they considered him a genius, not unlike a savant. At age twenty-six, Lester not only wanted to advance in rank; someday, he wanted to make a run for the sheriff's office.

Lester knew he had problems and was dead-set on fixing them. His first problem was hearing loss. Raised in Mountain Pine, Arkansas by parents who were caring but dirt poor, he had a severe ear infection at age two and lost part of his hearing. When he was five, he was riding in his parents' car without a seat belt when a pickup truck t-boned them. Mrs. Lilly McFarlin, pregnant with Lester's brother, died along with the unborn baby at the hospital a few days later.

Little Lester had minor internal injuries, which healed quickly, and more severe head trauma which left his brain with residual impairments. He started school early in the morning and stayed after school to work with the teachers to keep up with his classmates. Although he took part in class discussions and appeared to be intelligent, he could barely read, even in high school. He passed tests given to him orally, but had trouble pronouncing and recognizing words. His teachers knew he had severe dyslexia but were not equipped to help him. They tried using a special font, but it didn't make things better. Since Lester's dad had no health insurance, he could not pay for long-term treatment by speech and hearing specialists. Without sustained treatment, Lester would not be able to improve. Adrian McFarlin, Lester's dad, had worked part time at the Weyerhaeuser plywood mill in Mountain Pine until the plant closed in 2006. Afterwards, he worked as a day laborer and sometimes earned income as a fishing guide.

A family friend helped Lester land a job at the Sheriff's Department and kind instructors coached him through the training academy. Finally, twenty-one years after the car accident that caused his head injuries, group health insurance, combined with his personal savings, would cover the cost of the medical care he needed.

The day after the shooting in Royal, he saw an ad in the paper.

Although he couldn't read the ad completely, he saw a pretty girl and translated her name as Debi Green. The word "dyslexia" in the ad looked like "aixelsyd" until he used his mirror to reverse the letters. He had seen that word his whole life. When he called to make an appointment, the lady on the phone was pleasant and faxed him a medical history questionnaire. She said to fill out what he could, and she would ask the rest of the questions in person.

I think she wants to see just how fucked up I am.

* * *

Lester went to her office the next day and sat down in a waiting room decorated in modern chrome and butter-yellow leather furniture. By calling customer service, he found his group health insurance would pay for everything except the co-pays. Even though Lester couldn't read most of it, the brass sign outside her office stated, "Debi Green MMSLP, Speech, Language, and Pathology." She had started her speech therapy business just a month earlier at age twenty-four, and was eager to recruit new clients.

At first, she thought Brad Pitt was in her waiting room. She directed Lester into her office, blushing when he shook her hand. His tall stature, thick mop of blond hair, broad shoulders and deep blue eyes almost caused her to freeze. His smile was engaging, with a slight crookedness at the corner of his mouth. *A man that good looking should be a lawyer or actor.* She squirmed in her leather chair when she addressed him.

"Uh…Mr. McFarlin, I want to thank you for trying to fill out your medical history form…was it difficult? Please know that I used the OpenDyslexic font to make it a little easier."

"Everything in print is hard for me…always was. I'll show you a secret weapon I use," Lester said. He pulled a scratched metal mirror out of his back jeans pocket.

"What I do, you see, is look straight on first and then turn the word to the mirror and read the mirror as the backward print next. Sometimes, between the two looks, I might know it or can figure out the word."

"So, Lester, you have been told you have a mirror form of dyslexia."

"Ma'am, I've been told that I have every form of it available to get. Between my hearing loss at two-years-old and the car wreck that killed my mom and busted my brain, I'm pretty fuck—I mean, messed up. Sorry, I hang around a bunch of cops."

"That's okay. I'm going to give you some exercises to work on that might help with simple words and phrases. I'd like to schedule you for a hearing test and an MRI. You okay with that?

"Yes…I guess so."

Lester might have bathed in acid if this pretty girl suggested it. He would have the two tests completed later in the week. As he walked to his car, he couldn't get over her beauty. She had coal black hair that flowed down below her shoulders, an olive complexion, and soft brown eyes that made him both comfortable and horny. Lester wanted to kiss her lips—and they were spectacular—movie star lips—big and somewhat pouty—especially her upper lip. He was willing to risk arrest just to kiss her once. Debi had an hourglass figure with adequate breasts pushing hard against the top of a purple blouse. Surely his friends at the department could get him off from a little sexual battery charge. There was a good chance she was single as the only ring she wore was a dinner ring on her little finger. On the bookcase behind her desk, Lester had seen a picture of her and some guy in a tan summer suit. He knew there wasn't much of a chance he could ever be with her. However, he didn't plan to stay a lowly deputy and be perceived as a loser. She most likely wouldn't be in his life when the changes happened, but whatever it took, changes were going to occur. He couldn't wait to be in her office again—across from those lips. She had given him cards with words and pictures that he would quickly memorize.

* * *

Lester was Debi's last patient for the day…and her only patient. The office space she had rented a month ago with her dad's help was close to a hearing aid office and an optometrist. She had completed her

Master's in Speech and Hearing at the University of Arkansas, where she had met Brad Thomas. He was a Sigma Chi and she was a Tri Delt, which meant something then but very little now. They were pinned in college, but Debi gave the fraternity pin back to him after graduation. He had become an intellectual property attorney with a large firm in Dallas. Brad wanted Debi to live with him and set up her practice there. She didn't know anyone in Dallas and imagined herself at home with screaming kids while he entertained clients (male and female) at night. Her life would be a horror movie. Although her parents and friends were in Hot Springs, she didn't know anyone to date there. Lester was probably the best looking man she had ever seen…even compared to the herds of preppy fraternity guys she knew in college.

Brad was the last man she had sex with, and that was almost six months ago. She knew she couldn't date Lester. The client-therapist clause in her professional license contract would cause her to lose her practice just as it was beginning. Debi could sense the pheromones floating in the air between them while he was in her office. She knew what steps had to be taken if there was even a chance they might go out someday, but wasn't sure she should do it yet. Maybe it would never happen. *Forget it,* she told herself. She locked up her office and headed to her empty apartment.

Chapter Two

"Here's the report on the two guns we picked up after the shooting," Becca Valdez said, placing the report on Lester's desk. She walked away, swaying her hips so he would notice. Lester had taken her out a few times and might again when horniness overtook common sense. Some in the department thought she was actually a "professional" who did police work on the side. Lester wasn't sure, but she hadn't charged him...yet.

He turned in his chair and handed the report to Little Richard, who wasn't little. His name was Rich, but nicknames flew freely in this department of cut-ups. Rich Roberson was huge—linebacker huge—and black. He had finished college at nearby Henderson University in Arkadelphia where he was an all-conference linebacker. His dad was a state policeman in Little Rock and Rich wanted to follow in his footsteps. The reason he came to Hot Springs was to learn from Lester, as did several other officers. Lester was a cult hero to many in law enforcement.

"Would you read this to me, please?" Lester asked. Everyone knew he couldn't read and why, so most didn't give him any grief. They also knew he was the best investigator on the force and in the city of Hot Springs...probably in the whole state. Local police would ask to "borrow" him on big investigations. Little Rock police had driven to Hot Springs ten times to get him for murder cases. Dallas flew him there for a case which he solved in just a few days. He saw crime scenes the way a blind person uses a heightened sense of smell, sound, and touch. Lester visualized a scene frontward and backward all at the same time. Most cops are lazy, wanting to bag the bodies and go for coffee. Lester solved many crimes because he worked his ass off chasing down minute details and investigating areas most cops would never dream of following. He had a kit for collecting tiny pieces of evidence. White plastic sticky sheets in various sizes picked up items from beds, floors, parking lots, and of course, bodies. He collected so many samples that his "kits" had to be stored in bins until all the items could be processed. Prosecutors loved him. From pubic hairs to DNA from toilet seats, he never provided too little evidence. Maybe he worked extra hard to make up for his dyslexia, or maybe he was just damn good at what he did.

If he were a supervisor, not only would he have to read his officers' reports, he'd have to write his own reports in a language only he could understand and decipher. Around the office it was called "Lesterese," and there wasn't a Rosetta Stone on earth to help with translation. He sure as hell couldn't read anyone else's report. His mirror technique only worked for a few words at a time and was painstakingly slow.

Little Richard began reading. "Both guns were registered to a small gangster wannabe from New Orleans named Tony Evola. Some arrests for petty crimes but no convictions. Don't know much about him but will check further."

"That goddamn Katrina washed a lot of badass people into Arkansas after 2005. I guess some good ones, too," Lester said. He knew local artists and business people who had moved to Hot Springs after the storm and actually contributed to the city.

"Can I do some research for you, Lester?" Rich always wanted to help solve one of Lester's cases, but so far this wasn't a case. The sheriff had named the file *Domestic Shooting by a Jealous and Estranged Ex-Husband*, and closed the matter. Done, go on to something else.

"Yeah, Rich, go interview the sister with the orphaned baby—see what she knew about the weapons in the man's house. Where Quince bought—or stole them. As a felon, he got them from an individual or maybe a gun show. Find out more about this Evola guy. We know Quincy was a dealer, so I'm going by his rent house to see what I can find. Don't tell Sheriff Adams what we're looking for because he'll go bat shit."

Lester ordered people around and gave assignments at will. He was known to both solve crimes and share the credit. Many officers had gained their ranks on the backs of Lester's investigations. Since budgets were more on the mind of the sheriff, he wouldn't spend scant resources on a crime that appeared to be solved. If Lester found a bigger crime, the sheriff would okay further investigation, but until then, pursuing this case had to be a clandestine activity.

Lester stopped his patrol car in front of the rented white shotgun house in Crystal Springs. He had turned onto a dirt and gravel path that meandered through a new growth of pine trees. The house looked unoccupied, and the only vehicle there was an older model Ford F-150 pickup truck parked under a large red oak tree. A hoist was hanging from a huge limb attached to an engine that was either coming out or going in. Lester walked up the wooden steps and stood on a porch that wobbled and creaked under his feet. A broken stove sat next to a recliner covered with a ripped and stained wedding ring quilt. He had checked out Quince's keys from the property room and tried to guess which one would work the deadbolt on the door. Since the occupant had been killed in a shootout, he figured there was probable cause to enter without a warrant.

After a few tries, he heard the lock click. Slowly, he opened the door and yelled, "Police! Anyone in the house?" He heard only the sound of a mouse scampering and rattling through paper, to the right in the kitchen.

Lester had a highly developed sense of smell. He shut the door and stood in the living room and let the floating particles of scent come to him. First was stale beer...then male body odor. Dust was next, along with decaying food and cheese. He walked to the kitchen and found pizza slices partly eaten and a trash can that overflowed with discarded food. A carton of spoiled milk sat on the counter, and dishes were piled high in the sink. Most on the right side were washed, with a dish towel laid over them as protection from the filth elsewhere in the room.

Lester guessed he was the first to enter Quince's house since the shooting two days earlier. Had the case been more than a domestic dispute gone bad, the sheriff's men would have taped off the house and done a search. Lester went from room to room looking for evidence that might suggest Quince was a drug dealer. In the bedroom dresser were underwear and socks, neatly folded. Shirts and other clothes were the same. He had seen this before: military men, especially Marines, could not unlearn the neatness beaten into them in basic training. The bedsheets were made up with hospital folds at the corners.

Guns, not clothes, occupied the closet. A rack at the rear held an AK-47, M-16, a Barrett .50 caliber, and several automatics Lester had never seen. Cases of ammo were stacked next to the guns. Lester put on gloves and loaded weapons, plus ammo, into the rear of his patrol car. Exploring more of the house, he found a hall closet filled with handguns, machine gun pistols, hand grenades, and a rocket-propelled grenade launcher with five rounds. He loaded those next.

Of all the papers and documents he examined in the house, two struck him as out of the ordinary: a small box in the bedroom closet packed with stacks of hundred dollar bills, and a business card on the dresser.

The card read, "S.G. Crystals, P.O. Box 14733, Mt. Ida, AR 71957" and below the heading were the words "Wholesale Only." Lester was able to pick out a few words. He took out his mirror and held it over the card. "Mt. Ida" were two and three letter words which he had seen many times. He looked at the words with and without the mirror—yes, he was sure. "Wholesale" was impossible to read and the S. and G. made no sense. "Crystal" looked like "latsyrC," but he recognized that word because Mt. Ida was the crystal capital of the world. Maybe the card was for one of the rock shops or crystal dealers.

Lester knew several crystal mine owners in the area but was aware of someone who could translate this card and shed light on anything related to crystal mining. It was almost lunch time, so he decided he would drive the twenty minutes to Mt. Ida and seek out a good friend at the Montgomery County Sheriff's office.

Jake Thomas was the high sheriff in Mt. Ida, and although he only had four patrolmen, his little army held crime in check. His office was directly across Highway 270 from the Mt. Ida Cafe. Lester parked next to a patrol car and went directly to Jake's office.

"Hey, Jakester! How 'bout I buy your lunch?" Lester extended his hand and felt the pudgy fingers of Jake's hand in his. Sheriff Thomas looked exactly like the southern country lawman depicted in most movies. He was short, fat, bald, and red-faced, and a damn good officer. Lester and Jake had hunted together and even shot sporting clays once. "He just doesn't miss," Lester said of him to his friends in Hot Springs.

"Don't turn down free lunches," Jake said and grabbed his hat.

They walked across the street to the cafe; everyone greeted Jake. Most people were just friendly, but a few said they had something to discuss with him. He waved them off and told them to come by the office. He figured Lester had business to talk about or he wouldn't be in town.

"Jake, you heard about the mobile home killings in Royal a couple of nights ago?"

"Yeah, three people dead. Jealous ex-husband, I heard."

"Seems that way. Well, I went out today and poked around the ol' boy's rent house. Didn't find any drugs but found a ton of guns. I'll show you when we go back across the street. Other than a felon having enough guns to arm the Chinese Army, the place was clean. I don't know where he was working out of or who he was working for. Let me show you this."

Lester pulled out the business card. "I couldn't read much but 'Crystals' and 'Mount Ida.' What else does it say?" The sheriff looked and scratched his head as though it would help his train of thought. Quartz crystal mining was a major industry in Montgomery County and most had been around for years. Jake knew all the owners. He read the card to Lester and told him what he knew about the firm listed on the card.

"Never heard of it by name, but there's a new outfit back in the woods between here and Joplin. Huge place. Has a giant fence around it. There's a guard station—checks cars going and coming. Never been in it. Some folks have said most of the workers come from Louisiana. Not open to the public. Would you like me to check it out?" Jake asked.

"Yeah, but I want to be with you, if you don't mind."

"Hell, I insist since you'll see things no one else will."

They ordered their lunch and gasped when a waitress brought a huge burger to a man who looked like a lumberjack. The burger had two or three patties of meat, a fried egg, an enormous onion ring, and cheese. A butcher knife stuck through the top held the monster together. Jake had a BLT and Lester had his usual salad. Both left a nice tip for their attentive service, as they were known to the wait staff. On their way out the door, a man in a suit who had arrived before Lester and Jake was waving his menu in the air, still hoping to be waited on. Apparently being known by the waitresses proved helpful.

They walked across the street. Lester looked around to make sure no one could see in his trunk, and raised the lid. Jake said, "Holy bat shit!" and reached down to touch the RPG. Lester quickly closed the lid.

"If the people inside that fence had anything to do with these weapons, we better get the state troopers to go with us," Jake said in an excited voice.

"If we just show up they won't let us search the place. If we get a warrant, they'll hide everything," Lester said. "I suggest we make a visit because we want to welcome them to the community. Offer them Mount Ida and Hot Springs security for their business. See how they react."

"When?"

"Give me a couple of days to check ownership on these weapons and I'll call you," Lester said and got in his car. Jake tapped on his window, which Lester lowered. "If we make a big bust, we both are going to have one of those burgers with the butcher knife stuck in it," Jake said, laughing.

As Lester drove back to Hot Springs, he wondered what he would find in the big building, he thought about Debi Green and what she would look like naked, and he contemplated the possibility of eating one of those giant burgers.

Chapter Three

Debi was anxious to see if Lester had worked on the exercises she had assigned him the previous week. He was to memorize the words and pictures on large index cards. She wanted to go over the results of the hearing test and the MRI with him. She was just eager to see him.

Over the weekend she had visited her parents, gone to a movie with a girlfriend, and watched a preseason Dallas Cowboy football game. They lost. She told herself that preseason didn't mean anything. In a few weeks the Razorbacks would start their season with three straight cupcake teams. Wins with these small college teams meant little more than a scrimmage; even so, she loved to go to the games but now had no one to go with. Her old boyfriend had season tickets on the 35 yard line only twenty rows up. Her parents sometimes had season tickets, but going with them was like reverting back to childhood. She ached for her own life independent of them. On this Monday her appointment with Lester was at noon.

Early that morning Sheriff Mike Adams had Lester in his office. "Why in the hell did you keep going on with this domestic shooting case? Now you've opened up a huge can of worms! I've heard from Jake in Mount Ida, the state police, the feds and God knows who else," Adams said, with only a hint of irritation in his voice. Mike Adams was actually proud of Lester, and if truth be told, he wouldn't have been reelected without Lester's great work. Little things became big things once Lester was free to investigate a case.

"Several agencies have asked to help, but I told them they'd be getting in your way at this point. However, according to the arsenal of weapons you found, you may need the 101st Airborne Division before this is over. Keep me posted on what you and Jake find at that crystal mining outfit. We're making this a joint county operation with the state police as backups. If we make a raid, then we'll have Feds with ATF forces and maybe the DEA if you guys find where Quince got his drugs to sell." There was concern in his voice. He had a bad feeling about an organization that had easy access to automatic weapons and rocket-propelled grenades.

"Uh—I got the picture. Would you mind letting me know when you guys finish with the traces on the weapons? I'd like to know a little more before me and Jake make our call on S.G. Crystals," Lester said.

"Will do," the sheriff replied.

"Becca going to be the one working on them?"

"Yes, and maybe Little Richard."

"Have Becca deliver them to me in person so I can watch her walk away," Lester said.

"You better quit tapping the women in the office. You aren't supposed to date anyone in the office without getting approval first." Mike sounded stern, but he was smiling. More than one girl in the office had gone to the sheriff, crying, because Lester had dumped her, or as he put it, "didn't want to go out with her anymore."

Lester noted the time and decided to show up at Debi's office a little early. If she wasn't with a client, maybe he could take her to lunch. He called her on his cell.

"Yes. Debi Green speaking."

"Hey, Debi, this is Lester McFarlin. How are ya today?"

"Very well, Lester, and you?"

"Fine, I guess, except I have to go to this doctor to have my brain examined, and I just can't do that on an empty stomach. Would it be okay if we talked about my brain over lunch? If that's all right, I'll pick you up in five minutes in front of your office." Lester held his breath, knowing that she would be breaking protocol meeting a client out of the office.

There was silence for what seemed like a long time. "Well—I don't guess there'll be any harm in that if we pay for our own. But before you get any ideas, Lester, there's no way I can go out with you as long as you're a client. I can lose my license to practice. Do you understand?"

"Yes, I totally understand, and I'd never put your license in jeopardy."

"Where are we going?" She really didn't care, but was conflicted, nervous, and excited at the same time.

"Park Hotel. Quiet there, and they have good salads. That ok?

"Sounds fine—what're you driving?"

"Red Yukon—I'm here."

"See you—let me lock up and make a quick phone call." Debi grabbed Lester's file after the call and keyed the deadbolt on the front door. Lester was out of the car and holding the passenger door open for her. The big SUV required a high step-up to get in and was a challenge even with Lester's help. The tight, short red skirt she was wearing exposed her legs as she struggled to step up to the cab. He tried to not look directly at her long shapely limbs, but snuck a quick glance anyway.

"Sorry this dang truck's so high off the ground."

"It's fine. I love Yukons and Escalades. Not made for short dresses, though."

"Whaddya drive?"

"BMW Z-3—old one, 2005. Parents got it for me while I was at the U of A. Convertible top needs fixing. Fun car, though."

"I think BMW makes fine cars, and that little roadster is one good-looking car," Lester said as he pulled into the small parking lot next to the Park Hotel. Since he was early, he found a slot for his big Yukon. He went around and took her hand and helped Debi to place her foot on the running board.

"Your hands are so soft," Lester said.

"I don't do carpenter work, Lester."

Lester held her hand as long as he could but finally released it and placed his hand on the center of her back to guide her up the steps to the hotel entrance.

* * *

Debi felt intense emotions throughout her body when Lester

held her hand as he helped her out of the truck. The feelings were too intense, she thought, for someone she barely knew and was one of her first clients. Whether pheromones had floated in the air around them or she had experienced pure animal lust, Debi didn't know. Being so attractive to another human would be exciting if it wasn't so damn illegal. Her goal was to hide it and be professional, but she knew what had to be done and already made a call before she left her office.

Both stood at the threshold of the restaurant, which was just to the right as they entered the hotel. They were quickly seated near a rear window in a private area. They admired the workmanship of the old tile from floor to ceiling. Debi laid a large manila envelope on the table sliding it to her left. Lester responded by placing his 3 x 5 cards on the table and matching her move by pushing them to his left and smiling in a teasing sort of way. Debi laughed and began the conversation.

"My father is a radiologist and because of that I was able to get a copy of your MRI. I also have a copy of your hearing test."

A pretty waitress wearing too much makeup delivered menus and asked for the drink order. Both asked for water and opened the menus.

"Does it say grilled chicken salad anywhere?" Lester asked.

"Let me see. Monkey brains—lizard gizzards—goat hearts—no, don't see—yes, there it is. Forty dollars seems a bit steep for a stupid salad." She and Lester both laughed.

"I can't believe my therapist—one pledged to make me well—would make light of my unfortunate mental deficiency. It's so sad and discouraging," Lester said, with mock seriousness.

The waitress was back, pen in hand, ready for the order. "We do have a luncheon special. Shrimp linguini in a light cream sauce with a side of asparagus for $9.95. Have you decided what you want?"

"Debi would like the forty dollar grilled chicken salad, and I'll have the same," Lester said, grinning.

"I believe it's only seven ninety-five," she said.

"My bad—must have read it wrong," Lester said.

"Would you like a glass of wine for lunch?" asked the waitress.

"Debi, would you drink a glass of chardonnay?"

"I guess…don't have another appointment until four." Debi waited until the server had walked some distance before she continued speaking.

"Lester, I'm going to be very blunt with you. I'm going to transfer your records to Sydney Carter. She's a great speech therapist in Little Rock. I've already called her office. After today I'll no longer be your therapist. I just feel more comfortable if you saw someone else for your condition. I don't want any suggestion of impropriety. I hope this doesn't make you mad."

"I'm sorry if I did something to upset you," Lester said.

"Lester, I think we see ourselves as beginning to be friends— friends that have lunch together, and if I guess right, you'll continue to try to develop that friendship. I'm not stopping you, but in no way is this pointing to a professional relationship."

"I understand, and I'm glad you're not stopping me. Can we go ahead and finish going over the information you brought?"

"Certainly, but it and your entire file will be transferred to Mrs. Carter by fax later today," Debi said.

"I've been fired as a client!"

"Your reward for taking me to lunch."

Having ordered wine, a dangerous substance for an illegal relationship and sure to add fuel to any lust lying below the surface, they decided to get down to the business of Lester's disorder.

"Here are my memory cards where you have written words against pictures. Obviously I know the pictures, but I don't see words like you do. Somewhere in my brain, the normal filtration of letters and words go through a sort of Enigma machine and they all come out in a secret code. I know the code, but can't always translate your words to mine. Let me give you an example: you gave me an Apple Card. I only know because there is a picture. The letters appear to me as EPLPA. When I write reports they're full of coded words like that. I've learned over time what my language means, and I can identify many words by looking and placing a mirror by them. Two-letter and three-letter words are easy but still backwards. Large words are mostly impossible. I'm not stupid and use every means available to educate myself. I listen to audio books every day and have readers for me at work for reports. Numbers are easier since there're only 10 numbers moved around. Sixes and nines are difficult along with equations and plus and minus numbers. I'll truly do anything you say to fix this problem. I want to go to college and be a professional at something. Maybe law enforcement since I'm good at it—maybe something else." Lester spoke with such intensity, flawless grammar, and sincerity Debi was shocked and almost speechless. He had lost the "good ol' boy" slang.

The wine and salad arrived at the same time. Both had ordered dressing on the side, which they poured on their salad to fill the silence. Debi took a gulp of wine and looked in Lester's eyes.

"Lester, first you need to know that both Einstein and Steve Jobs had dyslexia. Having dyslexia is in no way a measure of intelligence. You're an amazing and brilliant man. However, I've never seen or heard of a case as severe as yours. I think I know why. Here's a copy of your MRI." She slid a multi-colored electronic picture from her envelope.

"This should be reviewed by your doctor, and you need to discuss it with Sydney, but I thought we could at least see the issue and then you can go into detail with a neurologist." Debi pointed to a spot on the colored picture. Another large swig from her wine glass was in order.

"What is that spot?" Lester asked.

"My dad couldn't be sure, but believes that the car wreck that killed your mom injured your brain, and caused either a blood clot or scar tissue right on top of the area of your brain that controls certain speech and word functions. The cerebral cortex processes language and symbolic representations. Two sections within this region that are vital for human communication are the Wernick's area and the Broca's area. Some recent studies showed the less dominant right hemisphere participates in comprehension of words either written or heard. Your anomaly sits right on top of this area." Debi looked up to see what his reaction would be. He put his finger on the spot and rubbed it as though he hoped it would go away.

"Einstein? Steve Jobs? Cool!" He looked Debi in her eyes and said, "You're a very smart lady. I'm impressed that you got your dad to read the MRI so you could explain the findings to me rather than dumping me off to a neurologist who might not care about me as a person." Lester reached over and squeezed her hand. He noticed she had tears in her eyes.

"You okay?" he asked.

"Yes. I'm sorry, but that was a sweet thing to say." Debi blotted her eyes with a white cloth napkin.

Lester laughed and said, "I suggest we eat our salads and drink wine until this place closes."

"Lester, I don't think there has ever been anyone who had surgery to correct dyslexia. Your case may be an exception. If you did have that scar tissue or blood clot removed, there's the possibility that you would have to re-learn everything you know. Of course, it would be a hell of lot easier, but still…"

"Does your dad know the best neurosurgeon in the state?" Lester asked.

"I'll ask, but little is known about specific areas of the brain. Much has been learned by accident. A man gets shot during a war, and while he is operated on to remove a bullet on the brain, the doctors notice that a certain part of his speech is affected, and that is noted. A woman has a stroke and they remove the clot on her brain, and they notice she can speak but no longer can read. They put that in their notes. This has gone on for centuries to where we have collected a pretty extensive body of work," Debi explained.

"The hearing specialist said a hearing aid for my left side would help me some."

"Yes, I'm sorry I didn't bring that up. My guess is that you read lips at times from conversation coming from your left. The device will help you, but I don't think your dyslexia was affected much by your hearing loss. You can ask your new speech therapist her opinion."

"Is she as pretty as you are?"

"She's about sixty-six-years-old, very attractive, and very married."

They finished their salads and had another glass of wine before they left. Lester gave her an envelope with his $40 co-pay and insisted on paying for her meal. He explained that he was paid more than even the officers at the sheriff's office since the sheriff paid him as a special investigator. He earned bonuses for his work with all the other police departments.

When he dropped her off at her office, he said he would wait to hear from her dad on a recommendation for a neurosurgeon. Lester went around the SUV and held her hand as she exited the truck. Some sort of electrical energy ran through their hands and it took them a while to disconnect. Lester stood by as she unlocked the office. An awkward moment followed.

"Uh...are you going to set up my first appointment with Mrs. Carter?"

"I'd be glad to do that for you, Lester."

"Debi -would you—uh—have dinner with me Friday night since I guess we are legal now?"

"I would love to, but I wonder if there is a residual patient-client thingy—what do we do about that?"

"You only date past patients who're police officers and also have scar tissue on their brain—no other former patients?"

"Got it—call me later and we'll also discuss my dad's advice on brain doctors."

Lester drove off, wondering if she had accepted or put him off.

Chapter Four

Monday—Mt. Ida

A black Hummer blew past the guard office at S.G. Crystals and slid to a stop in front of a door marked "Employees only." A striking blond woman with radiant green eyes moved quickly from the vehicle to the door without looking around. Her skintight leather pants exposed a shapely young body enhanced by boots with three-inch heels and a gun holster under her left armpit. The door barely slammed shut when she started shouting angrily.

A tall young man with long brown hair tied in a ponytail was pressed up against the wall. His face was only inches from the pretty blond-haired woman. Spit peppered his face during her tirade.

"Stick—you idiot! Why in the fuck didn't you go to Quince's house and pick up those guns?"

"I didn't hear about him getting shot until two days later, and the cop had already been out there," Stick said.

"Where were you that you didn't hear the news on TV or your goddamn radio?" More spit blasted his face.

"Deer stand…we went to deer camp to build stands. No TV there, and nobody called me. Sorry, didn't know all this was going to happen. I talked to Quince and invited him to go with us. Said…had things to do. Didn't know that meant—killing his wife and her boyfriend." He stared her straight in the eyes.

She moved away from where she had him pinned to the wall and looked at the group of about ten people in the room.

"All of you better be prepared to have this place searched. Go underground with the operation and seal and perfume it from drug dogs. Make this place look legit if it means you buy ten tons of crystals from everybody in town. Get a crew working the old Waggner Mine we bought and get several truckloads dumped in the back of the warehouse. I can fucking assure you they will be around. Lester McFarlin is as good as they get simply because he don't miss a trick. Most cops would have scratched this up as a domestic case and went for coffee and donuts. Not this guy. In a couple of days he'll be here and maybe also in New Orleans. Prepare your ass to be investigated."

She left, slamming the door again, and jumped into her Hummer, fishtailed down the gravel driveway and out the guard gate. Angel Gambini's thoughts mostly centered on her decision to move her operations from New Orleans to the Arkansas sticks. *Damn deer hunters—so goddamn important here.* Katrina wiped out her production facilities that were located in the ninth ward in Orleans Parish. She had little hope of starting back up anytime soon even though she had tried for a long time.

For years her family came to Hot Springs for summer vacation and in the springtime to bet on the horses. They had a houseboat at Mountain Harbor Resort and loved to go dock it on an island for swimming and fishing. Compared to the swampland in southern Louisiana where most trees had water beneath them, this was paradise. Lakes in Arkansas had gravel bottoms surrounded by rock cliffs. Angel had never seen a rock in Louisiana. Parking lots, roads and driveways were paved with oyster shells. Without oyster shells, cars in New Orleans would sink below the surface, and only boats would be left to take folks around town. Angel had been told this, but wasn't sure how true it was.

She came from families who might not be trusted to tell the truth. Among her distant Italian relatives were names like Marcello, Carollo, Gagliano, and Giacona. Her parents were Matrangas, and she was pretty sure she was connected to most crime families in New Orleans and New York City. Her husband, Richie Gambini, had died in a car accident that ended in a deep dive off the causeway into a swamp full of alligators. The police first said he was driving too fast for conditions, but later reported his hands were tied behind him and a bullet was lodged in his brain. Angel insisted she had not taken part in the killing and acted genuinely distraught at the funeral. Later, people learned he had sampled too many of the amenities at the Royal Street Asian Massage Parlor he owned, now managed by Angel. The only thing she would admit was she moved out when she discovered her husband Richie had a thing going with a certain Asian hooker.

Crime families generate nicknames, and this family had such characters as Fat Frank Gagliano and Spider Gambini, for Angel Gambini. Since black widow spiders kill their mates, why not apply "Spider" to the only female underboss in an American crime family? Although Angel did not choose the Spider designation and denied any part in her husband's death, her cohorts stuck her with the name just the same.

She and Richie had a son, Frank Marcello Gambini, fifteen-years-old and attending a boarding school in New York. Plenty of family in the area to keep an eye on him, and if he gave his full name to anyone who had a sense of history they would surely give him a wide berth.

Spider was thirty-seven and every bit as beautiful as when she was a nineteen-year-old contestant in the Miss Louisiana beauty contest. As second runner up, she had some animosity toward her parents for not paying the right people to get her the title. Her talent on the stage was tap dancing, but her real talent was using guns, a skill the judges didn't get to witness. She didn't see many men on a social basis, as most were a little put off by the array of guns she took to bed with her. However, she had casually met Lester McFarlin at a Hot Springs charity event and talked to him about crime fighting and some of the cases he had solved. She told him she was a writer and might want to interview him further. She really liked what she saw. Spider said she would call to set up an interview but never did. In the back of her mind she had some fear that if he found her out and then she would have to kill him.

* * *

On this Tuesday morning, Becca saw Lester sitting at his desk and came by, walked completely around him, and moved some papers for a landing place for her shapely rear.

"Doll, got your report. Except for the RPGs, assault rifles, and grenades, they all came from New Orleans—same guy. Reports say he's a gun runner for the mob there. Little Richard interviewed the sister and she reported that Quince's wife had stolen the Glock from her estranged husband since he had plenty. Automatic weapons most likely were ripped off from a reserve unit near Shreveport—rest from overseas—most likely Pakistan—can buy a tank there, so I'm told."

"Do people whisper those things in your ear during intimate moments?" Lester asked.

"Come over tonight and I'll whisper something in your ear."

"Get back to you on that."

Little Richard was sitting at a desk behind Lester and was a little put off that Becca had given part of his report.

"Rich, can you get me the New Orleans police department on the phone? See if they have an organized crime department—if not, the people who work that crap," Lester said.

A few minutes later, Lester was talking to a captain by the name of Hank Campanella who headed a vice unit. "Captain, this is Lester McFarlin with the Garland County Sheriff's office in Hot Springs, Arkansas. How are you today? Great. Would you be so kind as to check up on a Tony Evola for me? Seems to run guns and a few of them floated into Arkansas after Katrina."

"Don't have to check—know him well," Captain Campanella said. "He buys guns for most of the mob here. Has his own sporting goods store and participates in every gun show known to man. For the most part he keeps his nose clean, but we all know he's dealing arms under the table—just can't catch his ass."

"Found a closet full of automatic weapons, RPGs, and grenades. All the legal guns were registered to your man Evola. Tell me about your crime families there. Got a feeling some of them are on permanent vacation in my lovely city," Lester said.

"The old families—the Marcellos, Carollos, Giaconas, and the Gaglianos all died out—but their kids, grandkids, cousins and uncles still operate quietly. Many in legitimate businesses. I did hear that one may have moved to Arkansas."

"Who is he?"

"Not a he. It's a she, and a damn good looking one at that. Mean as a snake, and please don't send her back here."

"Give me her name. I think I may have dated her," Lester said, laughing.

"If you did, you're lucky to be alive. Angel Gambini—a.k.a., Spider Gambini. Kin to every gangster that ever lived. Big time drug dealer. Keep her. And we've heard of you, Lester—started to hire you for a big murder investigation, but the department didn't have the money to spare. Good luck on your investigation."

"Thanks. If I come to New Orleans for this case maybe I can help you with something —no charge. If you've a picture of Angel, that'd be helpful. Rich'll give you the fax number."

Lester handed the phone to Little Richard and got up and walked to the sheriff's office. Lester had made the freebie offer to the New Orleans police department without consulting Mike Adams, which Lester knew would not go quietly into the night. Sheriff Adams was on the phone to the quorum court concerning completion of a new jail that had been funded by a tax increase. Remarkably, there were $2 million in reserves that had not been anticipated since the tax generated an excess in revenues. Lester was aware of the giant slush fund and was not shy about dipping into it.

When the sheriff hung up, Lester said, "Mike, I'm just warning you that I may need to go to New Orleans for this investigation." Lester loved dropping these bombs, and then he would sit back and watch the sheriff self-destruct. Mike Adams did not disappoint him.

"Why in hell do you think because you're Lester McFarlin you can go anywhere…investigate anywhere…spend my whole fucking budget in a day or two—can't do me that way!" Sheriff Adams stopped for a minute to get his breath and let his blood pressure drop back below stroke level.

"I had to take one of my clerical staff down to part time the other day because of my budget, but because you want to be a hero you can spend thousands of dollars chasing pussy in New Orleans." Mike was now just grabbing airtime.

"Mike, I know you can put your clerical staff under the jail budget and take that person back to full time if you want to. Two million will pay for a secretary that will type a hundred words a minute and blow you at the same time. I'll get back to you on the 'chasing pussy' trip to New Orleans, and believe me when I tell you this case will make you famous."

Lester didn't wait for a reply and excused himself, stopped by his desk to pick up a faxed picture of a very attractive gangster lady, and walked out the door to his patrol car. As he cranked up the engine he glanced at the black and white picture. He knew this lady from somewhere. While driving toward his church, he tried to place the woman. Ah, now he had it! She was at the Levi hospital fund raiser, and she said she was a writer or reporter. He had looked forward to an interview, but she never called. He was beginning to understand why. He looked at the picture again. God, she was beautiful. A one-on-one interview with her would have been trouble.

Chapter Five

Church and Gunfire

Lester's church wasn't really a church, but rather a cafe in the tiny town of Kirby in Pike County. It was Arkansas. It was America. It was the soul of the universe. Near a table by the front window, the molten core of the earth surfaced and wrapped itself around Lester. This was his religious pilgrimage. If his funeral were to take place in that small room, joy and peace would surround him. He rarely ate with anyone since this was his prayer time—not in the conventional bowing of one's head and muttering words—but more esoteric—in a way only Lester understood. Usually he drank black coffee and listened to the real world preach to him. Deer hunters talked of their cameras picking up a huge buck crossing to a feeder. Farmers exclaimed their excitement about the rise in beef prices. More than likely, a couple worried over paying bills or lamented friends getting a divorce. Men talked about the coming football season, while women discussed weddings and parties. It was all so damn real. It was life on Earth. The cafe was the world compressed into one room. After church, he peacefully drove his cruiser back to Hot Springs refreshed, cleansed— his spirit renewed. The air he breathed seemed sweeter, and the things that bothered him had now drifted off somewhere.

Sitting at his desk in the office, he didn't really want to talk to anyone. Sheriff Adams walked by with the mayor at his side and gave Lester the finger behind his back so the mayor wouldn't notice. Lester smiled and resisted returning the gesture. He was still in his religious frame of mind. It was afternoon and he was also in a Debi Green frame of mind. He decided to call her. He was a little nervous but was really comfortable around women, and they sensed it.

Confident men can be very sexy, Debi thought as she toyed with Lester on the phone.

"Just because I don't have any more patients today doesn't mean I can go riding around with the first cop who calls me. Maybe I've got things to do…and didn't we have lunch together yesterday?"

"Since I'm the first cop to call you today, maybe I get some credits for being…in line first. And remember, you fired me yesterday. I'm traumatized and in need of counseling. I'll be by in the shiny red car in five minutes."

Debi was waiting outside her office, smiling. She leaned towards the approaching car as though she were excited about the trip. Lester got out of the car to help her, but this time she wore pants, so the awkward short dress affair was avoided. He put his hand out to help Debi step into the elevated SUV.

She felt that same magical electrical feeling as Lester squeezed her hand to assist her. Debi really wanted to get out of the office. She really wanted to be with Lester today and wanted desperately to hide that from him. In a playful manner, she started arguments with him and disagreed with everything he said. Debi was more attracted to him than to any guy in her past. What she wanted was a relationship—the relationship—that would shape everything they would ever do in their lives. Her goal was to hold herself together until then and not blow it.

"Can we drive out to Ouachita and look at the lake, maybe get a bite to eat at Shangri-La? Just get away for a while and not be at work," Lester said, waiting for Debi's reaction to see if she was game.

"Well, I guess, but I was hoping to see you shoot somebody today. Have you gotten around to that yet?" Debi said, holding back a laugh.

"If I just wounded you—would that count?"

"Too easy a target. Tell me about some cases you're working on, or would you have to shoot me if you told me?"

"I may have to go to New Orleans for a gun dealer case. Want to go with me?" Lester cut his eyes at her and flashed a goofy grin.

"Do I get my own room or would I be required to sleep with the head investigator?"

"Well, that'd be Captain Campanella. I'll call and ask if you can sleep with him. I think he's married but I'll call to see…" Lester reached for his phone and acted as if he were dialing when Debi took the phone from him.

"When is this trip?" Debi asked.

"Right now Sheriff Adams is a little cool to the idea, but in a few days—months—maybe years—he'll give in."

"What else do you have a little closer to home so that I don't have to sleep with a New Orleans cop?"

"Possible drug lab posing as a crystal mine. And that's all I'm going to say, or I'll have to kill you, and I'd hate to do that on an empty stomach."

Debi laughed and wondered about the world cops lived in. She knew their jobs could be dangerous, and maybe she was attracted to guys who liked a little danger. Her ex-boyfriend was a scuba diver and sky diver. She loved scuba diving but refused to leave a plane that was still airborne with the engines running. She liked motorcycles if they were girl-sized, such as trail bikes. Big Harleys—not so much. She had shot trap with her dad at his gun club and was getting to be better at busting the clay targets. Maybe Lester would like to go with her.

"Lester, would you take me trap shooting sometime?"

"Will you have a gun, too?" Lester couldn't hold back the laughter and then noticed a fist coming in his direction.

Debi reached over and slugged him on the shoulder. She had come up with something slightly manly they could do together, and he had made fun of it. *Typical male,* she thought.

Realizing he may have been a little harsh, he reopened the game. "Debi, I'd love to go trap shooting with you, and I'll go a step further— I'll take you to shoot sporting clays if you want to," Lester said in his most sincere voice.

"Maybe…but now you've pissed me off, and I might just shoot you by accident."

"Whatever. There's a bait shop before we get into Montgomery County where we can get some beer or wine to take with us. It's a dry county at the lake. That be ok?" Lester asked.

"Yes. Can I tell you what kind of wine I want? I prefer a Jordan's cab—maybe a 2008 or 9. If not, a Cakebread chardonnay with some nice Havarti cheese."

"Debi—it's a bait store."

"How nice of a bait store?"

"It ain't a Neiman Marcus bait store!"

"Well, shit. I'll go in with you and pick out what I want."

Lester laughed and wondered if she had ever been in a real bait and tackle store.

They kidded around about the type of beverages they expected to find and whether worms, minnows, crickets, or beer would be the best use of floor space. Nothing had been solved when Jody's Bait Store came into view on the right. The side of the small white building was covered in huge letters that said, "Beer, Bait, and Ammo."

"Oh, they're using my floor space for ammo, I see. Most effective— high return during deer season, I bet," Debi said.

Lester had gotten quiet. He reached under the seat and pulled out two black cases. Without looking down he removed two pistols. One was a Sig Sauer .45 caliber automatic and the other a Berretta 9 millimeter. He slid shells into chambers, released the safety on both and handed the Berretta to Debi. He put an extra clip in his pocket.

"Don't point this at me and if you have to use it, just aim and pull the trigger as fast as you can."

"What the hell is going on, Lester? I'm scared!"

"So am I. Do you see that pimped-out car parked sideways in front of the bait shop?" Lester asked but didn't expect an answer. "Pretty sure the place is being robbed. When I pull in I'll park the Yukon in front of their car. We'll get out and take cover behind our car and wait to see what happens. If I get hit, just point the gun at anyone that comes near you and empty the magazine."

Lester pulled up the big SUV and pointed the front towards the highway, blocking an older model Chevy with thin tires and expensive rims that spun while the car was stopped. A black man with a knit ski hat pulled down over his face sat behind the steering wheel. The motor was running. Lester jumped out, pulled Debi across the seat and placed her in a squatting position near the ground behind the rear wheel well.

"Stay there and keep your head down!" Lester yelled as he moved to the front wheel well. He rose up with his gun directed across the hood. The Chevy's driver started opening his door at the same time a gunshot rang out from inside the bait store. Seconds later a skinny tall black man ran out of the shop.

He carried a plastic bag and yelled at his friend, "Let's get the fuck out of here!"

Before he could take another step, a blast from inside the building blew out the front store window, spraying buckshot and glass on the man's back. He turned to fire at the store owner.

"Sherriff's Department! Drop the gun or I'll take your head off!!" Lester expected what would come next since most robberies were committed by people who were fried on drugs and didn't care if they lived or died.

"No way, motherfucker!"

The man wheeled around and started firing his pistol on full semi-automatic. Bullets zipped by Lester's head and burst through the windows of his car. Brutal metallic sounds pierced the air when the bullets slammed into the door and hood of the car. Most cops fire off a lot of rounds because they are fueled with adrenalin, but Lester stood up, Zen-like through the chaos, and fired one shot centered almost perfectly between the man's eyes. A halo of pink appeared at the rear of the man's head as brain matter exploded. The man crumbled into an awkward pile of legs and arms.

The driver was up behind his door and began to spray the SUV with automatic pistol fire. Lester realized he was using a machine pistol like an Uzi or a Mac-10. Bullets were flying everywhere. He glanced at Debi and instead of looking scared, she looked mad. Lester dropped to the ground and motioned for Debi to do the same. She was so sexy with a gun in her hand—like a Vogue cover girl or maybe a model on the front of a hunting magazine. Lester told her to shoot at the legs of the guy standing by the car door from under the Yukon. Debi took aim and fired through the tight space under the carriage of the Yukon in the general direction of the shooter. She hit near his legs and through his door. That was all the distraction Lester needed. He stood erect and took aim at the little bit of the knit hat that showed above the door. The bullet entered the man's brain through the hat and he too slumped into a weird position.

Debi and Lester rushed with a first aid kit to the front door of the bait shop.

"It's the police. Don't shoot. It's Lester McFarlin, Jody. You okay?"

"No, I'm not okay. That black motherfucker tried to kill me. Come on in."

Lester and Debi ran to his side where he had propped himself against the counter while seated on the floor. His right chest area had a bad bullet wound. Blood was pumping out but slowed by a large stash of paper towels Jody had stuffed in the hole. Lester and Debi put on rubber gloves and worked on the wound with gauze compresses and bandages while they dialed every emergency vehicle in two counties. He could survive the wound, but loss of blood was a concern. Lester asked his blood type and added that to his telephone report. A Lifeline helicopter with type O Positive was on the way. Debi noticed blood running down Lester's shoulder and raised his short-sleeved polo shirt to find a small hole where a bullet had entered and exited his upper arm.

"Just a flesh wound, my dear. Don't hurt much." Lester grinned, but Debi didn't believe the not hurting part. She cleaned the wound and put a gauze dressing on each side with an ample amount of antibiotic she found in a tube.

Jody appeared stable when the paramedics arrived. Before they loaded him in the helicopter, Debi said she needed to ask him a question. "What is it?" he asked.

"Can you recommend a nice red wine from your collection here at the bait shop?"

Jody laughed out loud and whispered something in her ear.

"What did he say?" asked Lester, who was being re-doctored by paramedics from Mt. Ida. They praised Debi's first aid work but added stiches to his wound. Debi ignored Lester's inquiry.

Police and sheriff cars started pulling up. Sheriff Jake was one of the first to come from Mt. Ida. Lester introduced Debi.

"Debi, I want you to watch how a group of cops can screw up a crime scene," Lester said.

They both watched as state police, sheriff deputies, and others strolled over the entire crime scene—stepping on footprints, leaning on doors and counters and placing their hands on everything and everywhere. One by one, they walked up to the bodies and poked around in pockets. They stepped in blood and picked up empty cartridges without properly marking them. The actions would have been comical had the crime not involved Lester and Debi.

Sheriff Mike Adams pulled up and shooed everyone out of the area except for Little Richard and the photographer. The sheriff came over and introduced himself to Debi. Rich then followed Lester's protocol. He interviewed Lester and Debi—separately. Later, he would interview Jody when he was stabilized at the hospital. He collected all the weapons, including Lester's two pistols, while wearing gloves. He issued instructions to the coroner. He collected evidence inside the store and on the grounds. He started to put up crime scene tape and Debi asked him to give her a minute. She ran inside and came out with a bottle of wine. She told Little Richard to tell Jody about the wine.

"Lester, why is he being so thorough on this crime scene? It's cut and dry. You saved Jody and took two criminals off the streets," Debi said, perplexed.

"Cops are investigated on a tougher standard than bad guys." Lester had been a part of cases on both sides of the spectrum.

"I'll be suspended with pay until I'm cleared. My car can't be fixed until the authorities check it out. First thing they'll say is I was racial profiling when I pulled in front of a black guy parked at a store with his car running and wearing a ski mask in August. Maybe the guy fired at me to defend himself. Maybe Jody tried to rob the black guy when he went in to buy some beer. Maybe the machine pistol was a Christmas present," Lester said without much emotion.

"Horse shit! How in the world does anyone ever become a cop if they are treated that way?" Debi was furious.

"Really, the investigation is done to satisfy the relatives of the dead robbers and the general public. I know the results will be favorable, especially because Little Richard is doing his job. We all go through this and can just hope Internal Affairs works quickly because I have work to do. By the way, you were great under fire. I'll think twice from now on before making you too mad."

"Let me see if I can borrow a car since I'm off duty now."

Little Richard said he would ride back with the sheriff and lent Lester his patrol car, assuring him he would stay until Lester's car was towed.

Lester turned onto the highway and headed to Shangri La Resort. Once he pulled up to the restaurant, Debi got out on her side, holding the wine close to her body. The manager, Sam Barnhouse, knew Lester and had heard about the shooting from a customer who had passed the crime scene. The staff gave them a round of applause as they walked in.

"Would it be possible to drink our bottle of wine here?" Lester asked. "I don't think Sheriff Jake will arrest me."

"Lester, you can open a saloon here if you want after what you went through today," Sam said.

Still hiding the wine from Lester, Debi ordered fried shrimp, while Lester found a large chef salad on the menu and added shrimp as a topping. After they ordered, Debi carried the wine to the kitchen and asked them to serve it when the food came out. Seated at the table, both sipped water and gazed at each other.

So much had happened since Lester called her for a little drive by the lake. They were having fun before the killings. Now they stared and said nothing. Debi reasoned they had earned the right to lock eyes. Hell, they had been in a gunfight. Bullets had flown by their heads. One had torn through Lester's arm. They had stopped the bleeding on a man who might have died if they hadn't come into the bait store. They both had blood on their clothes. She had shot at a man who had a machine pistol and was spraying bullets all around them.

Debi wondered if the good times of sparring with each other and dancing around the mutual attraction had disappeared. The phoniness was now gone. How long could they keep looking at each other? As these thoughts moved around in her head, the food arrived and both blinked. Directly following the food, Sam lovingly carried a bottle of wine wrapped in a towel. He was holding two beautiful wine glasses Debi imagined belonged to a local household, maybe robbed for this occasion. Sam placed the glasses in front of them and peeled the foil from the top of the bottle, exposing the cork which he removed like a pro. The "no alcohol law" possibly had been ignored many times before. He poured a small amount for Lester, who swirled the wine around in his large glass and viewed the rich red color. He sniffed and tasted the smooth, bold, and complex beverage. Sam poured a glass for Debi and then filled Lester's glass. They each sipped. Both acknowledged the wine was very good. Debi pulled down the towel, exposing the label on the bottle.

"Let me read the label, Lester. Jordan's Cabernet Sauvignon—estate bottled—2005." Debi smiled at Lester. "It appears that ol' Jody is a wine freak and only too happy to share his private stock. He made this a gift for helping him." Debi was beaming.

Lester took Debi's hand, leaned over the table and kissed her on the lips…not too long, but not too quick. He stopped for a minute and savored her breath—then kissed her again.

In one afternoon, they had bonded more strongly than some people do in a lifetime. He held both of her hands and whispered, "Baby, where do we go from here?"

Chapter Six

St. Bernard Parish, Chalmette, Louisiana

One visitor to the Louisiana Sportsman's Super Store in Chalmette gave a statement to the New Orleans Times Picayune, "Dey's enough guns in dere to start and win World War III—twice."

The huge gun store was a cavernous building that featured stuffed animals ranging from rabbits to a rhinoceros. They were placed in settings much like their own habitat next to animals which were normally close associates before they were all shot, skinned, and sent to the neighborhood taxidermist. Live alligators were in an enclosure along with a few turtles and fish. Whole chickens were thrown to them during a well-announced and posted feeding time.

"Attention Super Store Guests! We will be feeding the alligator in fifteen minutes. Find your way to the center of the store. While you're there, please notice the sale on Alabama rigs for only fourteen ninety-five. They won't last long at that price. Thank you for shopping at our Sportsman's Super Store."

Suddenly there was a loud murmur as everyone pushed in to watch alligators fighting for dead chickens. Adjoining the gators was a big glassed-in display of water moccasins squirming around in a swamp setting replete with Spanish moss hanging from tree limbs. The place had a *Night in the Museum* feel to it until you noticed that every room held weapons. A dizzying array of rifles, pistols, bows, arrows, and ninja throwing knives were for sale. If the United States were attacked by any country smaller than Russia or China, the place could easily hold them off for a good while.

A more remarkable collection of weapons rested behind a concrete bunker hidden in back of a false wall in the rear of the store, its contents lovingly cared for by Anthony "Tony" Evola. Tony was in his sixties, short, round, and partly bald with a comb-over effect going on in a last ditch effort to cover an emerging shiny skull. He had a large Italian Catholic family—five sons who worked in the store and a daughter who was a doctor in the Memphis area. It was unlikely that Mr. Evola had ever been hunting or knew anything about it. He, however, knew guns and this store was his second. Katrina took the first one.

He also ate at the same restaurants, such as Mosca's in Avondale and Salvatori's in Fat City, as did local mobsters, but denied being connected to any of them. When asked about the notorious restaurants, he said, "Great Italian food for a reasonable price. My wife and boys love the manicotti."

The idea of an underground facility for his automatic weapons was abandoned when he rebuilt his store in 2007.

His contractor said, "Tony, if we dig down five feet we hit water. There's no way to keep it out since we're below sea level here."

The bunker was then cleverly hidden behind an indoor pistol range at the rear of the store. The only way to enter was to walk down to the end of the range and access a seamless door. These weapons in the bunker were designed for combat where bullets were counted in terms of rounds per second or minute. The federal government prohibited these weapons from being owned, except for the magic and elusive special permit for automatic weapons. Tony and his lawyers knew all the laws, all the ways around them, and methods to get the permits legally. He had made strategic gifts to all the right people to keep his Class 3 federal firearms license current.

The local sheriff had signed off for Tony's license application way back in the 70s, and in turn, Mr. Evola had bankrolled the expenses of each sheriff's election every year since.

Chalmette rested close to the Mississippi River and was a lovely spot for off-loading anything needed to keep an attractive array of firearms for Tony's customers. Many of those customers were just twenty minutes up the road in New Orleans.

The crazy thing was that just about anyone could buy a machine gun if he or she followed the paperwork requirements that Tony's lawyers had developed. It required the client to form a trust which bypassed their local law enforcement officer's sign off. Once that was complete and a $200 federal permit was purchased, the expensive part of the transaction was to follow. Tony even put on seminars in the evenings or weekends. He would preach to the enthusiastic audiences until their eyes slammed shut. He truly loved guns and made the following statement at each meeting:

"By law, only automatic weapons manufactured before 1986 can be sold and owned. Since no new ones were in the marketplace, the law of supply and demand has driven the prices through the roof. The price of one M-60 machine gun can cost here at the store up to twenty thousand dollars. AK-47s and MAC-10s are much cheaper. Since we are the dealer, we must clear every person's licensing process before they are allowed to leave the store with it. If they wish to sell the automatic weapon, it must come back through the store until the new permit holder is cleared even though it's not our sale. Just remember, anyone can own a machine gun—it just takes money and paperwork."

Over the years Tony made it known throughout the US that he was a buyer. Behind his concrete bunker wall was a collection that would make small countries larger countries. Of course, his biggest and most profitable sales were when he bypassed all the rules and regulations and sold unregistered automatic weapons of any manufacture date to those who paid the most. They remained anonymous.

In August of 2005, Katrina had flooded Chalmette with over 15 feet in certain areas. Tony loaded tractor trailer trucks and sold his entire legal inventory to a large sporting goods store that had just expanded in the Fort Worth area for $2 million, a full thirty percent off of normal wholesale prices. The automatic weapons, both legal and otherwise, were stored in a dry warehouse until he could rebuild. The trailer with the contraband weapons was worth ten times more but had to be placed in the hands of buyers he would be assured kept their origin secret. With $1.4 million as a down payment for his new store, he built the biggest sporting goods store in Louisiana and a concrete bunker for the largest number of illegal weapons in the United States. The grand opening was held in 2007. The water moccasins were added in 2010.

* * *

There were a few dry leaves blowing across the highway, mostly due to stress from the hot days of August. Lester and Debi were quiet on the drive from Lake Ouachita, and both felt warm around their temples from the wine they consumed at Shangri La. The month was ending, and soon it would be time for football games, hunting season, fall events, and cooler temperatures. A time of change. Lester thought about the operation that would remove an object that sat directly on the facilities controlling his ability to read words like everyone else. How long would it take him to relearn everything? Should he wait until his relationship with Debi was stronger so maybe she would be there for him after he was transformed into a total idiot? Would the doctor be willing to operate? Who was this doctor her dad was going to recommend? He looked over at her and squeezed her hand as it rested on the console next to a pump shotgun racked upright between them. They were in Little Richard's patrol car, identical to Lester's back at the sheriff's office.

Debi smiled at him and squeezed his hand as well. "Can I shoot Little Richard's shotgun?" Debi asked, just making conversation.

"Not yet—wait till a deer crosses the road."

Debi believed that they were returning to something like normal. Her parents certainly didn't feel normal when they heard about the shooting on the news. The first statement made by her mother was classic.

"You don't need to be dating some cop who takes you on shootouts with him. He's going to get you killed!" Susan Green said this as Debi held her cell phone to her ear and Lester's big paw in her other hand during dinner. They spent most of the dinner with their eyes locked on each other. Debi had tried to explain.

"Mother! How many times on a date do you pull up to a bait shop while it's being robbed by two dudes and one has a machine gun?" Debi said, exasperated at the thought that the focus of their date was looking for robberies in progress.

"You would be safer with Brad. He always takes you to safe places," Susan said.

"Yeah, like his bedroom," Debi said sarcastically.

"Just saying," her mother said.

"Mother, I'm done with Brad. No lawyer for a son-in-law. Get over it." She ended the conversation with her mother with a scowl on her face.

Susan Green had also been a Tri Delt sorority sister while at the University of Arkansas and had married well—something that seemed to be required of her. This challenge had been drummed into Debi's head most her life. Besides wanting grandkids, she wanted her daughter to marry someone with a good income so there wouldn't be a financial burden on her and Dr. Martin Green. A lowly corporal in the sheriff office did not figure inside the picture she vividly painted in her mind for her daughter. It didn't matter that the cop was famous.

Lester had overheard part of this conversation but didn't say anything until they were driving back to Hot Springs. He figured he wouldn't be too popular with her country club parents.

"You know, Debi, I'm never going to be truly welcome at your parents' house unless I get my problem fixed and make something more of myself. It might take a while, but I'll do that; I promise you."

"Lester, I like you and feel totally comfortable around you. You've done a tremendous job educating yourself, and if you never get over your problem, I'll still like you. And guess what? My parents don't choose the guys I date—I do. If they want to see me, then they get to meet the people I go out with—like it or lump it," she said forcefully.

"I'll start out in the 'lump it' category and see if I can work my way up."

In about a half-hour, Lester pulled up next to Debi's car and got out and opened her door, partly to be nice, and selfishly, so he could kiss her goodnight without leaning over Rich's shotgun. She stood by her car after she had pressed the automatic lock release on her key chain.

She turned towards Lester, and for a few seconds they just stared at each other, smiling. He kissed her, and this time it was much different than the kiss over the table at Shangri La. It was deep, passionate, and involved tongues that danced around each other and sent warmth to the lower parts of both their bodies.

"Good night, Debi. I'll call you tomorrow about the doctor your dad might be recommending."

Both went home with one overriding thought in their heads, but it wasn't time for that yet. Lester checked his mail at the apartment complex's group of receptacles. The tape he had been waiting on was there with raised braille lettering next to the printed text. He had learned braille several years ago and had an adapter for his computer and printer which featured a stylus attachment for either raised dots for braille or black and white dots adapting braille for the sighted. Lester found out many years ago that schools for the blind could be a great resource to help him. The Hadley School for the Blind had turned him onto *The Learning Ally*, which featured thousands of audio text books.

He rushed to his apartment, grabbed a cold beer and placed the first CD into the player. The speaker introduced the person reading the book with some soft music playing in the background. Lester readied himself and placed a small braille stylus maker in his lap. He used it to type notes which he could read back by feeling the impressions made by the stylus on special paper. "How the brain learns," started the reader. Lester waited on every word and at times stopped the player and went back to hear facts again. It was an eight-hour book and Lester listened to it all that night. The only break was when Debi called.

"How are you doing—how is the arm?"

"Fine. Getting a little sore where it tore through some muscle—but you know I have so much of it, it's hardly missed," Lester said, laughing.

"I'm sorry you got shot, but I'm glad I was with you."

There was a pause, and then out of nowhere she said, "Yes."

"Yes—what?" Lester inquired.

"Yes, I'll go out with you for dinner Friday," she said with a muted laugh, answering the question that had been asked of her a couple days ago.

"And my dad has made you an appointment with Dr. Steve Arrison next Tuesday at the University of Arkansas for Medical Science in Little Rock. He has your MRI, so be there at 10 to fill out your medical background. Your appointment is at 10:30. They know to verbally get your info. My dad likes you and wants to meet you, so prepare yourself to be invited over real soon. Seems like you're like a folk hero to him."

"And your mom?"

"You have work to do there. Two out of three ain't bad for starts," Debi chuckled.

"So's your mom have any hobbies or special interests?"

"Uhh...she's in a garden club—likes roses mainly. Why—you going to win her over with gardening tips?" Debi said sarcastically.

"No, but I hope to know something about roses by the time I meet her."

"Where do you order all these audio books?" Debi asked.

"Blind schools."

"Oh, my God! You can read braille, can't you? It would be a perfect learning tool for you. I never thought about it."

"Yes."

"Why didn't you tell me?"

"It didn't really come up, and you never asked me."

"Did you take courses with them?"

"Yes."

"Why do I have to pull this out of you? It's amazing what you did!" Debi said, slightly exasperated.

"Did you take college classes and if you did—how many credits do you have?"

"Yes and sixty-six hours. But Debi, they're correspondence courses from a blind school. It's not exactly something I want anyone to know. You're the only one I've ever told about it. It's been a very private way for me to learn. I can feel words but still can't read the black and white dot version or regular English."

"Wow! Wow! What in the hell are you going to do to amaze me next?"

"I'd say win over your mother, but that might take a while. I better get back to my book so I can get some sleep. Thanks for calling, and I'm looking forward to Friday."

"Me, too. Oh by the way, what audio book are you listening to?"

"*How the Brain Learns.*"

"Jesus! I'll talk to you tomorrow. Good night, baby." Debi hung up, wondering what other surprises Lester had for her and then realized that she had just called him "baby."

Lester showed up for work a little late on Wednesday since he was determined to finish the book. What he had learned about the brain only created a desire to learn more. He put in a call to the Garland County Library to see how many books they had on roses and asked them to hold a couple for him. Sheriff Mike came by and told him they were finished processing his car and had towed it to Golden's Body Shop for repairs. He patted Lester on the back and said the department would pick up the deductible on his insurance, and if they raised his premiums, he would pick up the difference. In fairness, Lester thought the department should have picked up all the expense so that no claim was charged to his insurance. Maybe Mike wasn't being as generous as he appeared. Had he been in a patrol car, all the damage would be paid by the sheriff's office.

The suspension would be over on Monday since there were no findings so far on Lester's part. He was free to use the patrol car, but no active assignments. Jake had called about the visit to the crystal mine, and Mike Adams told him he thought next week would be okay. Mike wandered off to glad-hand a visitor wearing a suit who had entered the office.

Lester asked Little Richard to read some reports that were on his desk. One pertained to the two weapons used for the bait shop attempted robbery. The guns had been bought from individuals who had purchased them legally from the Louisiana's Sportsman's Super Store. One was a .40 caliber Glock semi-automatic pistol and the other was a MAC-11 automatic pistol. Lester knew the specs on this weapon and had fired it and the 9mm MAC-10. The smaller MAC-11 used a .380 caliber and a 32 round clip that could be emptied in two seconds if the trigger was held down. To own one, an application fee of $200 would have to be paid and there would be a background check at both the local and federal levels.

"Rich, call down to that gun store and find out what paperwork needs to be done to buy one. Tell 'em you're a member of the Mountain Valley Sportsman's Club and the club wants one for their range. Then find out what they cost. My guess, they're between three and five thousand. No way could that dude afford one unless he was either furnished the gun or stole it."

Rich made the call and finally got to the manager, who was one of Tony's sons. He told him that he was representing the gun club and that they wanted automatic weapons to have special shoots for club members.

"If you're serious I'll send you the paperwork. In lieu of a local sheriff's sign-off, you can have the gun owned by a trust set up for your gun club, which for a fee we'll draft. You pay a two-hundred dollar fee, and pass the federal application process. The gun needs to be manufactured before 1986. What kind of weapon do you want?" asked the manager.

"MAC 10 or 11. We've heard the .380 MAC 11 is cheaper than some of the others." Rich was working on his academy award speech, Lester figured.

"I've some of both, but the MAC-11 will run you thirty-five hundred dollars."

"Do you have an indoor range where I could fire it?" Rich asked.

"Yes, but you pay for the ammo."

"Please send the application to Mt. Valley Sportsman Association at ..."

Then he gave his home address and thanked the manager for his help. Rich was a member as was Lester since they had an IPA range for pistols and great trap shooting bunkers for shotguns.

"I'm going to guess that Tony Evola has a herd of attorneys that've made this application process very easy. Let me know what they send you," Lester said.

Lester drove to the library to check out some books on roses. He hoped someone would help him learn to identify species and forms of roses and give him an excuse to call Debi.

Chapter Seven

Tony Evola knew exactly when the local UPS trucks were being retired and sold. This only occurred after extensive work was done to remove proprietary logos and equipment. Great care was taken to grind off any identifying UPS signage. Even more work was required to place all those logos back on the trucks after Tony purchased them. They were the older model trucks without automatic transmissions and improved ventilation systems but worked just fine for delivering anything Tony desired. A UPS truck could pull up to the Louisiana Sportsman's Super Store and load up boxes containing Uzis, AK-47s, and BARs without question and drive them around locally or to neighboring states where they would be placed in the hands of the buyers.

The drivers used quick-change license places after crossing state lines to avoid questions from local UPS employees who were avoided like the plague. Rarely do UPS trucks make left turns as it is more fuel-efficient to make only right turns, so Tony required his drivers to follow this protocol. In the event of an accident, real license plates had to be flipped and the UPS uniform top had to come off. As soon as the police arrived at the scene they would find a used UPS truck with current insurance, tags, and a legitimate registration to Chalmette Speedy Delivery Service, which was owned by Nicco Evola, Tony's older son.

"We haven't had time to take off the logos since we bought it," would be the explanation to the police. All the paperwork was in place, so hope was there would be no further investigation. However, when these trucks started showing up in Hot Springs, Arkansas, it would only be a matter of time before they were noticed by Lester McFarlin.

* * *

Drugs, weapon sales, and prostitution were the only ways Spider Gambini knew to make money. She wasn't really good at anything else. Had she won the Miss Louisiana beauty contest, her life might have been different for a while. She would have toured the state, gone to charity events, and maybe met an eligible suitor other than Richie Gambini. Maybe a doctor, lawyer, or rich guy would have asked her out—but there would have come the time she would bring them home to meet Mom and Dad—Sam and Mary Matranga. Sam was a cousin to Charles Matranga who had retired as a major crime boss in the 1970s and turned his empire over to "Silver Dollar Sam" Corolla. If the suitor called again after that encounter, he was either connected by family, or he was a total moron.

A date with Richie Gambini was actually set up by relatives, and everyone had their eyes open and arms held out for a "family union." They were married in a Catholic ceremony with hundreds in attendance. Long lines of black SUVs lined the streets in front of the church, each one guarded by a couple of goons with flowers in their lapels and machine guns under their coats. Trust of other families was not an abundant asset on that day.

The Matranga family did business in Orleans Parish and the Gambinis in St. Bernard Parish. Katrina had affected them all and there was great interest in what Spider was trying to accomplish in Hot Springs. Not so much concern for her success—they just wanted to know where she was in case her past activities back in New Orleans needed to be rectified.

She had quietly come to the Spa City a few years back and bought out two strip clubs and an Asian massage parlor. Spider's call girls worked at all three places and had beautiful websites. All the city laws were followed for the strip clubs, and generous and identifiable donations were given to the sheriff's boys' ranch and the police charities. A manager for these places was brought from New Orleans as were a stable of sexy girls for the clubs and extracurricular activities. The former owner, Vander Usterhoff, had employed several girls, yet most of them were just butt ugly. He still owned a big escort business in two states based out of Hot Springs, and it was a constant source of irritation for Spider to make sure her girls didn't sneak around and work as escorts for Vander's operation. She had tried in vain to buy the escort business.

"Spider, I'll sell all the girls, limos, guns and drivers to you for one million in cash," Vander told her a couple years back.

Spider refused. "Vander, there are escorts and there are whores. Your girls barely qualify as the latter. Go fuck yourself."

However, the new girls she brought into the strip clubs caused quite a stir in town among patrons. She brought a few dealers with her and they fanned out in the community to find out the drugs of choice. The reports that came back to Spider were: pot was number one, followed by meth, cocaine, and heroin. The import and manufacture would follow that basic need structure. The S. G. Crystal Mine would be the storage, manufacturing, and distribution center. As much as she hated it, the operation was put in one of her employee's name.

Guns were a particularly profitable shelf item, and now about $60,000 worth of guns and ammo had been confiscated by the sheriff's office. They belonged to Spider and Tony jointly, and somehow they had to be replaced. A discussion needed to take place.

"Your fucking retarded Arkansas idiot got my guns snatched! What are you going to do to replace them, Spider?" Tony yelled.

"I lost the same amount you did, Tony. We move on and make it up in gun sales. Five M-60s and ten AKs and we recoup our losses," said Spider. She had her ear buds plugged into her cell phone while she touched up her fingernails with a bright orange color. "I need inventory whether you go in or not."

"I tell you what—you find a good place to store them, and I'll think about it. No damn rent house in the middle of the woods. Capisce?"

"Capisce. Talk to you when I find a place."

Spider put her cell phone down next to her plate which held an omelet too big for her to eat. She carved off about half of it; she would take the rest home with her. Spider was in Hester's Café, which was filled with tired furniture and décor but was a spot that mostly blue-collar patrons found comfortable. Smoking was not allowed, but a residual smell lingered in the air from the twenty or thirty years that it had been a favorite activity. Looking down at her coffee, she wondered if there had been a conscious attempt to match her hair color with the amount of cream she had added to the hot liquid. Coffee was something she drank for the effect but really liked the cream and sugar better.

She pulled a newspaper up to the table from the booth seat, and the front page headline blasted through her brain: "Shoot Out at Local Bait Store Leaves Two Dead."

"What the f…!" she started to say out loud and realized there were kids in a nearby booth.

"Lester McFarlin, an off duty sheriff's deputy interceded in a robbery and attempted murder of Jody Woodward, owner of Jody's Bait and Tackle store yesterday in Joplin, Arkansas."

She then read the names of the two deceased robbers and recognized them as recent gun clients and part-time dealers. If they had also used her whorehouses—well, that was yet another loss.

As she read further, she realized that Jody's place was closed until later notice. He was still in St. Vincent's hospital in fair condition. A thought rushed through her head… *What if he would sell his place?* It would be perfect if she had a buyer whose record was clean enough to get the liquor license transferred. She might add on a bunker on the back for the guns. Her next call was to the real estate lady who sold her a nice condo on Lake Hamilton.

"Lauren, this is Angel Gambini. How are you today? Listen, it was terrible about Mr. Woodward who owns Jody's Bait and Tackle being shot and all. His place is over in Joplin. Do you know it? Good. I wonder if he would be willing to sell. I know it's a terrible time for him, but he just might want to get out of the business. It said in the paper that he was sixty-six years old, so maybe he'd like to retire. I know someone who would run it for me. Would you be so kind as to call him? See if he has a figure in mind and tell him we want it now before his inventory goes bad. Thanks." When she thought about the inventory, she could see minnows going belly-up and crickets dying of whatever crickets die of.

Spider gathered up all her things, including a box for her half-eaten breakfast, paid her bill and walked back to the table to drop a dollar tip on the table. She had planned to go back to her condo, but did not want to be alone tonight. She would call Stick to see if he would keep her company for a while. He would never be her first choice for any long-term relationship, but for an hour or so of sex he would do. Hopefully, she would hear from Lauren, and if the news was good she would have the last part of her empire in place very soon. She was also glad that Lester McFarlin had been suspended. She could relax for a few days. Spider fantasized that it would be much nicer if Lester were coming over instead of Stick.

Chapter Eight

In her best professional voice, Debi answered Lester's call as she saw her last patient and expressed an interest in talking to him afterwards. Truthfully, it was the call she had waited for all day.

"Lester, we seem to talk every day. Don't you think we'll get tired of each other?"

"Never—you're so interesting and one of the best kissers I've ever known."

"Who was the best?"

"Molly Lockwood—sixth grade—made my toes curl."

"I'll work on the toe-curling technique someday. What'd you call about? Or did you just feel a need to make me feel bad about Molly having superior kissing skills?"

"I need your help on a book I'm trying to read."

"You've always found a way before."

"They didn't have this one on audio books or braille and it has lots of pictures."

"Enough suspense—what's it about?"

"Roses."

"I see—for impressing my mom? Couldn't hurt, but might not help. Show up as a nice plastic surgeon and you'll have a better chance. Okay, where do we meet?"

"My place…or your place if you think we can behave ourselves," Lester said, thinking there would be a long pause.

She replied immediately. "Your place—I want to see the bat cave!"

Lester gave her his address, which she already knew from his case file. His apartment was also on Lake Hamilton near the Twin

Points area and overlooked the main channel. He watched the Belle of Hot Springs go by most nights and hoped the tourists on board were enjoying themselves.

Lester rushed home and tidied up, unpacked some groceries, and opened a bottle of wine for his visitor. He didn't need to stow away the porn videos or magazines because he didn't have any. Lester starred in his own make-believe adult movies, and many girls clamored to have a supporting role of enjoying his company. Remnants of his frequent visitors needed to be removed like the aftermath of a minor crime scene. All he needed was for Debi to find a pair of panties in a drawer in the bedside table or a bra hanging in his closet, or condom wrappers that had missed the trash can. About five o'clock there was a knock on his door, and he hoped to God it was Debi.

She stood outside his door with a bottle of wine in her hand. She was wearing shorts and her tan legs were so sleek and sexy, but Lester tried not to stare. Someday Lester wanted to stare at Debi's body—all of it for as long as he wanted.

"Will you eat salmon?" Lester asked.

"Love it. Are you going to a lot of trouble?"

"No—just cooked enough to top a salad, if that's okay?"

"Of course. Do you need some help?"

"Well, I'll put the salmon on the top of the salad but you can add the other stuff. I have those little oranges, walnuts, avocados, and tomatoes, pine nuts, capers, etcetera, so here's your plate—have at it."

Debi created her salad and picked up a glass of wine that Lester had poured, then sat next to him at a small dining room table. Music played in the background. Debi recognized it as Bruno Mars and heard "I will jump on a grenade for you."

"I like some of his music, but the hip-hop parts—just not my thing," Lester said.

"Lester, I like your apartment. It has a man cave feel to it, but it's clean and comfortable. Your artwork is mostly black pen and ink—not a lot of color. Some big photographs of old buildings and women models—some nudes but mostly artsy fartsy and very classy works."

"May I look around?" she asked.

"Help yourself. Be careful looking in closets—there may be girls hiding in there."

Debi took her glass of wine and walked into the bedroom and noted that the same style of brooding art work flowed into that room. "So this is where all the fun occurs: women are slain, virgins are de-virginized, and honest women are...well...most of us aren't honest anyway."

"You make my life seem so—one dimensional. I do have a job in addition to de-virginizing young girls. However, now it seems boring after you described my love life."

Debi returned to the table and leaned over and kissed Lester lightly on the lips before she sat in front of her salad. They finished their meal and drank another glass of wine while sitting on Lester's couch with the book of roses. Lester got up and went to his closet and came back with a strange device that resembled an incomplete typewriter.

"Okay, Debi, if you would be so kind to read me the names and species under the roses where I have placed page markers, I will use this stylus to print braille for me to study later."

Debi went through floribundas, shrubs, hybrid teas, grandifloras, climbers, ramblers, and then Lester's favorites, the English Roses and the Bourbons. As she read the names of roses and their classifications to Lester, he typed braille using the stylus, then removed the paper and placed it with the page. He did this on about ten different roses, then asked Debi to read certain pages which he had memorized. He then took the rose book from her and pulled her over to him on the couch. He laid her across his lap and looked down at her while he ran his hands along her beautiful face. He traced her lips with his finger and then said, "Damn, I should have washed that finger." Debi laughed, and he bent down and kissed her softly at first, then deeper and deeper.

She looked up at him and said, "Do you want me, Lester?"

"You know the answer. Of course I do. I dream up reasons to call you and be with you. I can't get you off my mind. You're beautiful, smart, funny, and I'm guessing you look good in the shower," Lester laughed.

"I feel the same way. I can't wait until you call me, and I know it shouldn't be possible this soon, but I'm falling for you more than I should at this point," Debi said.

"Besides being crazy for you, which is easy, I also want to be your best friend. Someone you can trust and depend on to be there when you need me," Lester said.

"I can't believe we've known each other about one week, and we're having a conversation that normally is months away. Is it scaring you away?" Debi asked.

"Not at all. Is it making you nervous?"

"No. If we talked about kids, buying a house, religion, money, and family, would that make you squirm?"

"I want to have kids and buy a house. I want to put together a swing set. I want to be able to read stories to my kids and put them to bed at night. I'm not traditionally religious, probably because my parents were Pentecostal and way too conservative for me. But don't get me wrong: I love my dad. His name is Adrian McFarlin and hopefully you'll meet him soon. He's just a hard-working guy with a great sense of humor. Someday I'll take you to my church. Money is important to me because of its power, I guess. Tell me how you feel about these things."

"At least two kids—maybe three. I love that you'll read to my kids and put together their swing sets. I'm Presbyterian, but our family doesn't take it seriously. Money's important so we can take care of our family, drive a nice car, and go on a cruise once in a while," Debi said.

"My God. If I marry you, I get to go on a cruise. Hot damn!"

"Lester, is there anything about me you don't like?"

"No. Nothing at all. Well, I haven't seen you naked yet, so I don't know what might be lurking beneath all those clothes, but I'm guessing you are put together very well and probably work out to keep your figure. Would you like to go with me sometime to the Y or do you go to one of the fancy gyms?"

"I go to one of the fancy gyms, and I don't want you to see me sweating—not from working out anyway," Debi said.

"Is there anything about me you don't like or would like to change

about me, as long as we are opening ourselves up for ridicule?"
Lester asked.

"I worry you're going to be killed by some wacko, but you're so
damn good at what you do I wouldn't ask you to give it up. Help you
pass your exams at the sheriff's office—that's on my to-do list, along
with learning to read if the operation happens. Also, I haven't seen you
naked yet either, so I have to withhold judgment there. Since I have
three beautiful breasts, I'm kind of hoping you have three balls so I
won't be the only freak," Debi said, laughing.

"I hate to discuss this, but maybe we should get it over with—other
sex partners?" asked Debi. She knew she was bringing something up
that was way too early in their relationship, but he was easy to talk to.
She was pushing it a little. She was curious as to the history of a man
who had a reputation of being a womanizer. It was eating at her and
had bound her emotions. She wasn't sure she should get involved any
deeper without knowing.

"You first…and are we really ready to go there?" Lester said, a
little irritated that he was being investigated.

"For the last couple of years—no three years—it has mainly been
Brad. We broke up a couple of times, and there were two other guys
during those interims. I always used protection except for the last few
months Brad and I were living together. I always used birth control
pills as well and still do. How about you?" Debi spoke quickly because
she wanted to get to the good stuff.

"This will be a lose-lose proposition for me. For one, I'm four years
older than you, so I've had longer to be single. If I'd married and gotten
a divorce or two, then I'd be marked down for that failure. If I had a
couple of long relationships—then why didn't I marry one of them?
If I had a series of short meaningless relationships then maybe I'm
shallow and not capable of commitment. Also, if we're counting the
number of times we each had sex—you might win that competition
since you actually lived with Brad for a while. I've dated a lot of girls
and for the most part, very attractive girls who were sweet, nice, and
smart, and I slept with a lot of them. You need to know I'm still friends
with most all of them. I treated them very well, and some I still see
periodically. I just never met one I thought I could really fall in love

with until you came along." Lester took a deep breath and frowned. "I won't count them and you don't have to count the times you were intimate with Brad."

"Okay, Lester, I gleaned from that bit of evasive rambling that you've slept with lots of pretty girls and never allowed your emotions to get in the way of your fun. You're also comparing my sleeping with Brad to your numerous sexual encounters. Is that really fair?" Debi wasn't mad but a little defensive.

"Debi, yes, I dated some beautiful ladies who've by now made good life partners for some lucky men. But as they got serious, I bailed—very quickly before anyone got hurt. If I had the same feelings for them as I'm beginning to have for you, I'd be putting swing sets together. You have to know that I have very strong feelings for you and don't want it to end—ever. Once I commit—that's it," Lester said in a shaky voice, as he knew how strong the loss would be if she were no longer in his life, even after such a short time.

"Then there's the issue of Molly Lockwood. You know, the toe curler," Debi said, smiling. She'd decided she'd heard all the sordid sex history she was going to get from Lester and sensed friction between them for the first time. It was uncomfortable, but she felt better.

"It's possible with a lot of effort you might bounce her out of first place. I'll warn you—it'll take a lot of work." Lester got up and pulled Debi off the couch and into a standing position.

"When can I start?" Debi asked as Lester drew her towards the bedroom.

"Tonight," Lester said with a huge smile.

"Tonight? How much time will I have? You know it'll require a long session and great concentration," Debi said grinning, as she stopped his forward motion and started unbuttoning his shirt. Lester pulled her blouse over her head. Her breasts were bulging out of her bra.

"You only have two tits. Did you know that?"

"I must have miscounted," she laughed. "Will I have time tonight to count your balls? I'm hoping for three."

"You have all night!"

Chapter Nine

The only redeeming quality Spider Gambini found with Stick Hennessey was they had interlocking sex organs. It was unlikely they even kissed during the activity. Once this convenient pairing was over, she sent him on his way. Stick left with a smile on his face, and Angel, still undressed with her feet propped over an arm chair, smoked a long, brown, skinny cigar and longed for a likable lover.

She had liked Richie—no, she had loved Richie. They were parents of a son but didn't have more kids because of his affairs. She confronted him, and they had violent arguments—physical arguments which produced no clear winners. Fed up with his less-than-discreet affair with one of the Asian hookers at the massage parlor, Spider moved out of their house. Most people thought that she ordered the hit on Richie, but that wasn't the case. Richie had moved some of his dealers into a parish controlled by a weak underboss who had experienced infighting with his people. Richie thought he had taken over, but a bullet in the back of his skull proved otherwise. The fall-out wasn't pretty. He was connected to several families, and almost all of them believed Spider was involved, and there was talk of a contract on her. She waved good-bye to the Big Easy about three years ago and headed to the wilds of Arkansas. New Orleans had not recovered much from Katrina and it was apparent it might never be the same. Later, the truth came out when the underboss admitted that Spider had nothing to do with the killing. The word finally got back to Richie's family and they actually called Angel to say they were sorry to have blamed her. It all came too late to get rid of a nickname and too late to recall all of the money she had invested in Hot Springs.

Since she spent most summers in Hot Springs and usually a trip during the horse racing season, it seemed like a second home. LSU and the Saints were her favorites even in the land of the Razorbacks and Dallas Cowboys. She would always be torn between the two cities, but couldn't believe her luck at starting her businesses in Arkansas. If just a few more things would go right, there would then be respect from the other bosses. Spider dreamed of sitting at the big table at Salvatore's with all the other family heads as they listened with great interest to her success.

She had received a text from Lauren that Jody wanted to sell, and the price was better than she had hoped for. Now she had to put the ownership in the name of someone who didn't have an Italian last name and had a spotless record so the liquor license transfer would go smoothly. Maybe Stick—maybe not—maybe there was no one else.

Angel Gambini missed her son. She called him every week now that he would accept her calls. After his dad died, he suspected his mother's involvement and refused to speak to her for almost a year. He later learned she had nothing to do with the hit and warmed back up to his mom. She dialed the number of his cell. While the phone rang, she wondered what he would do for a living. Maybe she would let him have some of her business in Arkansas. He was only fifteen, so there were a few years to decide anything. Maybe he would make his own connections in New York City. Many of the crime bosses in New Orleans learned their trade in the Big Apple. She hoped his memories of Arkansas would sway his decision, and he would come to Hot Springs and bypass the mob.

"Hello, Mom. How are you?"

"Oh, Frankie, it's so good to hear your voice."

"You, too."

"Tell me about your love life. Who's the lucky girl this week?"

"Like I'm goin' ta tell you that."

"Have you thought any more about coming to New Orleans for Thanksgiving?"

"Mom, will you feel safe there? There may be some that don't believe you didn't help in Dad's murder," Frankie said.

"If they're going to do anything to me, Hot Springs isn't an insurmountable distance for them to drive. We can stay with my parents and things will be fine. Even Richie's parents want to see us. My mother makes great oyster dressing and everything you like for dessert. You do remember her Key lime pie?" Angel said, a little shy of begging.

"Okay. It sounds fun, and I need to catch up with my friends there. Are you still coming out to visit next month?"

"Oh, yes. I have the tickets already. Make me a wish list on Amazon, and I'll pick one or two of them for your birthday. Let's see: it's sometime in the first week of October…I'll look it up."

"Mother, you're so humorous. Call me next week. Love you."

"Love you too, Frankie," Angel said as she wiped her eyes.

She thought about turning all her businesses over to something legitimate. What if she went to prison—what would happen to Frankie? If she had everything in someone else's name, maybe that would help. New Orleans was the home of some of her other businesses that she and Richie had operated. Some she sold to come to Hot Springs, but she kept her massage parlors so she could move the girls around when there was a raid or when business was better in other areas. During racing season, many girls were added to her stables in the Spa City. She was so damn good at what she did and had no idea what kind of legitimate business she could run. They all seemed so boring. Then she thought about the things she liked. Mentally, she started listing them: sex, guns, money, jewelry, clothes, big houses, cool cars, spas, massages, shoes, airplanes, scuba, and boats. *Boats – boats*, she repeated to herself. She grabbed her phone book and looked for boat dealers. It was there, and she was upset. Someone already had the Sea Ray dealership. After reflection, Angel figured that larger boats would be too hard to move to and from Hot Springs. Real estate might be okay if she owned the properties; sales could be made without requiring a license. If she got a license, it would open up a whole new world. Maybe that would be something to check out tomorrow. She had to talk to Lauren anyway about the bait store. Soon she would quiz all her employees to find those with clean records. She didn't hold much hope for spotless behavior.

* * *

It was early on Thursday, and Lester woke up and kissed Debi lightly on the lips, but she didn't wake. He pulled the covers back and started kissing her breasts and down her stomach to her navel.

"Is this the way I will be awakened for the rest of my life?" Debi asked without opening her eyes.

"No, it's the way I want to be awakened each morning for the rest of my life."

"Can we take turns?" Debi asked.

"Sure. Look, I can cook your breakfast, and you can take a shower while I'm slaving away. I guess you have clients, so you'll need to dress at your place. Eggs, bacon, oatmeal, toast, fruit, or pancakes?

"Lester, you can always cook my breakfast, and I can always cook yours, and I will. But we haven't taken a shower together, and that's what I want for breakfast." Debi opened her eyes and pulled Lester next to her. She smiled and kissed him lightly. "Toothpaste and toothbrush? Can't kiss you with road-kill breath."

"They both await you in the bathroom. You go in and brush your teeth. There are about ten new toothbrushes in there, the toilet seat is down, and get the shower adjusted. Call me when you want me to join you."

Debi appreciated the privacy. Brad would always come in and talk to her when she was drawers down in full stream. There should be some boundaries, and it appears that Lester respected them.

They took a shower together and made love again with Lester picking her up and letting her wrap her legs around him. Once they were done, they washed each other very slowly. Lester finally got that long look at Debi's body and was amazed at how beautiful it was. Her breasts weren't large, but they were shaped beautifully and certainly adequate. Her waist was small, and she had a perfect, flat stomach with a belly button that was set in a long concave area of the stomach that caused Lester to drool. Her long legs were smooth, tan, and beautiful all the way down to thin ankles. She was perfect, and Lester wondered how Victoria's Secret modeling agency had missed signing her. They dried each other and talked about plans for the day.

Debi had to go over to her parents that night for dinner and would ask if Lester could come. Unless they had several other friends over, it should be all right. Introducing a new boyfriend at a bridge party or some special function might prove to be awkward, but Debi felt this was just family.

Debi dressed and kissed Lester as she left for her apartment. Her head was spinning. She was so excited about this relationship. Her feelings were getting to that tipping point of no return, and it was a little scary to be so exposed emotionally. The alternative was to be numb inside—she had been there and didn't care for it. On the other hand, the mystery of having sex had been resolved, so now the work of building a relationship could begin in earnest. She would call her mom later to see if Lester could come with her for dinner tonight. There would be an uncomfortable conversation, but many of her talks with her mother required an antacid afterwards. Susan Green had a rough childhood and she reminded Debi of it every chance she got. Debi's brother, Ray, escaped to California as soon as he was out of college and now came home only for special occasions. Debi missed her brother but kept in touch with him and his family on Facebook and by phone. He had two kids, so the grandchildren pressure wasn't squarely on Debi's shoulders.

Today would be busy, as she had two new clients on top of the three she picked up earlier in the week. The income was reaching the point where she could make payments to her dad and have some money left over. Things were working out, yet there was a nagging doubt about the outcome of Lester's surgery, and it wasn't even clear he would have it. She would call him after she talked to her mom.

Lester dressed and called the sheriff's office to inform them he was going to Little Rock to talk to the FBI office there. One of the special investigators, Jim Webb, had some information on the infiltration and migration of crime specific to Katrina. Lester thought the FBI was great at collecting information but slow to act. He had an alternate plan to visit Cantrell Gardens which he had called earlier in the week. They had a few English roses.

Chapter Ten

Stick Hennessey had been called Stick since grade school, but his real name was Hunter. At six foot seven, he towered over everyone in school. When he played basketball at Cutter-Morningstar High School, shot blocking made him famous, but he never filled out his frame enough to play college ball. He didn't really try, since a couple of stints in Afghanistan with the US Army took the place of higher education. On his last mission, he was wounded three times. One bullet tore through his midsection and out his lower back, barely missing his spine. Another round smashed a kneecap, and the last one landed dead center of his right hand. He filed for a service-related disability and received an award of seventy percent, giving him a little more than a thousand a month. To a twenty-year-old guy, it seemed like a lot of money, especially if he could supplement it with other work. However, most unskilled jobs such as high-paying construction work, required heavy lifting, and he found he couldn't meet the qualifications for other unskilled positions.

But he could shoot. He could really shoot.

After he qualified at the expert level with every weapon he fired, his superiors shipped him off to a seven-week sniper course at Fort Benning, Georgia. He learned "detection by the enemy" meant a death sentence. Stick did well.

On his last mission in Afghanistan, his mountain patrol was ambushed. Two of Stick's fellow soldiers were killed. Another died on the helicopter after he was medivaced. Stick, wounded severely and bleeding profusely, located the source of incoming fire and crawled to get in firing position. Once he found them in his scope, he killed six Taliban soldiers with six shots. After his collapse, the medics loaded him on a helicopter and started an IV. He died four times on the way to the hospital, but the crew kept bringing him back. They refused to give up on him. He was given a Silver Star for his action. He probably should have had the Medal of Honor.

The residual pain, coupled with a likely case of post-traumatic stress syndrome, caused Hunter Hennessey to struggle with civilian life. Some of his army friends had killed themselves. Stick had overdosed on pain killers, only to be saved at the last minute at a local hospital. Heavy drinking and drug abuse had led to some arrests. Because he was a war hero, all charges were reduced to misdemeanors and wiped from his record. He was going nowhere. When he answered a newspaper ad for a security guard with military experience, he was headed for serious trouble.

The S.G. Crystal facility was under construction. When Stick showed up for his interview, the front office had been framed. The sheet rock was up, but it had not been floated. A single wooden desk had been placed on the concrete floors, along with a couple of folding chairs. Behind the desk was the prettiest woman that Stick had ever seen. He quickly realized she was business—all business.

"Hunter, you have a good service record, and I like you've qualified with a lot of weapons. I checked your arrest record and it seemed pretty clean, but it seems you got away with some drug and alcohol arrests. You don't need that shit—so stop it. What I need here is someone to guard this place, me, and my employees and not ask any questions. Can you do that?" Spider asked.

"Yes, ma'am! Can I ask what it pays? And I don't know your name," Stick said.

"My name is Angel Gambini and your pay is one thousand dollars a week. Vacation and all that shit—just ask, and I'll see if I can do without you for a few days," Spider said. She got up from the desk and had a bookkeeper take her chair to get Stick's information for employment.

After working closely with Stick for a couple of years, she had periodically invited him to her condo for a drink, and seduced him so many times that he was now on call.

He wasn't a bad-looking man, but he dressed with shirts that had the sleeves cut off in "wife beater" fashion. His face was chiseled, with a strong chin and muscular jaw, softened by bright blue eyes. Since being released from the army several years ago, it was unlikely that he had cut his hair, and that added to his shaggy appearance. However, he always took a shower before going to see Spider. He knew she wanted no part of a dirty, smelly redneck.

Stick didn't think she was really his lover, but more like a beautiful woman with a scheduled maintenance need. Stick thought if Spider had a warranty book, he should be stamping it on each visit. Her beautiful body was all his for a while, but there was no hint of romance, and rarely did she kiss him unless it enhanced the moment of intense passion. He was treated much like an escort. That was fine by Stick.

"Thank you, Stick. I'll see you tomorrow at S&G," was her typical after-sex conversation.

Gradually, he had learned about her businesses, and it scared him. Not the prostitutes, not the guns, but the drugs worried him. The moral part wasn't an issue, but dying over bad drug deals was a real fear. Angel paid him for referrals on hookers, gun sales, and dealers, loading his pockets with unimaginable cash. He refused to sell drugs, believing doing so would end badly. Hunter Hennessey was sucked into these enterprises without an avenue of escape. Afghanistan was dangerous, but at least he got out alive. This seemed to be a dead-end street.

* * *

Lester went through security at the West Little Rock FBI building. Since he was officially still under suspension, he didn't carry his weapon anymore, so he avoided that hassle. He was directed down a long hallway to a small waiting room, where a security guard sat behind a curved counter. A clipboard with a form attached was extended to him. Lester handed it back to the guard and asked him to read what he wanted.

"You can't read?"

"No, sir."

The guard frowned as though he didn't believe him. He read the questions anyway.

"Who you here to see?"

"Jim Webb."

"Your name? Okay sign here. I'll tell him you're here," the guard said. Lester scribbled gibberish he used as a signature.

Shortly, Jim came through the door. He put on his dark suit coat to match his dark pants. Jim had agreed to lunch if Lester paid. Lester knew FBI guys had expense accounts and hoped Jim would do the honors. Jim drove his agency car and laid a large manila envelope on the seat between them.

"Look in there," Jim said. He pushed the envelope towards Lester.

"I hope there are a lot of pictures. I don't read very well," Lester said.

"Open it up to the diagram on the second page."

Lester pulled out a report that was stapled at the left corner. After flipping over the cover sheet, there was a diagram of New Orleans and Hot Springs. There were several boxes with arrows pointing to other boxes in New Orleans, and further down, to boxes back to Hot Springs. Lester had his mirror out, working it feverishly back and forth between names and titles to each block. He did find S.G. Crystals pointing to five other boxes.

"What are these boxes? Do they represent criminals and their businesses in Hot Springs and New Orleans?"

"For someone that doesn't read, you figured most of it out quite well," Jim said. He parked his car in front of P.F. Chang's restaurant.

They found a booth towards the back against the wall and ordered lunch. Making sure no one was near or within earshot, Jim began to explain the boxes.

"It appears that one crime family has moved into your lovely resort town and has started a little dynasty there, or at least she's trying to."

"You mean Spider Gambini?"

"Yes. Here's what's in some of her boxes so far. She bought two strip clubs—the Player's Lounge and the Southern Exposure Men's Club—but of course, not in her name. Here are their boxes. This box is for the Asian Spa. Notice the lines leading down to the Royal Street Asian Massage Parlor in New Orleans from all three. There's an empty box next to them which we expect will be her yet-to-be-named escort service. She may own them now, but since they're illegal, there's no public record of the sale. They're listed in the Hot Springs phone book by various names. Now, notice the S.G. Crystal box, where we both suspect drugs are made and distributed. There's another empty box that has a line running down to Chalmette, Louisiana to Tony Evola's gun operation. You picked up one big haul, but we feel sure they'll reload." Jim took a breath then started again. "I guess you know the guns used at the bait store shooting were sold to someone from his store in Chalmette?"

Lester shook his head. The report had not been delivered to him yet.

"Lester, once we get enough evidence we can raid all of these at one time and clean them up. This Spider woman is a genius at building a crime organization, and by God, she has the bloodlines for it. Her son carries Marcello as his middle name. The only reason she's here is that all the bosses aligned with Richie Gambini's family thought Spider killed him. By the time she was cleared, she'd built a Mafia kingdom in your backyard. Now, you and I know that prostitution, drugs, and illegal gun sales all existed before she got there. A new coach is in town. Left unchecked, that bitch'll build and build until it'll take all of our Navy Seals to clean it up."

"I didn't know about the clubs being purchased by her. Ownership passes hands without being public record. I've heard prettier girls were being brought into town. So, I guess she moves them from New Orleans when needed," Lester said.

"Not only from there, but she gets the 'closed down' girls from various part of the country where raids have taken place. All they need to do is call her and send a picture. She has them shipped to one of her clubs. You know, when you have money and a big enough operation, you also grow by acquisition. In another year or so there'll be enough call girls to supply the United States out of Hot Springs," Jim said. He put the information back in his envelope when the food arrived.

"Lester, do you have someone in your department that is a computer whiz? I mean, really knowledgeable?" Jim said.

"Little Richard has set up stings on child molesters by posing as a thirteen-year-old girl."

"Ask him if he knows about the deep internet sites…you know, the dark sites that don't have IP addresses."

"I've studied it myself, and know a little about the search engine TOR and Onion. The Silkroad was just shut down, and that guy was arrested. Richie talks to me all the time about it," Lester said.

"Good. Gambini and Evola use it. Pay attention to automatic weapons, drug, and prostitution sites. Learn everything you can about bitcoin, feathercoin, and cyber-currency," Jim said.

"Okay, but it's a creepy place."

"Think we don't know that? We can view all the criminal activity and can't do a goddamn thing about most of it. It's all non-traceable and all of it is encrypted," Jim said.

"You're aware that Jake and I are going to S & G on Monday. Just a friendly welcome call. I don't know if Spider will be around. Sheriff Jake called me yesterday to tell me he'd put out some surveillance cameras that look like game cameras, except they take a digital picture every minute. We'll have those to look at before we visit. My guess is that it's all underground for now. I don't think you can cook meth without ventilation. We'll look for anything that's out of place," Lester said.

"Keep me in the loop," Jim said.

"Hell, you are the loop."

After lunch, which Jim picked up after considerable complaining, Lester headed for Cantrell Gardens. He asked a pretty young hippie-looking girl to help him with some roses. She was very attractive without makeup—very natural, with perfect features and a great figure. Her blond hair was streaked with shades of light brown, and she wore torn jeans that fit nicely over her shapely body. He had seen Debi now without makeup, and she was still pretty. Lester knew the kind of beauty that existed when a girl washed up on shore somewhere and still had a pretty face was rare. Her nametag said "Ribbon"—a real live flower child.

"Ribbon, were your parents hippies?" Lester asked. He blushed a little, after he realized he shouldn't have asked without first getting to know her.

"Yes, and I guess they still are. They live up in the Ozarks in a house that's built into the ground. They grow tomatoes on the roof," Ribbon said.

"Do you have brothers and sisters?" Lester asked.

"Have a brother—his name is Cloud."

"Cool. You are very pretty. Uh, can I see some David Austin English roses, please?"

She looked directly at Lester, locked eyes for a short while, and smiled. She liked him and the way he looked, but so did most girls. She walked out of the main building and led him to an outdoor aisle lined with roses. Many had not been priced and were huddled in circular clumps, waiting to be displayed.

"Did you have some varieties in mind?"

"Abraham Darby—own root, if possible."

"Here's one, but it's grafted—I think all of ours are that way. You may have to order one on the internet to get it as an 'own root.' Let me call for you," Ribbon said. She pulled a small two-way radio from her belt and chatted with a supervisor. She talked for a minute or two before she walked over to where the large shipment of fall plants were stacked by the aisle, and started checking labels. In a few minutes, she smiled and handed Lester an 'own root' Abraham Darby rose in a gallon container.

"Is this for you?" Ribbon asked. Again, she looked directly into his eyes, much like a child would do.

"It's for the mother of my new girlfriend. I'm trying to win her over."

"The mother or the girlfriend?" she said, laughing.

"Both!" Lester said, with a huge smile.

"Just take it to the front desk to pay. I hope you come back."

"I guess a pretty girl like you is already married."

"Was. Didn't work out. Single again. If the roses don't win her over, come back to see me," Ribbon said, and locked eyes again.

Lester thought about her all the way back to Hot Springs. He had always had this problem with girls. It was just too easy for him. He loved to flirt, and he loved the chase. Now, he had to give that up. He hoped he could because he didn't want to lose Debi. As that guilty thought was crawling around in his brain, his cell phone rang. It was Debi.

"You're on tonight, big guy. It's going to be fun watching my mother eat you alive."

"I'll just hang with your dad—he likes me."

"Where are you and what are you doing? Or is that secret police shit?"

"I'm driving back from Little Rock with Abraham Darby."

"Who's he? Oh, I remember—the rose. Hope it works, but don't hold your breath. I will be by at six to pick you up. We don't need a sheriff's cruiser parked in front of our house."

"Can I bring my gun?"

Chapter Eleven

A black Cadillac Escalade pulled up to the secured gate to Whispering Oaks subdivision and the driver keyed in a code. There was a dinging sound, signifying he had hit the jackpot number that caused the ornately designed iron gate to swing open. The driver was a large African American man wearing a business suit. His passenger was a young woman with a tight dress and too much makeup. They didn't drive far before they turned into 179 Spanish Oak Drive, and pulled in the rock-lined driveway.

The woman in the tight dress got out and spoke to the driver before going to the door. Dr. Farley Simpson, a wealthy widower in his early sixties, answered the door. He was also lonely and very horny. So much so, he had called one of the listings in the phone book for Wild Girls Escort Service. The girl, who looked like she was born for the job, was at the door. He was beyond excited.

"Hello, Farley! I'm Destiny Jones. Are you ready for a good time?" she said. She stepped inside the huge house and gave Farley a kiss on the cheek.

"You bet, my girl. I've been ready for a while," Farley said. He patted the boner he had worked up from taking two large blue pills an hour before.

"Can we get the pesky paperwork and payments out of the way before we get started?" Destiny said.

Dr. Simpson led her to a large couch that looked out on his deck at Lake Hamilton. She didn't really have any paperwork, and it was doubtful a piece of paper with the name of the escort service existed anywhere on the planet.

"My services for your party tonight will be two thousand cash. I assure you it will be worth it."

"What the hell? Your people told me it would be one thousand!" Farley yelled.

"Now, Dr. Simpson, please calm down. I guess they failed to tell you that the agency gets a thousand, and I get a thousand for my services. They do a piss-poor job of explaining it sometimes," Destiny said, trying to sell the extra payment.

"You know, Destiny, I can fly to Vegas and screw myself goofy for that much. If you want to work for the amount the agency quoted me, fine—otherwise I'm going to ask you to leave."

"It doesn't quite work like that, Doctor. You see, we have expenses for coming out here, so we don't leave until you pay. You aren't taking us to court, because we don't really exist, and it would be an embarrassment for you to tell anyone. So if you'll just pay me, I'll be in your bedroom or on my way. One thousand to leave and two thousand to stay," Destiny said. She pulled her two-way radio out of her pocket and hit something that made a buzzing sound.

"Fuck if I pay you a goddamn dime!" Farley said, and walked to a small table in the hallway, opened a drawer, and pulled out a 1911 .45 automatic. Before he could look at her again, the front door burst open and a large black man stepped in holding a machine pistol.

There was a loud noise from the couch area, and a round fired by Destiny's 9mm Berretta struck the doctor in his right ass cheek and slammed him into the wall. He quickly fired a shot at her. The bullet broke her right humerus, and she screamed. The black man had opened up with his machine pistol, spraying Farley and everything around him, but Farley was firing in his direction. The doctor got off six shots before one of the machine pistol rounds found his right temple. Two of the doctor's shots struck the man in his right chest, and brought him to his knees.

With only one good arm, Destiny helped him walk to the Escalade, leaving a long blood trail and all their weapons. After helping him into the front seat, she headed to the National Park Hospital Emergency room. Her former driver was dead on arrival at the hospital, and she was rushed to surgery in an effort to save her arm. Police were at the hospital within minutes, and soon were swarming all over the crime scene at Dr. Simpson's house.

Neighbors called the police about the small war that had just taken place in their normally quiet and peace-loving gated community. There didn't appear to be a mystery to solve—only a mess to clean up. The city police called the last number punched in on the doctor's phone—no answer or recording. Phone records identified it as Wild Girl Escorts at the same address as the Asian massage parlor. The next day, it would no longer be a working number. A couple of the coroner's attendants sported big smiles as they rolled Dr. Simpson's body to the waiting ambulance. A huge erection made a nice tent effect on his ride to the morgue.

Lester saw Debi's Z-3 pull up in the parking lot of his condo. In seconds, he climbed in next to her with a container in his hands and accepted a long kiss before he settled into his seat. When she ended the kiss, the briefing began in earnest.

"Call my mother Susan and my dad Marty...his name is Martin. My mother is a Democrat and my dad is a Republican. Mother was a cheerleader for the University of Arkansas and both are huge Razorback fans. They have season tickets for everything...probably ping-pong if we had a team. Mother is in a garden club...but probably more for the wine they serve than for the flower info. You could have just bought her a vase of cut roses, a bottle of cabernet, and done just as well, but of course your attention to detail is a sickness. My mom is from a Greek family—the Polycrons of Little Rock...the reason for my olive complexion and dark hair and eyes. Dad is a typical European-mutt origin and his mom also lives in Little Rock. My grandfather passed away last year. Dad is a duck hunter and has two labs that rule the house—Bongo and Hershey—the chocolate lab. We came to Hot Springs when I was very young because the hospital needed a radiologist. My mother works in the real estate business. And there you have enough information to ease your way through the mine field," Debi said, without taking a breath.

"Jesus...I hope you didn't leave anything out—like your parents' favorite positions or turn-ons and turn-offs—you know like the centerfolds of a Playboy Playmate of the Month interview."

"People who spit when they talk and rude drivers who give you the finger?" Debi said.

"You read *Playboy* magazine, don't you?" Lester asked.

"Only for the articles," Debi laughed, and swung her car into position to head towards her parents' lakeside home.

In a few minutes, they turned into the driveway that led to a three-car garage. Dr. Martin Green was outside one of the opened doors of the garage, closing the lid on a green ceramic smoker while nursing a beer held in his other hand.

"You must be Lester. I'm Marty Green. Nice to finally meet you. I've followed your career for years and have to say I'm a big fan," Martin Green said. He smiled and took hold of Lester's large hand.

"Nice to meet you, Dr. Green. Want to thank you for getting the MRIs so Debi could go over them with me."

"No problem—and it's Marty, please. Understand you are going to Little Rock to see the Doc next week?"

"Yes—can't say I'm excited about it—but needs to be discussed," Lester said.

"If anything can be done, he's your guy—best in the country I'd say," Marty said.

Debi walked over and hugged and kissed her dad, and led Lester to the front door. She continued into the house and yelled for her mom.

"Mother! Cops are here! Better hide your dope."

"Already flushed it, dear. Is he packing?" Susan said.

Susan Green walked into view. Lester was in shock. There stood a slightly older, but almost identical version of Debi Green. She smiled, not just to be friendly, but because she knew a handsome face when she saw one. She held out her hand but instead decided to hug him. Debi frowned at her mother.

"Mother, he's taken, so don't get any ideas."

"Lester, my daughter is always dragging home handsome guys, but you might just be the winner," Susan said, laughing.

"It's nice to meet you, Mrs. Green. I can't believe how much you two look alike."

"It's Susan, Lester, and what do you have in your hand?"

"Debi said you liked roses, so I thought I'd bring you a peace offering. I'm so sorry that Debi had to be exposed to that incident," Lester said. He decided to go directly to an issue that he knew was festering in Susan's mind.

"Boy! You don't dodge an issue do you? I know you didn't plan your date with Debi around a gunfight, but I do worry that you'll never back down from one in the future. I'll just ask to always consider her safety first before you start shooting up a place," Susan said.

"I promise to always do that, Susan."

"Thank you, Lester. Now, what kind of rose did you bring me?"

"It's a David Austin English rose called Abraham Darby. I hope you can use it. I also offer to be the hole digger, if you need me," Lester explained.

"I love it. I had one before but lost it to a virus," she said. She held the container and flipped over the tag with her other hand.

"Own root. Wow! You do know your roses. Own-root ones rarely have viruses. The one I had was grafted," Susan said, and an enormous smile emerged on her face.

"Lester, you're amazing, especially how you've educated yourself. Debi told me about the college credits you earned by correspondence from a blind school. It seems whatever problem is placed in front of you, you find a way around it," Susan said. She walked through the kitchen and out the rear door to her garden, and placed the rose container on her potting table. Lester followed, and she took his arm and led him to her rose garden. Once there, she let go of his arm and raised a rose from the top of a bush and placed it in his hand. It was buttery yellow with a cupped shape, displaying an ample number of petals.

"Graham Thomas or Golden Celebration?" Lester guessed.

"It's a Graham Thomas, and again, you continue to amaze me, especially since I know you just learned all this for my benefit," Susan said.

"Hey, it's made me a big fan."

"Good. Then you don't mind coming over and spraying for black spot for me every week," Susan said.

"Mother. Enough on stealing my boyfriend's time. Can we have a drink?"

They all went inside, and Susan poured wine. Lester excused himself to go help Marty at the grill.

Lester approached Marty while he was poking at a big pork loin on the grill. "Can I be of any help?" he asked.

"Grab me a beer out of the fridge over there in the garage, if you don't mind."

Lester found a Shiner Bock and opened it for Dr. Green.

"Did Susan chew on your ass about the shooting?" Marty asked.

"I brought it up first and tried to just put it out there."

"She loves people to be direct. And you won a couple of points with the rose. Let me warn you though—I've been married to her for thirty years and can't ever please her," Marty laughed.

"Marty, you have a beautiful wife and daughter. Debi's a very special young lady," Lester said.

"Debi is crazy about you, even if she did fire you as a client. And you two certainly make a good-looking couple.

"Do you have any questions about your doctor's appointment next week?"

"When you talked to him—any indications as to whether he was willing to operate?"

"I think he will ask you if the risk is worth the reward. You've done so well by going around the system, so to speak, to educate yourself without formal reading skills. What makes it so important to you?" Marty asked.

"I know it's a risk. I may have to start all over with learning, but I think if that's the case, I can accelerate the process. I've wanted a degree, or degrees, for years, but it's so difficult to complete outside the traditional methods. Law school or a criminal justice degree has been a goal for a while, but afterwards I might stay in law enforcement since I have some skills there. I want to make enough money to adequately support a family as well. My dad has struggled so hard since the

Weyerhaeuser plant shut down, and I'd like to help him out to make his life a little easier," Lester explained. He also believed the family part explained his intentions with Debi.

"Well, I'm jumping ahead here, but I know my daughter pretty well, and if she gets any more serious about you, I'll have grandkids a little closer to home before too long. If you guys stay together, and when and if the time comes, I might be able to lend you a little money to help you with your school. I want to see you get that degree as well."

Two labs ran through the garage and headed for the men standing by the grill. Bongo and Hershey slowed down and jumped up and around the two men, with tails going into full-fast wag. Marty told them to calm down, but it didn't seem to help much. Susan and Debi called them and put them back in their pen in the side yard.

"Great dogs," Lester said. "And thanks for the offer to help with school. I'm hoping for scholarships and grants—that isn't for sure, so it's nice to know I might have a fallback plan. If I did accept help, it definitely would be a loan. Thanks again for the offer." He was a little shocked that Marty would offer to help on his first visit, but it might have also been his way of saying, "If you want my daughter, then you better, by God, get a degree and a real job."

Susan brought out a serving platter to retrieve the pork loin, and Lester followed Marty inside to find a beautifully set table. Susan and Marty knew the look on their daughter's face while she talked to Lester during the meal. It was as though they were already married and had been for years. Susan had made her peace with Lester. Marty continued to be a fan and was even more impressed once he had actually talked to him.

Debi ushered Lester to the car after a short period of after-dinner drinks. She had other things on her mind.

She shed her clothes as soon as they walked in the door of Lester's apartment, leaving a trail of shorts, tank tops and panties right up next to the bed. She wanted on top and he didn't object. Both finished far too soon but marked it up to a build-up of emotions. They grabbed robes and moved to the deck, where they shared a couch. Debi laid in Lester's lap, and she looked up at him while he stared down at her beautiful face. They were talking quietly when Lester's cell phone rang.

"Lester, Mike. Hot Springs police want to talk to you at the scene of a murder at Whispering Oaks subdivision. The body's been moved already. Another died at the hospital. An escort is still alive with a bullet in her arm. Your suspension is over. Get over here, pronto, before the local police screw up your crime scene. FBI said they needed to talk to you as well. The whore has already lawyered up."

Chapter Twelve

"Jim, are these people part of Spider's organization?" Lester asked when he got Jim Webb on his cell phone.

"Don't think so. Three guns left at the crime scene—one an Uzi—a quick check by your local police shows no connection to Tony's store. No serial numbers on the Uzi. The nine millimeter registered to a Molly Gonzalez—the real name of the whore. The .45 was the Doc's. If Spider didn't buy this operation before, she sure as hell will pick it up for pocket change now. We need to find active landlines and tap them, if possible. I'm sure they talk to each other on burners, but we'll try anyway. Sent a crew to Hot Springs as soon as the local police called us. They'll be there soon. I'll keep you informed," Jim said.

"Did we get the hooker's cell?" Lester asked.

"She didn't have one on her, according to the police."

"Bet she dumped it on the way to the hospital. I'll do a search," Lester said.

Lester pulled up to Dr. Simpson's house, and was met by Captain Larry Boshears at the door. He showed Lester the three main areas of blood stains, and where the doctor's body was found. They walked the scene and followed the patterns of gunshots.

"The hooker was on the couch, and fired one shot at the doctor. He returned one shot. Doesn't really matter in what order. The driver came through the door, firing almost a full magazine at the doctor before the shot that killed him. It appears most of the shots just messed up the décor. Why would she shoot a customer? Maybe she was jacking the price? If he refused, she was going to either extort money or just plain rob his ass. He went for his gun, and she fired at him. He returned fire, and the big gun came through the door. Not complicated, but strange that no money ever changed hands."

"Any credit card charges? Anything happen on his computer recently?" Lester asked. The captain told him they were checking, but the doctor did have over a thousand cash in his pockets.

"Captain, can you spare some men to do a search for a possible tossed cell phone?" Lester asked.

Captain Boshears ordered the search. Lester directed the men to look only to the left side of the road, since the girl was driving with only a good left hand. He had them walk the area starting on the other side of the gate entrance. The four officers took only thirty minutes to find an iPhone intact, with a charge still on the battery.

"This call girl just had to have a smart phone instead of a burner phone," Lester said. He asked the captain to check her recent calls. Vander Usterhoff came up quickly, followed by calls to the Asian massage parlor. Many other calls were to other girls, listed on her phone with apparent aliases. He decided to hand over the phone to the FBI men that Jim Webb was sending to rig up the wire taps. This was going to be done quickly, but Lester figured that the important calls had already taken place. He was right.

"Vander, this is Angel. Heard about your problem. Want to sell your call girl operation?" Spider asked.

"Maybe," Vander said, trying not to sound anxious.

"Tell me what I'd be buying besides your sites, phone numbers, vehicles, and the names of the girls on contract. Have a feeling some of them are already my girls."

"Not many. Pulled those girls when you bought the strip clubs and massage parlor. I have thirty girls located in Arkansas and Oklahoma. None as stupid as the one that got shot tonight. I think she tossed her phone. So far, they haven't found it. If they bring in McFarlin, there's a good chance he'll look for it. Get ready for a tap on every landline listed in her database. You'd also get the web sites and the encryption software. I took down the Wild Girls' number, but the other two escort services listed in the phone book are mine as well. So, you get thirty girls, website, ads in phone book, five limos, five machine pistols, and ten…no, make that nine, part-time drivers who were issued the weapons. Sell it all to you for a hundred thousand. It brought in a half million last year," Vander said.

"Jesus H. Christ! You might have to pay me to take this crap off your hands. All of them will have to be retrained, and this shit of changing prices and holding people up won't happen in my operation. I'll have to redesign the website, change all the ads in the phone books, and change the titles on the limos. I'll give you twenty-five thousand dollars for the whole operation," Spider said.

"No fucking way! But I'll let you have it for seventy-five large, because I think they'll impound the limo and it's new."

"I'll go forty thousand and that's it. You may be in prison and have to use the money to buy body guards to keep from being some nigger's bitch. I'm going to hang up in five seconds and won't entertain an offer after that. You need me…I can steal all this from you in time, anyway."

Silence extended through the full five seconds. "Holy shit, I'm getting fucked in the ass—okay, do the conversion on feathercoins and send them to my Jeweled Ladies' account listed on Tor," Vander said. He knew he would clean out all the cash in that account before he transferred it to Spider.

"Ok. I'll have to go cyber mining to find them. The transferring account will be Mama's Automatics. You'll get half the money, and the rest when you send me all the info. Once you get the money, I'll need the contact numbers for all the girls and limo drivers. Send all limo titles, ad charges, inventory of weapons, vehicles and their locations, and other miscellaneous items to my S.G. Crystals' P.O. Box in Mount Ida."

Spider was thinking about the steps to find enough cyber money to purchase and then transfer to Vander. It wasn't like going to a bank; instead, you bought either bitcoins or feathercoins in the cyber fund network at whatever prices you could negotiate, but the transaction would avoid being recorded. They could be converted to real cash by selling them to an eager market anytime. The value was so great, many were now sold by fractions of a coin.

"I should've sold everything to you when you bought the clubs. Now I have to dodge cops. May be out of touch for a while... Caribbean sounds nice." Vander hung up, and Spider could imagine the wild scrambling going on to put everything in order, so he could fly off in his private plane to escape the local law. Spider supposed that as long as Vander had an internet connection, he was okay to survive just about anywhere.

* * *

Stick clicked off his cell phone and headed to a meeting with Lauren Bell at a local title company. The sale of the bait store had been accelerated, cash distributed, and an alcohol permit sent off to hopefully be approved. It had been a few years since Stick had had any problems with the law and all had been expunged, so maybe he would pass the process. Angel Gambini's police report wouldn't allow her to sell lemonade in front of the bait store, so her name was not on anything, but her money backed the check Stick wrote for the transaction. Once the keys were handed over, an out-of-state contractor would begin to add a concrete room at the rear of the store, where orders for Mama's Automatics could be filled. The dark net would come to life in Garland County, Arkansas.

Spider had plans to expand the garage behind S.G. Crystals to include the escort limos, the UPS trucks, and her private Lotus sports car. Guns sold on the dark net could be delivered all over the Southwest by her trained uniformed workers. Everything was falling into place to grow Spider's backwoods crime network, located apart from most of the world, into a major player. Her chances of bypassing scrutiny by law enforcement were fading rapidly. Lester and Sheriff Jake were about to make a friendly first-time visit. Even the yard man who cut the grass at S.G. Crystals knew there was no such thing as a "Welcome to Mt. Ida" visit from these two lawmen.

Lester drove to his office and stuck his head in Mike Adams' door. He didn't speak when he saw the sheriff look out the window and curse at the person on the phone. Lester proceeded to the evidence room and checked out a piece of evidence from the Quince Jackson shooting case. It was a small cardboard box the size of an old VHS shipping container with the words, "Don't open without permission of L. McFarlin" marked on top. Lester signed for it and walked back to the sheriff's office.

The cursing had ceased and he was downing a cup of coffee that had cooled during his long phone conversation.

"Mike, can I have a minute?" Lester asked.

"Shit. I guess, but it better not be some international smuggling ring or something that takes all my deputies from their jobs."

"No. It's simple. If I can find a way for the department to pay for the repairs on my Yukon without going through my insurance company and outside your budget, would you entertain it?"

"Maybe—if it doesn't get me arrested," Mike said.

"Remember when I found all those guns at Quince Jackson's place?" Lester didn't wait for him to answer. "Along with the guns, I found a box of money, and there's no longer a need to hold it for trial. I heard from Golden's. My car is fixed, and the tab is six thousand dollars. There's twenty-four thousand, three hundred dollars in this box to use as general funds, since the money is a confiscated item." Lester smiled and handed the box over to the sheriff.

"Did you tell me about this money before? I don't remember it."

"It's in my report, but a little hard to read. I got busy and failed to record this for Little Richard to type up. Anyway it solves our problems. Me and Jake are going together to S&G and I need my car." Lester smiled and hoped the Sheriff was too busy to fight him on this.

"Goddammit, Lester! I'm not sure we're allowed to do this. Let me bring in the property clerk." He dialed her number, and she showed up almost immediately. She was pretty and had dated Lester in the past. Lester had moved on when she started getting clingy, but neither had hard feelings.

"Peggy, I want to pay Lester for his shot-up car—six grand, I think—hell, you know all about the shooting. He found a box of money with the guns he brought in on the Jackson case. Should be our money now since it's illegal—owner's dead—all that shit. If you agree it's abandoned or confiscated property, then log this money out, list what it's for, and put the balance in our operations account. Get receipts." Mike handed her the money and Lester followed her to her desk. She took care of the transaction, did the paperwork, and recorded everything so that Mike and Lester wouldn't be cellmates.

"I hear you're seeing the new speech therapist in town. Is that right?" Peggy asked.

"Yes. Word gets out I guess," Lester said. He smiled, recalling that he and Peggy had some pretty intense nights together.

"You don't date cops anymore, do you?"

"Nope, you cured me of that."

"We had some good times," Lester said.

"Yes, we did. It just didn't last on your part. But I wish the both of you well," Peggy said. She had him sign a receipt for the cash. "Please bring me the invoice from Golden's Body Shop. And good luck with Jake today. By the way, you know this money should go through the courts first. I won't tell, but be prepared to have your ass chewed out someday soon."

"Thanks."

After getting a ride from Rich, Lester learned there was news from New Orleans.

"Lester, I got that application back yesterday—filled it out—faxed it to them. Got a phone call today saying it's approved for the 9mm MAC-11—three thousand, three hundred and fifty dollars and it's mine. Should I talk to Sheriff Mike about it? We now have that money you got from the gun seizure."

"Rich, that's great, but I want to go with you to sell this to Mike, if I can. We need to contact ATF to see if there really is a violation. Find someone at ATF and send them a copy of your application to check to see if it's legal. Don't let them do anything yet. If the application is clean, we need to see if we can get them to step over the line when we go down there. Hold tight, but tell the gun dealer that we want to shoot it first and that we're planning a trip to New Orleans soon. Also, how do you feel about taking Becca? I'll take Debi so it'll look less like a couple of cops coming to investigate."

"Oh, my God! Do you have a bottle of Viagra I can borrow?" Rich asked.

Little Richard let him out at Golden's Body Shop and headed back to the office.

On Lester's way to Mt. Ida, his cell phone went off.

"Hey guy, you on your way?" Debi asked.

"Yep! Got ol' red back—good as new."

"Great. See you tonight, sweetheart."

"Looking forward to it, babe."

Lester smiled as his SUV blew past Crystal Springs and headed towards the community of Joplin. He wouldn't be able to see S.G. Crystals' operations from the highway, as it sat a couple miles off the highway. Jake had agreed to meet him at the entrance to Mountain Harbor Resort, so he didn't have to drive another twenty minutes to his office. He did notice a "sold" sign on Joey's Bait as he went by Crystal Springs and wondered who bought the store. Shortly afterwards, he saw the sheriff's car parked at the grocery store by the turn-off to Mountain Harbor.

"Lester, I want to show you something before we get there," Jake said.

He pulled out a file and opened it, exposing several color pictures blown up to 8" x 10" size.

"Look here, Lester. They've got some interesting things in their garage," Jake said. The photos revealed a couple of UPS trucks, a limo, and a red Lotus sports car, as well as dump trucks bringing in material and backing into the rear of the large metal building.

The pictures had been taken from three game cameras around the perimeter of the compound that were set to take a digital picture every fifteen minutes. Also at the front of the building were several pictures of a black Hummer occupied by a pretty blond lady.

"You know, Jake, UPS trucks go back to their service centers every night. These're probably either stolen ones or fakes used to deliver whatever without questions by the drivers."

"This Spider Lady doesn't miss a beat, does she?" Jake said.

"It's scary how efficiently she operates. Give her time and the bitch'll take over the world," Lester said.

"It's going to take some help to bring her down," Jake said.

"Jake, are you ready to go? Let's take two cars to the turn off and then take your cruiser in. I can pick up my car on the way out," Lester said. He followed Jake back to the entrance to S & G.

Jake had called ahead to tell them that he was making a welcome call, and would be there in a few minutes. He could sense they were nervous. The facility was a distance off the road, so they left Lester's Yukon near the highway. As they pulled up to the guard gate, they noticed a black Hummer parked in front of the metal building. A tall attractive woman stood next to it, smiling.

Chapter Thirteen

"Vandy, where we going, sweetie?" Tammy Wallace asked.

"How does Venezuela sound?" Vander Usterhoff said. "It's warm all year and has great beaches."

"How's the shopping?"

"Great—everything's cheap." He smiled at her and glanced down at her well-tanned and shapely legs, then checked his instruments in the cockpit.

Usterhoff had been a pilot for years and found it an excellent hobby for times when his other occupations became unpopular with the local police. This was one of those times.

He had driven to the Hot Springs airport earlier that day after he called ahead to have his twin engine Cessna Excalibur 421 gassed and serviced. The plan was to fly to a small private airport in Louisiana, then island hop across the Caribbean until he reached Venezuela. His upgraded Cessna had a range of 1700 miles, but he wouldn't push it to the limit. He and Tammy had been seeing each other for a while and she really wanted to go with him.

"Tammy, we may have to apply for citizenship there so the U.S. can't come get us."

"What did we do wrong?"

"Well, you were a call girl—clearly against the law."

"No one has complained—especially you."

"You were among the list of my employees, and an unfortunate set of circumstances will put all of us at risk of arrest. One girl and a driver shot a doctor while on a call. He's dead, and she's being interviewed by the police as we speak," Vander explained.

"Wow! That's awful. But you had nothing to do with that."

"You're right. If your friend, Destiny, follows her attorney's—my attorney's—advice, she'll say the doctor shot first and she was just defending herself. Maybe she gets probation for soliciting, firearms violation, and God knows what else. If she gives me up—the attorney walks!" He reached over and slid his hand over her beautiful legs and kissed her gently on the lips.

"So, Venezuela will stop the US from sending us back to jail?"

"Here's the deal, Tammy: even though Venezuela has an extradition treaty with the US, they rarely give anyone up unless they are a proven terrorist. Nicolas Maduro took power after Hugo Chavez's death in 2013 and has proved to be a model South American dictator. He immediately moved Christmas to November in an unsuccessful attempt to jump start their economy."

"How can you move Christmas?" Tammy asked.

"If you're a dictator, you do desperate things. Inflation there runs above fifty percent, and oil prices have dropped like a large boulder. The country needs money, so they have this screwy citizenship buy- in rule."

"Why do we want to be citizens of a country that celebrates Christmas in November?"

"Once you're a citizen, it's close to impossible to be extradited. It will cost me about twenty thousand dollars for each of us. We'll live in a warm country with pretty beaches, good food, and nobody puts us in jail. Pretty cool, huh?"

"Sounds cool, but I'll withhold judgment until I check out the shopping."

"Don't you think we'll have fun wherever we go?" Vander asked.

"Of course, sweetie," Tammy said and kissed him passionately. Even though Vander was twenty years her senior, she really liked him. She also liked his money.

They were admitted as tourists after landing at a tiny airport in Maiquetia, Venezuela. Vander rented a hangar for the plane and took a taxi to Caracas. After he stopped to buy a cheap cell phone, he called an English-speaking attorney. They rushed to the attorney's office to get guidance in a country that hated Americans. It would be expensive guidance but would lead to getting the documentation they needed.

In a few weeks, Vander and Tammy had a small house in a mountainous area outside Caracas and new citizenship papers. Most of Vander's $2 million he had smuggled in was in the form of gold coins. They worked well for currency in any country. Some of the coins he kept with him, but most were hidden on his plane in a private hangar at a small airstrip in Caracas.

They got bored at times and missed the United States but could console each other when they realized they were free and not in prison. The age difference didn't cause a problem, since Vander kept in good shape and took Tammy all over the country to find places for her to shop—an activity she never seemed to tire of. If she left him, she wouldn't be lonely long. Horny men with money are everywhere, and she was beautiful. Vander would be forced to buy another girl in Caracas. For now, both were content.

* * *

Jake parked next to Spider's big Hummer, and both officers walked over to where the attractive blond lady stood propped against her vehicle. Everyone knew the visit to this fake crystal operation would eventually end badly. Today, everyone would smile and act as though it were a stroll through a Disneyland theme park. Later visits might be less blissful.

Spider greeted Lester and Jake as they exited the patrol cars.

"Great to meet you, Jake," she said. She shook his hand and introduced herself to the sheriff.

"Finally," he said, "I get to meet the lady I've heard so much about."

"Any small part of it good, Mr. Sheriff?"

"You're as lovely as billed," Jake said.

"Thanks, Jake. I try to stay presentable." She turned towards Lester; her eyes locked on his, and a broad smile lit up her face.

"Lester, it's been a while. I wish I had gotten back to you on that interview. Maybe we could've been closer friends," Spider said. She wrapped an arm around his back and gave him a little squeeze. Lester had only seen her in person once, but by now, he and Spider had learned a few things about each other. As he walked with her, he thought she was as beautiful as when he talked to her at the charity ball a couple years ago. He sensed she was attracted to him by the way she hugged him and stared into his eyes.

"Angel, I do believe we might've had a little fun—then killed each other. You know—don't some spiders do that?"

Spider laughed and held on to Lester. He felt as though she were depending on him to help her walk, as if her legs were weak.

"Lester, I hear you're dating a pretty dark-haired speech therapist. Is it serious?"

"Yes, I met her parents. How much more serious can it get?" he said, laughing.

"Well, there go my fantasies."

"What, you wanted to meet her parents as well?"

They both laughed and she looked into his eyes once more. They were in the building now, and she walked alone.

Sheriff Jake was living in the real world. He had no designs, or even fleeting thoughts, of bedding down with this master criminal. He had a chubby wife that he loved dearly and was intimate with her every week or so as directed by the occasional life that came to his rotund body.

"Mrs. Gambini, we just wanted to welcome you to our community and offer our services if you ever need us," Jake said, well aware that as those words left his lips, everyone knew it was bullshit.

"Well, I appreciate that, Sheriff, but I think we both know you're here to see what we're up to, and why we have a big ol' fence and guards around our place. The truth is, we have a patented and proprietary system of treating quartz crystal to color them. We wish to keep that method a secret. Would you like to see the operation?" Spider asked.

She led them through the front office to the main floor of the colossal warehouse.

"The building with the round leaded windows is where we radiate the crystals, creating some of the most beautiful and unique specimens in the world." Spider indicated a large enclosed metal building with small smoked glass portholes sitting on the warehouse floor.

Lester looked at a table not far from the building that held trays of large pink, blue, and green quartz crystals. He and Jake had seen the smoky quartz that had been transformed by radiation, but neither had ever seen anything like the transformation created by Spider's secret method.

"Are they safe to pick up?" Lester asked. He had a large green one in his hand and peered through the clear prism, until Spider could be seen magnified and a nice emerald shade of green.

"They are now. We soak them in a special solution for weeks before we release them."

Slowly, she took the green crystal from Lester's hand, while she let one of her warm hands slide under his. Spider picked up a nearby Geiger counter and flipped the switch. It buzzed and increased in intensity as she held it near a pink crystal. The range on the meter, however, stayed in the safe scale.

"We test them all before they go out, but we haven't sold many yet. We're waiting for the big rock show in Las Vegas to introduce our line of colored crystals."

"Uh—Angel, I understand some people believe these crystals have special properties. Do you think they do?" Lester asked.

"I keep several under my bed at home. Anytime you want to be a part of a scientific study—just come by and mankind will be the better for it," Spider said.

"I love science!" Lester said. He was blushing.

The building with the round smoked-colored windows had yellow radiation symbols plastered on the doors, along with a sign that said, "Authorized Admittance Only. Radiation Hazard."

Spider walked to the door with the sign and opened it for them to look inside. It appeared almost like a doctor's office with x-ray machines, leaded glass, and heavy protective clothing hanging over the low walls. Controls and monitors were located safely outside the rooms. Spider didn't invite them to enter, but didn't seem to make any attempt to stop them. Lester walked into one of the rooms, looked at the large overhead x-ray equipment and turned back to the door, seemingly satisfied with what he saw. He could see all the way to the end of the building and into most of the x-ray rooms, and made mental notes of ceiling and flooring materials. Most of the machines, chairs, and metal tables had wheels.

Spider led the two men out into the massive space of the warehouse which had almost 100,000 square feet of space. The floors were concrete, and one side had about ten piles of yellowish-colored quartz that appeared to be individual dump truck loads. The tire tracks leading out the back door appeared fresh.

The middle of the warehouse consisted of a large washing plant where ore was dumped in from two orange front-end loaders parked in the building. A large conveyer belt carried the quartz crystals and was sprayed with water as it rattled along. It dumped into a large holding tank with drainage hoses that ran out the back of the building into a grated sewer or waste water opening. Five or six employees picked out the specimens and placed them on a sorting table.

On the opposite side of the warehouse from the piles of ore were more sorting tables. At regularly spaced intervals along the warehouse floors, black metal tool boxes stood about five feet tall. These were multi-drawer units designed for auto mechanics. They appeared out of place in this setting.

Lester and Jake walked over to the wash plant and observed workers while they picked a few pieces of quartz from the conveyor belt and took them to the tables for processing. Lester reached in and pulled out a small crystal with two points on it, then placed it back and wiped the mud off his hands under the metal sluice. They walked outside and watched the muddy water flow down into the hole in the ground. They looked at the multi-car garage in the back, but only one door was open, exposing the red Lotus. Except for the two front end loaders, the washing plant, a few sorting tables, and the tool boxes, there wasn't any other equipment in the huge warehouse.

As they turned to walk back to the office, Spider led a tall, long-haired man over to be introduced. "Lester, this is Hunter Hennessey. He manages some of my operations. If you come back in the future, feel free to contact him. All his friends call him 'Stick.'"

"Nice to meet you, Stick," Lester said.

"I believe we've met before, Stick," Jake said. He shook his hand. "Mrs. Gambini, you may not be aware, but Stick here is a war hero.

Silver Star, I believe, for saving his patrol in Afghanistan." Jake was careful not to bring up his arrests for DWI and minor drug charges. All had been expunged by Jake and taken off his record.

"I was aware, Jake. One of the reasons I hired him. He does an excellent job of taking care of my employees," Spider said. She left out Stick's role of taking care of her when she had special needs.

"Angel, we're glad you let us have a tour of your facility. We can better explain now why you have a fence around the property. I hope you do well with your colored crystals in Las Vegas. Feel free to call either of us if you need us," Jake said, and handed Spider and Stick a business card.

"I would like to go riding in that red Lotus you have parked in your garage. My girlfriend wouldn't like it, though," Lester said. "It was good to see you again, Spider. You have an impressive operation here. By the way, have you contacted Vander yet about buying his business? I bet you could get it cheap."

She smiled and patted him on his back. He had just let her know her criminal enterprise was on his radar. "Who is this Vander guy, and what is he about to sell?" Spider displayed a puzzled look.

"Your loss, Spider. I'll be in touch. Thanks again for the tour."

Spider just looked at Lester and smiled again, then waved goodbye as he and Jake drove off. She turned to Stick as they left. "If anything was out of place, he knows it now. Make sure everyone is armed, because they'll be back."

Lester and Sheriff Jake drove out to the highway and parked next to Lester's Yukon.

"My God, Lester, that girl has the hots for you!" Jake said.

"Yeah, and that would be a lovely way to die."

"She isn't mining those large crystals she had on display," Jake said. "It looks like they went up to one of the abandoned mines and threw some ore in a dump truck and deposited in the warehouse for show."

"Did you notice the metal tool boxes that were placed at intervals around the warehouse floor?" Lester asked. "They're covering ventilation tubes from an underground operation."

"That radiation building is the above operation for cooking meth.

Did you see the ventilation pipes on the roof of that building? Ten-to-one those x-ray machines are fake and designed to roll out of there and be pushed to the side," Lester said.

"I saw you place a couple of listening devices. Do you think Spider will find them?" Jake asked.

"I hope nobody finds them. They're flat out illegal and could get my ass in a lot of trouble," Lester said. He got out of Jake's patrol car and climbed into his SUV. "See you soon, Jake. Thanks for letting me tag along."

"Thank you. I'll give Mike my report. Watch your back. Stick is a better shot than me."

"Damn, he must be good," Lester said, and drove his car back onto 270 and headed back to Hot Springs.

On the way, he dialed Debi's cell phone and left her a message. "Deb—on my way back—I'll stop at your favorite wine store in Crystal Springs. How about fried chicken and some chardonnay?"

Lester noticed that the glass from the front door of the bait shop had already been repaired. A part-time clerk who had worked off and on for Joey for years stood behind the counter when he entered.

"I'm Deputy Lester McFarlin," Lester said. "And you are?"

"Bennie Mosley—nice to meet you. Heard 'bout you. Purty famous, I think."

"Not really. How's Joey? I heard he was out of the hospital."

"Much better. Much better. Especially since he sold this place and can retire now in peace," Bennie said.

Lester found a less-cheap bottle of wine from the array of super-cheap wines. He assumed just about any white wine would be okay for Popeye's fried chicken. He took his prize to the counter, handed the clerk a $10 dollar bill and received several dollars back. In passing, he decided to be his normal nosy self.

"Who bought this place?"

"Some guy named Hennessey. He came by yesterday and wants me to stay on. Don't think he will work much. He has another job. Told me he's going to build an extension on the back for a storage room for some of his personal stuff. Didn't say what—I didn't ask."

Lester took his wine, now wrapped in a brown paper sack, and walked to his car. He sat in the front seat and dialed Jake.

"Jake—Lester. Stick just bought the bait store where the shooting took place. He's building a storage room on back. You and I know he couldn't buy an outhouse. It's Spider's, and guess what she'll be storing behind the bait store?"

"Automatic weapons, rocket launchers, and armored personnel carriers if she could get 'em into the storage locker," Jake said.

"Damn—Damn—Damn! Jake, we're going to have a hell of a mess to clean up before you know it. I'm going to call the FBI so they'll know what's about to go down here. We're going to need their help before long."

Lester called Jim Webb and filled him in on all that he had found out. Jim told him to just sit tight. Everything needed to be in place before the takedown. He informed Lester that Vander Usterhoff had flown out of the country, and most likely was going to a place where they didn't have an extradition treaty with the US. Apparently he hadn't been indicted for the shooting, since the call girl wouldn't name him. Lester had to ask Jim a hypothetical question.

"Jim, if I was to sneak into the warehouse at S.G. Crystals and leave a listening device, how much trouble would I be in?"

"To be legal, we'd need a court order and have someone posted for line of sight. But to catch a bunch of asshole drug dealers who are poisoning our kids and one of those alleged devices that might already be placed there by —maybe the CIA or somebody—we could use it, but not make it part of any formal report. Tell me what you think might have been used by some secret part of our government and where they're placed. We will get someone listening to them immediately," Jim said.

"Uh—the CIA may have left one under a table in one of the x-ray rooms and one under the conveyer belt in the sorting room. The secret government agency ran out of devices, or I believe they would have put one in the bait store. Oh, from what I could see, they are standard long-range NSA models. Don't know where the CIA got them," Lester lied.

"Gotta go. Good work today, Lester."

Lester picked up the fried chicken and placed the wine in his freezer when he got home, wanting to cool it quickly. He hoped he didn't forget it and blow the top off his refrigerator. He sat on the couch and waited on Debi to get home and wondered to himself if all of the things going on in Hot Springs would be resolved in one big simultaneous raid. Would the bad guys use all the automatic weapons they had available? How long would the FBI collect information before they did anything? A long time, he bet, since they were a part of the government.

Then, he remembered he had a doctor's appointment with a brain surgeon the next morning at 10:30. Suddenly, he forgot all the criminal activity and focused on this visit to the doctor. The door opened, and Debi stood there, smiling. She ran over, laid down in his lap, looked up and kissed him. Now, there were no thoughts of criminals or brain surgery—just getting Debi into bed. Would it be before fried chicken, after fried chicken, or before the wine exploded in the freezer?

Chapter Fourteen

Lester was early for his appointment at University of Arkansas for Medical Sciences in Little Rock. It took only an hour to drive there from Hot Springs, but he gave himself two hours to be safe. This was an extremely vital appointment for Lester. He contemplated taking Debi with him, but somehow, letting Dr. Steve Arrison examine him alone was important. He had more than an hour before the appointment started, so he filled out as much paperwork as he could, which wasn't much. Debi could have helped with the forms.

Lester began to think about what he had accomplished in his life in spite of his disability. He was a special investigator for the sheriff's department, which limited his duty to the most complex and crucial cases. No longer did he have to work traffic, domestic battery, burglary, drug possession, or home invasion. He was in demand all over the state and known all over the US. Occasionally, he was asked to go out of state to assist. One newspaper called him a "Redneck Sherlock Homes." That write-up made him smile.

Most people had no idea of the time and effort he had invested in his self-education. Very few nights or weekends went by that he wasn't listening to an audio book or typing with his braille typewriter. He had two computers and an iPad. He worked with Dragon Software to convert speech to written words but had no way to check them unless he had someone else do an edit. Sometimes he would dictate reports into Dragon and print them, but there were always many errors, which made the police report unusable in a court of law. For a while, he had used a dictation machine and paid for a transcriber to reproduce the reports. It was expensive and generally required an extra employee, which the Sheriff's department couldn't afford. So Lester had worked out a deal with Little Richard to type abbreviated reports from Lester's small tape recorder. Rich got a very short statement from Lester and typed it for him. This method seemed to satisfy Sheriff Adams since it didn't cost him anything, and it was accurate enough to take to court. Little Richard practically worked for Lester anyway since he had sought out the job to learn from the master.

Lester felt his biggest accomplishment so far was his relationship with Debi. How could a poor boy from Mountain Pine, Arkansas who barely finished high school and had a job as a lowly deputy at a small town sheriff's office be in a relationship with a really classy girl whose dad was a doctor and whose mom was a sorority sister from the University of Arkansas? Deep down, Lester didn't believe he could keep Debi unless he was able to correct this deficiency in his brain. If Dr. Arrison told him he needed to remove his head and vacuum it out before he reattached it, Lester would have said, "Let's get started." While contemplating that thought, he heard his name called and was led into an examining room.

The room had an x-ray reading monitor on the wall and unusually comfortable chairs for a doctor's office. The nurse sat next to him and started asking him the questions that had been left off his questionnaire, which were most of them, except for Lester's on-another-planet signature. Satisfied that she had his complete history, she weighed him and took his blood pressure. He asked about it, and she told him 223 lbs. and 117/78.

"Is that okay?" he asked.

"Perfect," the young nurse said as she smiled and made eye contact. She had a slight accent and was exotically attractive. Maybe she was Spanish or Egyptian.

"Where you from?"

"I'm Palestinian."

"Isn't the King of Jordan's wife, Rania, Palestinian? At least her parents were Palestinian even though she was born in Kuwait. She is very pretty, as you are."

"Thanks, but how would you know that?" the nurse asked, her mouth open at full gape, and the tone of her voice approaching condescending.

"Ma'am, I'm not stupid."

"Mr. McFarlin, not a handful of college-educated people in this state would know that. I thought you had a learning disability?"

"You have no idea how many audiotapes I listen to, and pretty women are sort of a hobby."

"You're amazing, Mr. McFarlin! Is Rania the queen of Jordan?"

"She's the queen consort, as Queen Noor is still alive and has the title 'the Queen Dowager.' Queen Noor, however, can't be called the Queen Mother since she is the stepmother of King Abdullah II."

"You really are amazing!" the nurse again exclaimed.

"The doctor will be here shortly. It was truly nice to meet you. And thanks again for the compliment." She left the room, shaking her head.

As she walked down the hall, she met the doctor heading toward the exam room. She stopped him and told him what Lester had said about Jordan's rulers.

"This guy is some kind of savant. To not have the ability to read, he has learned more than most people will in a lifetime!" she said excitedly.

"I'll try not to screw him up," Dr. Arrison said with a grin. He pulled the files from the receptacle outside the exam room and looked over them for a minute before he entered.

"Lester, I'm Steve Arrison. I'm a neurosurgeon, but wonder sometimes if I wouldn't have had more fun as a gynecologist," he said laughing, and Lester joined him to lighten the mood. "It's a pleasure to meet the famous policeman I read about in the paper. The *Democrat-Gazette* did a profile on you a couple years ago, and I became a fan back then." The doctor shook Lester's hand and sat down in a chair next to him, hoping to make him comfortable.

"They called me the 'Redneck Sherlock Homes,' which I thought was really funny. I think the unique nature of my type of dyslexia allows me to see crime scenes from a front and backwards perspective. So it could be I'm a little more thorough than some other investigators. But most of the success is from doing the work most cops won't take on. Also, I've studied some of the truly great detectives, such as

Pollaky, Lees, and Allan Pinkerton. And I've followed the work of J.J. Armes, who also had a disability that required him to use metal claws for hands."

"What is amazing for me, Lester, is the ingenious ways you have accessed this knowledge without the ability to read. Tell me why you want to read when you seem to have exceeded most folks' educational experiences with your unique methods."

"Doc, most educational opportunities at the advanced level are traditional brick and mortar universities. Helen Keller did something during her time that made her a superwoman hero for me. My disability is a minor stumped toe compared to what she had to overcome. However, today the blind schools' approach to advanced degrees is limited. I would like to attend law school, where I can take part in mock trials and have the law books at my fingertips, or online as I understand they are now. I guess the word 'normal' is what I'm grasping for," Lester said, with some emotion.

"Lester, let's talk about what is most likely scar tissue on your brain, the operation, and possible results. When you were injured as a result of a car accident twenty-one years ago there was a violent blow to your head. There was trauma and bleeding above the area of the brain that affects language skills. Three years before that, you had a severe ear infection that caused hearing loss on that same side of your head as the blow. It was the perfect storm for a severe learning disability, but since you had been blessed from birth with superior intelligence, you kept finding ways to learn outside normal channels available to most people." The doctor opened a large file that had been sent to him by one of Lester's childhood doctors, who was listed in the original file generated by Debi. He had requested those files, which had followed Lester around from doctor to doctor, but Lester wasn't aware of their contents.

"I know your mother, Lilly, was a school teacher, but doing a little research on her school history, which was part of your medical records, I see she was a member of MENSA and had a genius level IQ. Your dad, Adrian, apparently has a normal intelligence level but rarely got to attend class because his parents were so poor. Do you remember your mother?"

"I do, but sometimes think that I am manufacturing the memory from the few pictures I have of her. My dad has filled me in as well as to what happened with the accident. This information about her being a genius is new to me. People have always said how smart she was—my aunt and uncle, especially. She went to college when she was fifteen and got a BS degree in two years—I did know that from my aunt. I remember very little about the car crash since I was knocked out. I'm glad that I don't have to recall my mother being killed."

"Apparently you inherited some of your mother's superior intelligence, so re-learning or learning from scratch possibly won't be too difficult or take that long. I kind of think you would enjoy the process. I've met Dr. Green's daughter, and from what Marty says, she wants to help you. In my opinion, an outside teacher might keep you on task better during the language and reading process. However, since there is no record of an operation of this nature, we need to talk about it." The doctor got up from his chair and walked to the backlighted x-ray board, slid in a colored transparent piece of film, and flipped on the light.

"Here is your scar tissue." He showed Lester a dark mass on the right frontal lobe of his brain.

"It isn't just lying there where it can be picked up with forceps and removed. It is interwoven into that part of your brain that recognizes symbols and even some speech patterns. I'll have to cut some tissue below it in order to remove it. So, let's talk about risk and reward. Do you have any questions at this point?"

"Doc, in your experience do these scar tissue cases extend very deep into the brain?"

"Not usually. In most cases I'm able to remove them and merely scape off a few millimeters of tissue to get the residual scar."

"Okay. Let's talk about the good, bad, and the ugly," Lester said.

"The brain bleeds when you cut into it," Dr. Arrison explained "In your case, it should be minimal, but the operation will require a shunt tube for a few days to remove the blood and avoid a clot forming. Because of the location of your scar tissue we can go through the sinus cavity without drilling a hole in your skull. This makes the operation less invasive and normally results in less bleeding and a faster recovery time.

"You'll be in bed here for a couple-three days and will have light duty for a couple of weeks. After that you can resume normal duties except no long flights or scuba diving for a few months. Avoid fist fights—use your gun instead," Doctor Arrison laughed.

"Doc, if you were to guess a post-operative prognosis what do you see?"

"As soon as you come out of the anesthesia, most likely there will be some confusion and maybe some memory loss. Gradually you will be able to use that part of your brain from a normal perspective or left-to-right viewing angle. Letters won't mean much to you until you see them lined up correctly for a change. Before, as I understand it, the words from written script enter your brain and were scrambled because of the scar tissue interfering. Now you shouldn't have the interference, but you may have the memory of the way you viewed letters and words before. It's going to be a lot of work to re-learn it all, but you will still have the superior intellect to get through it all. Your post-operative pain will be headaches and soreness from having stuff crammed up your sinus cavity. There are no guarantees and plenty of risks—excessive bleeding, blood clots, stroke, and death. Any more questions?"

"Can you do it on a Friday so Debi won't miss so much work? I think my dad can stay a few days as well, if he's needed."

"Yes, I can do it on a Friday. If we get lucky, you might be discharged on Sunday or Monday. You would be off work, though, for a couple of weeks, letting the brain heal. Do you think the criminals will take over the world by then, Lester?"

"Good chance they already have. I'll see how many of them I can shoot before then so we'll be ahead of the game. Do I schedule with your front desk?"

"Yes, and you won't able to eat or drink anything after midnight the day before," Dr. Arrison said.

"It was great to meet you," he continued. "Of course, as I have already said, there are no guarantees with this operation, and there are always risks with surgery. Someone will need to read the consent form to you before you sign it. I'll do my best to fix your problem, Lester."

The doctor walked out with him and directed him to the front desk, where he found the pretty Palestinian girl waiting to help him.

"My name is Sari, by the way," she said. "Mr. McFarlin, do you have a day that you wish to schedule your surgery?"

"Next Friday, if that's possible?" He looked directly in her dark brown eyes and smiled. Sari smiled back. Then he used the line he always used when he met pretty girls.

"I guess a pretty girl like you is already married?"

"Engaged."

"To a doctor, I bet. It's hard to compete with them."

"Yes, to a young resident. You, sir, are a flirt, and I know you have a beautiful girlfriend in Hot Springs."

"I never know when she's going to run me off, so I have to keep making friends."

She smiled and slapped him on the arm. Lester thought about her dark body and how exotic she would look naked. He couldn't help himself. He was a guy, and that's just the way he was wired.

"You will be the first surgery of the day on Friday, which means you need to be here at 5:30 a.m. Let me see: I have your group coverage through the sheriff's department. The hospital will hit you up for the deductible later on. Whoever brings you in on Friday needs to read the consent form to you. They will ask if you have a living will.

"I hope things go well for you, and we'll see you Friday morning."

"Will you be there to hold my hand during the surgery?"

"Sorry, I'll be in bed with my boyfriend, but thanks for thinking about me."

Lester turned and waved goodbye to Sari and went to his car. He sat there for a while and contemplated the scope and importance of this operation. He knew it would be worth it to take a few steps backward in order to move forward with his life.

Calls had to be made, starting with his dad. Normally he wouldn't be able to call until after five since his dad didn't have a cell phone. Lester had bought several of them for him, but he either lost them or crushed them in some type of work accident. The truth was that he didn't like them. If people needed him they could call him at night when he got home from work.

He decided to call Debi first, but before he could dial her number, his phone rang. It was her.

"Lester—babe—what did he say?"

"He'll do it. I'll be in the hospital about three days—then off work for two weeks—no fighting—scuba diving—airplanes rides— for a couple months. Sex is okay if you do all the work. Early Friday morning. Can you take me and stay with me? I'm sure my dad can come relieve you," Lester said. His excitement was evident in the rapid way he spoke.

"Sure, I'll be there. I'll move two appointments to next week. What did he think the results would be?"

"I'll be confused for a while and may not recognize people but should be able to learn normally after a while. He doesn't really know since he's never had a case like this."

"You coming home?'

"Yeah. Hey, we need to take my dad out to eat this week so you don't have to meet him for the first time in the hospital. He likes barbecue so we can meet at Stubby's, if that's all right?" Lester said.

"Okay. Today or tomorrow night?" Debi asked.

"I'll see if he can do it late this afternoon. I think his new job ends early. Do you have anything planned?"

"Oh, yes! But we can do it later after you get home. I want to make sure I get everything out of you before they start messing with your brain. You might not like me afterwards. Maybe you'll be attracted to fat black women or skinny Chinese women. Who knows? An inch cut there and it's heavy Hawaiian women. A slight cut a half-inch to the left and only blondes will satisfy you," she laughed.

"I already like blondes, Chinese, and black women, especially ones with big asses. A dark-headed, brown-eyed Greek woman just happened to show up in the nick of time. I'll call you after I talk to Dad and let you know about dinner. I have a get-acquainted interview with Mrs. Sydney Carter before I come home. You set it up for me, remember?"

"Yes, I do. Tell her I said 'hi' and be nice to her. Oh, I have a 5:30. Can we be done by then?"

"I think so. I'll call you."

Lester hung up and drove to his new speech therapist's office, which was only a few blocks away. Mrs. Carter was very professional, reviewed his file, and set up an appointment to see him after the operation. She didn't ask why Debi had dumped him but probably had figured it out the minute she saw him. Sydney was still very trim and attractive at sixty. If Lester had any desire for an older woman, she would do nicely.

Lester drove towards Hot Springs, ready to call his dad as soon as he arrived home. He decided he might pick him up and drive him to Stubby's since there were some things he needed to talk to him about in case this operation went badly. Lester didn't want him to worry, but a man-to-man talk needed to happen, and Debi didn't need to hear it.

Chapter Fifteen

Lester remembered that his dad had taken a new job with a construction company that let him off at 3:30. It was ten to four so he tried him.

"Dad, how you doing?"

"Well, hell, I can't get no better than I am. Saw on the news you had a big shoot 'em up at the bait store. I'm mighty glad ol' Jody weren't no more hurt than he was. He's a good friend and gave me a good deal on spinner baits for stripers the last time I was in."

"Are you coming by?"

"That I am, and I'm taking you to Stubby's for ribs. You're going to meet Debi. Might up and marry her someday. I'll be by in a few minutes."

"All right then. I'll put on a clean shirt and britches. Might even comb my hair. Want me to bring a date?"

"God, no! Dad, let's keep this simple until you get to know Debi." Lester knew most of his dad's girlfriends were picked up at Boot Scooters night club and were of dubious character.

Lester loved his dad, but knew he was a product of a very poor family who never placed much time or effort into formal education. He guessed his dad saw the quality of both education and beauty when he married a very pretty young flaxen-haired school teacher named Lil. Adrian hoped she might help refine him, but she didn't live long enough to cause the transformation.

Lester got some of his looks from his dad, who was tall and ruggedly handsome, and his softer looks and blond hair from his mom. His dad always walked with the certain assurance of a man who wouldn't back down from a fight and who maybe owned property or had money. He had little of either.

Adrian did own a small house in Mt. Pine, and it was paid for. He had received a settlement check from the wreck and paid off his house and a few bills with it. Also, he had enough money after paying off the house to buy a nicely-equipped fishing boat with outriggers. At the time, he wasn't aware Lester was going to have issues learning to read or he might have held off on the boat. The fancy fishing boat wasn't just for fun, as he was a professional fishing guide on weekends or whenever he could break away to do it. Mainly, he went after the big stripers that sometimes weighed over thirty pounds. This species of fish had acclimated from salt water to fresh water. Many people hated the stripers because they ate the bass and trout hatchlings placed in the water by the game and fish department. Adrian loved them and the $300 to $1000 a week he could make during the season, guiding a bunch of first-timers or even experienced fishermen.

When the mill closed down, his money earned as a guide kept him going. He mainly got clients from referrals but did print cards and a brochure. Once, after a particularly good season, he bought billboard space on Highway 270 going towards Lake Ouachita. He got a few clients from it, but primarily it expanded his pick-up ratio at Boot Scooters. He told Lester that he found higher-class women at "The Electric Cowboy" in Little Rock. When the time came for Adrian to bring a date to a function, Lester hoped the Little Rock club would furnish his dad with a woman that would embarrass his son just a little less.

Lester pulled up in the driveway of his dad's small white frame house and saw his Z71 Chevy truck parked under the carport. It was freshly washed and fell in line with the mowed and trimmed yard and well-maintained house. Adrian was always neat in appearance, and everything around him that he controlled was clean, combed, pressed and creased in all the proper places. He had been in the Marines as a young man, and their brand of discipline had been indelibly stamped on his psyche.

The front door opened and Adrian stepped out onto the porch and locked the door behind him. He climbed into Lester's SUV and extended a hand to his son.

"You okay? Something must be up for you to drag me out at short notice to meet your new girlfriend."

"Dad, I'll lay it out. I'm going in Friday to have some scar tissue removed from my brain. Got it from the wreck and they believe it caused my learning problems. I hope you can come to the hospital over the weekend to give Debi a rest. Dr. Arrison thinks he can get it without drilling in my skull, so a shunt will only be in for a couple of days. You okay with that?" Lester said. His dad knew there was more.

"You worried about something, son?"

"Don't know the outcome. Might be really retarded or a zombie or just stupid for a while. I think I will have to re-learn everything I know, but if it works I can learn to read like everyone else, then I'll be able to go to college and possibly law school—maybe make some real money. I just wanted you to know that if I'm really fucked up afterwards, then put me in a home somewhere and tell Debi to go on about her life," Lester said nervously.

"I doubt that's gonna happen, but if it does and you're a vegetable, I'll take ya to the best vegetable home around," Adrian said with a laugh.

After that, Lester and his dad mainly talked about fishing and other relatives that were still around but needed their statuses updated. They explored Debi's background, and Adrian had some questions about her parents, which Lester assumed meant he was speculating on how well he would be accepted.

"Sounds like they're good people."

"Her dad is really easy going, even if he's a doctor. Her mom doesn't like that I'm a cop. I brought a rosebush as a peace offering. She seemed to warm up."

"Think if I offer her a fish she'll like me?" Adrian asked.

"When we get to know them, we'll invite them on a striper trip. Her dad, Tom, is a big duck hunter, so in any case, he would enjoy it. Debi shoots trap so at least she does some gun stuff."

As they pulled up at Stubby's, they saw Debi parking her BMW. Adrian got out first and introduced himself to Debi. She shook his hand and stared at his face for a minute.

"Damn, you're as handsome as Lester," she said, shaking his hand with both of hers. "I'm not real sure which one of you to take home."

"He said you were a good lookin' young lady, but he really needs to do a better job of describing." Adrian chuckled and gave her a little hug.

"Dad, she's taken, so don't flirt with her."

They went through the line with their trays, picking up ribs, deviled eggs, and coleslaw. Debi wanted a fried peach pie, and as usual, Lester got a barbecue salad, which consisted of lettuce with chopped pork on the top, which they made especially for Lester since it wasn't on the menu. They chose a table nestled under a collection of license plates nailed on the wall.

"Dad and Deb, I just wanted you two to meet each other before the surgery. I will go in early Friday and hopefully by noon you should know if there are any issues. I truly don't expect any as it's a straightforward operation." He paused and left out the part where he could die.

"The aftermath is the big question, and how I will go about relearning everything. Debi has a good friend in Hot Springs that teaches second grade who's agreed to help. She's going to come by in the evenings to give me my lessons. Debi will help test me. I hope after I relearn the basics, I can take off from there."

"Sounds good, son. I'll be there Friday morning with Debi."

"Look at these ribs and how much meat is on them!" Adrian said as he took a large bite out of the center of a particularly large rib with pink meat over an inch thick.

"I'm taking most of mine home for later," Debi said. She looked at Lester. "Do you want me to drive you over on Friday?"

"Yeah—please. You know I've never had surgery. Is there something I should know or worry about? I've heard people wake up during operations. I hope that doesn't happen."

"Just tell the doctor hi. It'll scare the shit out of him and he'll knock you out again," Debi said, getting a laugh from both men.

"Everything will be fine, son. I'm going to guess this Dr. Arrison is one of the best in the state. I think he wants to be known for fixing the famous Lester McFarlin."

"He's one of the best in the nation," Lester said.

"I've got to run by and talk to the sheriff after I take you home, Dad. Are you ready to roll?"

"Yepsir. I'm taking a bunch of these ribs home, too," Adrian replied as they all got up to leave.

Lester kissed Debi and told her he would see her after work since she had one more late appointment. She had moved in with him for the most part, and he had seen his closet space diminish daily. Frightening objects like tampons and makeup now occupied space that he had left bare for no real reason except neatness.

Lester returned from taking his dad home to Mt. Pine and knew everyone in the office was working late. It wasn't by choice since the coordination of all the task forces was eating up normal working schedules. He knocked on Sheriff Mike Adams' door and didn't wait for an answer. He could see through the glass door that he was alone.

"Mike, they're going to remove my brain on Friday. Since I wasn't using it much, there might not be much change afterwards. My recovery will depend on how quickly I relearn the entire English language," Lester said, trying to make his operation seem insignificant.

"What the fuck! I didn't know you were planning this so soon. Please explain why you're doing this in the middle of the biggest organized crime take down in world history! Do you fucking notice everyone working late?" Sheriff Mike was clearly not in the loop concerning timing for the operation but did know about the scar tissue, the MRI, and the visit with the surgeon.

"Not a problem. Jim is setting up wiretaps and surveillance around the S.G. Crystal shop and the bait store. Also, they're trying to find out about the call girl business, and although I volunteered to test the quality of the ladies, they turned me down. The FBI is never going to get in a hurry when it's possible to collect enough information to fill a small library. I hope to be well enough to go with Little Richard to New Orleans in about a week to pick up our machine pistol. He can take Becca and I'll take Debi to appear to Tony's group that we're normal people. So really it is a perfect time to have my brain vacuumed and cleaned."

"Jesus H. Christ! I didn't okay any trip for a brainless investigator and his group of party animals to go to New Orleans. I need to think about this and see if we can afford it."

"Remember the new money you have. Oh, we need thirty-three hundred to buy the Mac-11," Lester said, with a huge smile.

"Get the fuck out of here. I'll contact the ATF people to see if they have any money so we don't use all of our new slush fund. And you don't know if they'll put your brain back in right side up, so we'll see how you're recovering."

Mike then calmed down a bit. "Lester, is there anything I can do for you during your recovery?" There was actually concern in his voice.

"No, just stay in touch with Jim Webb and Jake."

Next, Lester stopped by to talk to Rich and Becca about the trip. They were ready and said they would set up the hotels once they found out how he had survived the operation. Lester agreed to take his car since he wasn't allowed to fly. Rich would drive.

* * *

Lester decided to go to church before his operation. He was concerned, but not to the point of being scared. He loved his life now and wanted the part that included Debi to be the same after Friday. He called her late in the afternoon.

"I'm going to church. Want to go with me?" Lester said.

"If you can wait an hour, I'll go with you. Do I need to dress up?"

"No, it's not that kind of church. It's just a place that feels religious to me."

After picking her up at her clinic, they drove towards Kirby.

"Lester, tell me more about your church."

"Listen, Debi, I don't you want you to think I'm weirder than you already do. It's just a little cafe where you can feel the whole world—or at least I do. I just sit where I can listen to a lot of conversations at once. I somehow feel the spirit of Arkansas and America by just listening. We'll order coffee or tea but no food. We're not there to eat but to listen and meditate quietly. We won't stay long, but maybe it will calm me before the operation," Lester said, hoping Debi didn't have him committed to Happy Hills Mental Farm as soon as they got back.

"Lester, I mean this in the sincerest way—you are fucking nuts!" she said, giggling and shaking her head.

"Hey, it's no different than so many people who go to church and don't believe any of the tenets or the existence of a God, but go through the motions so their kids learn what the church considers right and wrong."

"I agree many people don't take it seriously but feel better that they showed up in church, hoping something spiritual has washed over them after the sermon," Debi said.

"I don't expect you to get as much out of this experience as I do, but I care deeply for you and wanted you to understand why I go there for my mental readjustments."

"I promise to behave myself and take it all in as best as I can. You're still fucking nuts."

In less than an hour they found a parking place in the limited space next to the modern yellow brick cafe. It wasn't fully packed yet as it was only five o'clock, and the work crowd hadn't all arrived. Lester and Debi entered the cafe and were greeted by Sherry, who recognized Lester. She took him to one of his favorite perches close to other tables and next to the long window which extended the length of the building. Lester ordered coffee and Debi had a sweet tea, something she rarely drank, but decided to get wild since this was going to be a new adventure.

Once seated, Lester listened around him and tried to separate the noise from the kitchen and the softer tones of conversations at tables near him. It was important to hear discussions from servers and cashiers as well, as they were all a part of the big picture. He always sat so his good right ear would compensate for the partial deafness on the left. After a few seconds a conversation among a group of men at a nearby table began to float through the air and pierced a hole in the extraneous sounds surrounding it. They all worked for a construction company, building houses.

One man was doing most of the talking. "I should have fired Travis years ago, but since I was responsible for getting him sober, I just couldn't let him go. He would show up for work spitting up blood— probably crapping it out, too. Had a bleeding ulcer and couldn't keep food down— and drank like a fish. I offered to take him to AA—told him he had to quit drinking or I couldn't keep him on the job, and he was probably going to die. He had a two-year-old boy he was helping take care of for his daughter. He said he would quit on his own. I told him it was too hard to do on his own. Here's what he told me: 'I was on meth real bad four years ago—just stopped and never had it anymore. I'll do the same thing with the liquor.'

"And by God, he did. Kept him on to this day, but he ain't the best hand I have. He's good at installing microwaves—can do it in twenty minutes. It'd take José two hours to put one in. Travis done it so much he knows right where to drill all the holes. Travis is good at laying tile, but I wouldn't let him touch framing. Just can't figure it out, so we always put him on something else. He's so little that you'd think he can't carry boards. He does it ok. Probably weighs about the same as my wife...'round 130, maybe 135. Wiry and all muscle, though. Came to work one day with one eye completely shut and the other black and blue. Said he got beat up cause he took out another man's wife. Then he said, 'You should've seen the other guy!'" The entire group roared.

"He's the guy you want in a foxhole with ya," he continued. "Doesn't back down to nobody—fearless, stubborn, and loyal."

Debi was concentrating on the conversation of two women at another table. One was a mother who was concerned her daughter was falling hard for a loser, and she didn't know what to do. The guy didn't have a job and was behind on his pickup payments. Her daughter was giving him money, and the boy just smoked pot and drank beer. The boy's dad was in jail for drug charges, and it appeared the son wasn't far behind him. She was afraid if she complained too much she would lose her daughter.

The two church-goers drank their coffee and tea, listened to the surrounding conversations and finally took in an exchange between two waitresses.

"Sherry, I got a birthday party Saturday for Evan. Can you work for me then—I'll owe you?"

"I can cover you until about six, Taylor, and then I'm going out with Donny. Can you finish the party by then?" Sherry asked.

"Guess I'll have to," Taylor said as she handed Lester the meal check.

Lester paid the bill and left a nice tip on the table. Outside, they got into the SUV and just sat there a minute.

"I get it, Lester!" Debi said. "You listen to people and how they go through life, then use it much like a sermon to learn good and bad from their examples. Yes?"

"That's part of it, of course, yet it is life going on—it keeps going on all around you. In that one space, the whole world comes together to teach you that people survive and dance and cry and laugh through heaven and hell every day to show up at the Kirby Cafe—then confess it all."

"Holy shit, Lester...there's a very deep side to you. Keep it up and you'll be a poet someday. Thanks for taking me to your church. How do you feel?"

"At peace, my dear—at peace."

Chapter Sixteen

A construction crew from Louisiana arrived at the bait store at the same time that a local lighting and fixture company pulled up to the side of the building. Stick was there to give instructions.

"Want a three-color neon sign—little larger than the sign is now. Maybe yellow-blue-red. Is that a good color combo?" Stick asked in the direction of a young kid who probably didn't know the roygbiv concept and most likely flunked art class.

"Lot of people doing purple, gold, and red," he said, trying to push out as much color information as he had stored in his nineteen-year-old brain.

"Fucking LSU colors with Razorback red thrown in! The bitch'll love it. Do those and get 'em made fast. Can you make the neon and install it by Monday?"

"No problem! Still want it 'Beer, Bait, and Ammo,' in that order?"

"Yes, let's leave it in the order it has been for 50 fucking years—we don't want to confuse our customers. Holy shit!" Stick stomped around to the back of the store, shaking his head and began barking out instructions to the construction crew.

* * *

The University of Arkansas for Medical Sciences was quiet at six o'clock in the morning. It seemed as though people and things moved slowly but with purpose and authority. A nurse met with Lester, having him sign a release and living will after Debi read them to him. The living will was the "vegetable form" that spelled out the pulling-of-the-plug process if your mind resembled an old head of cabbage after the operation. The nurse led them to a room where he was asked to put on a hospital gown. Lester's dad was not due there for a couple of hours since he wanted to come to the recovery room and relieve Debi for a while. Lester came out of the bathroom wearing a gown that looked two sizes too small for his big frame. Debi helped him tie it behind him and couldn't resist pinching his ass. He lay down on the hospital bed, trying not to show too much of his naked body to the nurse. More nurses arrived and hooked up an IV and EKG.

Lester had a few memories of the last time he was in the hospital; some were flashes of having tubes down his throat, then the news about his mom. He learned his mother had died by overhearing nurses talk while they thought he was asleep. He was only five at the time and started crying when they said he was the little boy whose mother was killed in a car wreck. Lester had been in a Hot Springs hospital for a short time, then moved to Arkansas Children's Hospital in Little Rock for several weeks. There was swelling on his brain back then, but they chose not to put in a shunt. It was decided to let it recede slowly, as it did after several weeks. He went home to a house without a mother, with a grieving father, and with a mind that didn't work right. Lester had survived and knew he could get through this.

More nurses and orderlies swarmed into the room, hooking up wires, putting a yellow substance around and up his nose, injecting something into the port on his IV. All were trying a little too hard to be jovial. They asked if he was ready for surgery and he groggily said yes. Debi ran over and kissed him, telling him everything would be fine and she loved him. He tried to respond but was drifting into drug land. He watched the sprinkler system and the ceiling tiles go by as they rushed him to the operating room. Still slightly awake, he noticed how bitter cold and metallic it was in the operating room. Lester felt as though he were going to have surgery in a refrigerator. They pulled his rolling bed next to what appeared to be a long thin metal slab. Several nurses and attendants slid him over on the narrow table, and a man in a plastic tent moved near him. It briefly reminded him of the ET movie. There were voices all around him and warm blankets were placed under him and on top of him. The man in the tent was moving above his head, and a peaceful darkness came over him. He felt nothing as an endotracheal tube was pushed down his throat.

* * *

Becca Valdez decided to enter the law enforcement field partly because she had been raped at age thirteen by a kindly, yet perverted, uncle—not just once, but on a recurring basis for three years. She was too scared and ashamed to tell her parents, and this man was family. He had been a favorite uncle, and she loved him as one would normally love a family member. He never threatened her or struck her, but to say he never harmed her would be a stretch. The uncle lived close by and would invite her to his home. She did what was expected of her, never complaining or resisting. She knew it was wrong but was too naïve to assess the magnitude of what was happening. Strange as it might seem, the experience was exciting at some level, getting to explore sex at such a young age.

Her uncle was a brand of sexual predator who used popular sexual culture Becca was exposed to from movies, TV, and the magazine rack as a way to make her feel good about the encounters. Her teenaged friends were talking about sex, but she was doing it. Knowing she was beyond curious, he used a kind approach, always making sure to be gentle so she would enjoy it. It wasn't until she was sixteen and told one of her girlfriends about the sexual activity that the shit hit the fan. The friend demanded Becca tell her mom. Her mother, Maria Valdez, now informed, put her Latino temper in overdrive, marched over to see the uncle, her husband's brother, and shot him between the eyes with a .357 magnum. She went to jail, and Becca's life changed forever.

After high school and a couple years at National Park Community College, she decided to go to the police academy. Women were always needed to handle women offenders, doing pat downs, looking after them in jail, and of course doing everything the men do in the normal line of duty. Becca took several computer courses in college as she wavered between being an internet technician or a cop. Those technical skills made her very popular at the sheriff's office, where she found herself in a sea of computer stupidity. When research was needed, she was the go-to girl.

When a guy needed a good time date, she was also the girl. It wasn't clear if the early sexual activity led to her promiscuity, but she certainly had a leg up, so to speak, in experience. She enjoyed men a little too much. She had not been able to maintain long-term relationships with men, primarily because she just didn't take romance seriously. Becca's experience with her uncle had twisted sex and love into a knot.

The real shame was that she was only twenty-three years old, smart, very pretty with looks just shy of J. Lo and Eva Mendes and a sizzling hot body. In spite of her formidable issues, she always expressed a bubbly, outgoing personality, which won her many friends—primarily men. Lester and Little Richard had both taken her out in the past, and neither was in a hurry to go out with her again since there was no chase—only the catch. "Too damn aggressive," both had said afterwards. Nevertheless, she still tried to get them back in bed, but with only sporadic success—except when horniness overwhelmed the two men.

When Rich approached her with the possibility of joining him and Lester on a trip to New Orleans to bust some gunrunners, she was thumbs up for the trip. After learning that Debi was going, she knew Little Richard would be the focus of her efforts.

* * *

Debi and Adrian sat next to each other in the surgery waiting room. Lester's dad had arrived about an hour after his son went in for surgery. They were waiting for the doctor to emerge and give them an update on the operation.

"I know you have to work some next week, Debi. Would you like for me to stay with him for a while during the day?"

"Adrian, I've moved all my appointments to be over at about 1 or 2 in the afternoon. I'll stay with him after that until the next morning. We have an ugly nurse lined up for any morning that I need her, but can use you anytime you are free in the mornings. I don't want you to lose work, though."

"I just hope that ugly nurse does the trick. What if she's giving him a bath in his apartment and he forgets what ugly looks like? Of course, it would be a short affair because when he sees you he'll know the difference." They both laughed.

After reading all the *Good Housekeeping* and *Southern Living* magazines for almost an hour, the couple noticed a tall doctor walking towards them. He was a distinguished looking man wearing blue scrubs. Dr. Arrison had met Debi briefly before the operation, and he headed directly to her. He was smiling, and his mask was hanging by strings under his bearded chin.

"The operation went fine, and Lester will be in recovery for a while. The scar tissue was a little deeper than I thought it would be, but on the positive side it finally came loose from the brain without much, if any, residual scar tissue embedded. Also, there was very little bleeding, so the shunt can come out tomorrow afternoon if there continues to be no blood loss. Because of the depth of the invading anomaly there may be some short-term memory loss—that is, memory loss that he will regain in time. He may not know you at first, so give him time.

"After he heals, I would expect no less than a period of rapid learning and relearning. There's no longer a barrier in front of his brain that blocks word and symbol recognition. With his IQ and people to help him, the world is his oyster.

"I'll give you some prescriptions when he checks out for his brain swelling, a blood thinner for clot prevention, and some pain medication. He will have headaches and sinus soreness for a few days. No flying or lifting for thirty days. He can drive in about a week or ten days, but I need to see him first. Make an appointment to see me in a week. He did great."

Adrian thanked him and shook his hand. Debi hugged him and kissed him on the cheek and thanked him profusely. They were told to go to the recovery waiting room and later he would be assigned a room. The recovery room had a few hunting and fishing magazines, so Adrian was thrilled. After a short time, they were ushered in to a room segregating patients with curtains pulled in a circle. The two took opposite sides of his bed and saw that his eyes were open.

"Lester, it's your dad. Do you recognize me?"

Lester looked up with a puzzled expression, but said nothing.

Debi leaned over and kissed his cheek lightly. "Babe, it's Debi. Remember me?"

Lester looked up and smiled. "You're beautiful. Is a pretty girl like you married? Are we married?" His "break the ice" and pickup line hadn't been carved out during the procedure, but his memory was not yet in place.

"No, we're not married, but we are seeing each other a lot," Debi said. She didn't really want to say any more because she wanted the memory to come back on its own and not be planted there by her.

Tears came to her eyes, and Adrian moved to the other side of the bed and hugged her and assured her that his memory would come back. Debi wondered if he was turned loose before he got his memory back, would he likely take up with the first pretty girl that came along. She felt the need to hang close to him.

The hospital stay was uneventful as Lester continued to recover physically. He had a few headaches and some pain from the sinus entry point. People came by from Hot Springs to visit but were told before they came in that they needed to introduce themselves and explain where they worked and how they knew him. Jim Webb came by but didn't talk about the case on which they were jointly working.

Little Richard and Becca came by and talked about going to New Orleans in a couple of weeks. Lester said it should be fun but had no idea about the purpose of the trip or who they were. Mike Adams came by for a minute to visit and asked Debi how she was going to reeducate him. She explained she was starting with a series of children's ABC videos and then he would have classes with a second grade teacher.

"Once he catches on and his brain is healed, he should learn at lightning speed. There will be no stopping him. I just hope his taste in women doesn't change," Debi said.

"Hey, I hear he thought you were beautiful. You'll be fine!" Mike said.

After Mike left, a reporter for the *Hot Springs Sentinel Record* came by and took a picture of Lester. She got some basic details but steered clear of any medical information that would have violated a privacy rule or might have embarrassed Lester if it were released to the public.

On Sunday afternoon he was released from the UAMS Hospital in Little Rock, and Debi drove him to his apartment in Hot Springs. He had learned, or relearned, some facts about her by the time he was home because he asked questions. She didn't say much about their relationship. He could walk okay but was dizzy if he got up quickly and not totally stable when he walked, so Debi got him a three-pronged cane to keep him from falling, which would be extremely dangerous.

His healing was progressing and there were some signs part of his memory was returning by Tuesday morning. He got a disturbing call from Debi. Her brother Ray had been seriously injured in a car wreck in Walnut Creek, California. He was in ICU with internal injuries and was given a 50/50 chance of surviving. Debi was going out immediately with her parents and would be back as soon as he had been stabilized. Lester wished her well and said he could do fine without her and not to worry about him.

Before leaving town, Debi called as many people as she could to alert them to take care of Lester. The special nurse was not immediately available, but could come in a couple days. Lester's dad said he could come by Wednesday as he had to work late on Tuesday. Little Richard would be on call if he needed anything and would let the sheriff's office know. Her last call before getting on the plane was to Lester, who still didn't realize the significance of their relationship or the attention he was getting from this pretty lady. She apologized for leaving him, and Lester expressed concern for her brother. Then inexplicably, he expressed his confidence in the medical community in Northern California and in particular the John Muir Trauma Unit in Walnut Creek. He wondered to himself how he knew anything about that subject. More and more he was finding out that he knew things but couldn't explain where the knowledge came from. Debi stared at the phone after he hung up. *"How in the hell did he know something I haven't learned yet?"*

Lester was feeling much better and rarely needed his cane for support. He was capable of cooking on his own but ate salads for most meals except breakfast when he cooked omelets or basted eggs, toast, and bacon from Coursey's in St. Joe, Arkansas. How did he remember where the bacon came from? He sat down with a late breakfast omelet and picked up the newspaper to see a front page article about his operation. Standing next to his hospital bed were his dad and Debi. He really liked her and wondered what kind of relationship they had before the surgery. Memories of his dad were coming back slowly, but they were to the point that he was sure Adrian was his dad. He hoped the memories of Debi would come back.

Chapter Seventeen

Spider Gambini was eating a late breakfast at Hester's Cafe. Her coffee was blond, her half-eaten omelet was tucked in a to-go box as usual, and she continued to read the local paper. There on the front page of the *Sentinel Record* was Lester's picture, head wrapped in a bandage, smiling from a hospital bed with his dad and that damn speech therapist standing by. She read the entire article, but it didn't give a lot of information on his condition except for his temporary memory loss. Running through her mind was whether he remembered her, and if she stopped by his place would he speak to her. For kicks, she might just stop to see him, but not if the dark-haired bitch was there. A call to the sheriff's office from a concerned friend was in order. Spider's informants had told her that Lester worked with Rich Robertson so she would start there. She got the operator at the Garland County Sheriff's Office and asked to be connected.

"Rich, this is Darlene McFarlin. I'm a cousin of Lester's in Tennessee, and I just heard he got operated on. How is he doing?"

"Darlene? He's never mentioned you, but I'm sure I don't know all his relatives. He's doing okay and kind of taking care of himself now. His girlfriend's brother was in a bad car wreck in California, and she flew out there to see him since he's in intensive care. I'm on call if he needs anything. There's a nurse that's supposed to go there sometime this week. So far he's cooked his own breakfast and is doing good. I call him every couple hours. Don't you have his number?" Rich asked.

"We don't talk much, and he never gave me his number. If you have it handy, I'll call him and then I can report back to all the Tennessee relatives."

Rich gave her the number, and the wheels started turning in her mind. She drove in the direction of his apartment, the location she had known for a long time. It was near her condo, so she would pick up a few things first and go over. How would she play this? So many ideas, and all of them were fun.

* * *

Debi and her parents rushed to the John Muir Medical Center in Walnut Creek, California and learned on the way that it was the only Trauma Center for Contra Costa County. After checking in at the front desk, they were directed to the ICU and told that only one family member could go in at a time and must be accompanied by a nurse. Tom made the first visit and met with one of the attending doctors. Ray had metal intrusion to his intestines and a punctured lung. His Mercedes had saved his life with several airbags having deployed when a drunk driver plowed into the side of his car as he sat at a traffic light in Lafayette. He had been shopping at a book store to buy a gift for his wife for their anniversary. His wife, Shasha, and their two boys, Eric and Ryan, were at home, so they escaped the crash. The doctor told Tom that all the metal had been removed and the intestines had been repaired, but an open colostomy would be in place until everything healed. A tremendous amount of work took place to clean the area of puncture. His lung had collapsed, but it was repaired as well. No other internal injuries had occurred, but he had a broken wrist and arm that were placed in casts. Other than scars from a few lacerations and burns from airbags, he should recover. The doctor reminded Tom that people with multiple injuries sometimes just crash because of the overall trauma to their system. For that reason they had placed Ray into an induced coma for a while to let his body recover. In a day or two he would be slowly released from that and given large doses of pain killers.

After Debi and Susan took their turns looking at Ray, replete with tubes and wires coming out of several orifices, they all went to his home to be with Shasha and the kids. It did appear he would live but would have a long period of recovery.

* * *

Answering a knock on his front door, Lester greeted a beautiful blond lady in her thirties carrying a large purse.

"Hello. Are you Lester McFarlin?" Angel asked.

"Yes, I'm that guy. And you are...?"

"Flo Blackman. I'm a nurse that was sent over to help you. Can I come in?"

"Oh, yeah. Debi said there would be a nurse, but you're too pretty to be a nurse. You do realize that you're beautiful."

"Lester, I was told you were a big flirt. So, you'll just have to let me do my job, and I'll try to ignore your comments," Angel said.

Spider took out a notebook and started asking him questions about his recovery. He answered them as best he could. She looked at his nose where the tube was inserted to operate on his brain.

"Lester, do you have a shower or a tub?"

"I have both, but don't use the tub much."

"I'm required to give you a bath. Now, I hope you aren't the modest type," Angel said with a stern facial expression.

"I think I can bathe myself."

"One slip—one dizzy episode—and wham! You hit your head and your brain could bleed and swell—erasing all the work the doctor has done, maybe even killing you." She sounded so serious and easily sold the idea to Lester.

"Now, Lester, I'm going to draw the bath and make sure you don't slip getting in and out."

"Okay." Lester was fairly bored hanging around his apartment by himself, and this was a nice diversion.

"You know it would be more fun if you took a bath with me," he said, only half-joking.

"Lester, you're such a flirt. What would you think of me if I took a bath with you?"

"I'd say you're a nurse that really cares about her patients."

"Let's get you in the tub first, and I'll think about joining you," Angel said. Lester assumed she was just saying it to please him.

Lester watched as she adjusted the water and laid towels on the floor so that he wouldn't slip. Once it had filled to an acceptable level,

Lester got undressed and with Angel's help he stepped carefully into the bathtub. After he was seated, he looked up at Angel.

"I won't tell your boss if you get in with me."

"Are you sure? I could lose my license."

"Promise not to turn you in," Lester said. He couldn't believe she was considering it.

He watched closely as Angel began to undress. After removing her fashionable slacks and sexy underwear, she stood facing Lester. She was gorgeous. Her breasts were tanned without a bra line, an obvious result of owning a tanning bed, and she was trimmed in the modern landing strip fashion right below a tight hard stomach with an elongated navel. She was a ten, and as she stepped into the bathtub Lester's mind was whirling. How did he get this lucky? Maybe he should get operated on more often. An image of Debi flashed briefly through his mind. He focused back on the creature that had just sat down directly in front of him. Angel was facing him while making eye contact and talking quietly with him. She asked about his police work and cases he was working on. He didn't remember much. He wanted to talk about her. She talked about a son in New York that she missed a great deal. Spider stood up and moved behind Lester and wrapped her long legs around him. He smiled and placed her soapy hands between his legs where he was ready for her touch. It wasn't long before Lester was spent and relaxed.

The water was beginning to cool so Angel got out first and helped Lester step out on the towels so he didn't slip. He helped her dry off and pressed up against her nude body, kissing her passionately for quite a while. Again there were flashes of Debi going through his mind. Suddenly he had a picture of Debi naked with him in the shower. He realized at that moment an intimate relationship had occurred with Debi.

After Angel dressed, she asked if Lester needed her to stop by tomorrow. Lester gave her his number and asked that she call first. As much as he would have loved for her to come back every day, he was sensing some other things were in conflict with his memory and emotions. He kissed the nurse and thanked her for coming.

She didn't call back, and the next day the real nurse showed up. Dorothy Cummings introduced herself as she stood outside Lester's door. She weighed in at defensive-line status and had a face with a masculine structure. Her mustache had not been properly trimmed and her hair style was somewhere between bedhead and wind-ravaged. Unattractive would be a compliment.

"I'm sorry, but I had a nurse here yesterday. Give me your number, and I'll call you if I need you," Lester said, knowing that time would never come.

Dorothy looked perplexed, but gave Lester a card and left.

Debi had called the night before, but he didn't mention the nurse. He wasn't so dumb not to recognize that if he had been in the shower with Debi, a relationship existed that would be shaken to its core by bathing with a pretty blond nurse. He didn't know when or if he would tell her, but it certainly wouldn't be on the phone.

The phone rang later in the day after the real nurse had been there.

"Lester. Just called to tell you they are slowly taking Ray out of the coma."

"That's great. How long will he be in the hospital?" Lester asked. He wanted to find out when she would be coming home.

"Once he's stabilized, Dad and I will come back, and Mother will stay to help Shasha and the kids. I'd guess in a few days. The hospital staff here is wonderful, so I believe he's getting the best care possible. By the way, did a nurse ever come to see you?"

"Uhhhhh—yes. One came by today. I'm not sure if it was a she or a he. Nice mustache, though. I really didn't need her, but I got her card." Lester side-stepped the issue of the other nurse, which he still hadn't figured out.

"Lester, she can help you, take your vitals, check on your meds, help you bathe so you don't fall—you know all the things that nurses do."

"Debi, did you happen to call any other nurses that might be a little more pleasing to the eye?"

"Are you nuts? I wouldn't turn a pretty nurse loose in your apartment with me not there to supervise. Why do you ask?"

"Uh—no reason. Just to let you know, I'm doing great and looking forward to seeing the doctor on Friday. Hope he'll let me drive. Rich said he'd give me a ride if you aren't back by then," Lester said, avoiding any more nurse questions.

Where did that blond nurse come from? He decided to call Little Richard to see if it was a prank initiated from the Sheriff's office.

"Rich—Lester here. Hey did you guys send out a nurse to see me this week?"

"Nope. Should be an ugly one coming. Debi said she hired one that would run a freight train onto a dirt road."

"Yeah, I met her. Did Debi just call and ask for the ugliest woman on earth? She had a mustache. I kid you not!"

"Oh, your cousin called from Tennessee—gave her your number. Did she get a hold of you? Said her name was Darlene McFarlin."

"What? Don't know if I have a cousin named Darlene from Tennessee, but maybe I just don't remember. What did she sound like?"

"If I had to place her accent I would say Cajun, or south Louisiana instead of Tennessee."

"That was her who came by—said her name was Sherry Jones. Really pretty. Helped me with a bath. Even got in with me."

"Ah, shit! You took a bath with your cousin. You pervert!"

"Hey, my mind might be fucked up, but I think I'd know if I had a cousin that good looking, wouldn't I?" Lester said, questioning himself.

"You didn't know me or who in the hell Debi was and she is damn good looking!" Rich said.

"Listen, Rich, can you bring me all the files we've been working on? I know I can't read them, but I might see something in there that might help me."

"Okay. I'll be there shortly. But I'm not sure anything will help you when incest charges are filed on your ass," Rich said, laughing.

"Screw you, Rich!"

The rush of emotions caused by the bath with the blonde and Rich's revelation about a cousin calling had awakened his senses. He needed memories, and they came flowing back in torrents. First his dad, and then his mother being killed. God, how he wished he hadn't remembered the details. Then his start as a deputy and how easy it was to solve crimes for the department. Memories of his listening to hours and hours of audio. How braille allowed him to type up his notes. Then, like a firestorm of colorful movies in his head—Debi—Debi was everything. Damn, he had been in a shootout alongside her, and he had very strong feelings for her. Stronger than just strong—he was in love with her! She hadn't told him much about their relationship because she wanted his feelings for her to come back on their own. It took the shock of being with another woman and learning he had been duped for it to surface. He had to call Debi, but not until he talked to Rich and looked over the reports.

The teacher was coming by later to start the instruction videos, and he hoped the learning process would go quickly. In about thirty minutes, Rich pulled up in a patrol car, causing a couple of teenagers by an adjacent building to move out of sight. He saw them and figured there was some weed action going on, but he didn't have time to chase them down.

The files Rich brought were building in girth since they first checked on the guns from the Quincy Jackson shootings. Lester was excited to see them and looked at the typed reports, noticing that the scattering filter in his brain that lined up words in a non-sequential order no longer behaved in that manner. He could see them in order but just didn't know how to read them yet. Pictures of the S.G. Crystals building and the bait shop were there and those memories flowed back in place. Then a picture—a black and white picture of a pretty woman laid on top of the pile.

"Rich, who is this woman?"

"You kidding me? It's Angel "Spider" Gambini. Don't tell me! She's your cousin. Not only did you get naked with your cousin but a kingpin crime boss all at the same time. This is fucking special!" Rich said, standing up and pulling on his short curly head of hair while trying to hold in his laughter but failing.

"Okay, asshole—have fun with this. You cannot breathe a word of this to anyone. Promise me!"

"Do you remember her now?" Rich asked.

"Yes. We met her at the crystal warehouse, and I had seen her sometime in the past as well.

"I'll tell you this—she makes a hell of a nurse, and I'll kill you if you tell Debi, but she does wash everything, and happy endings are sort of her specialty," Lester said, laughing.

"Not many men are alive that can say that got a hand job from Spider Gambini and lived to tell about it. You are a lucky, lucky guy. Why didn't she kill you like the spider woman she claims to be?" Rich asked.

"I don't know, but I bet she's laughing her ass off at what she pulled off on a poor man with memory loss," Lester said.

There was a knock on the door and Lester ushered in a middle-aged, sweet-looking lady armed with a video and a small stack of books. She was pudgy, short, and not at all sexy.

"Lester, I'm Tammy Fortis. I teach second grade at Oaklawn Elementary. I hope I can help you. Are you ready to get started?"

"Ma'am, you have no idea!"

Chapter Eighteen

Chalmette, LA

"Hey, Pops. I just got a call from Hot Springs, and that deputy sheriff, Rich Roberson, is coming down to shoot the MAC-11 next Friday," Nicco Evola said. "We got his application approved and a note from his gun club that they will actually be the owners. He's coming to New Orleans with some friends for a long weekend—asked about where to eat in the Quarter. I don't like that he's a deputy sheriff, but he seems to be clean and the gun club is one of the biggest in the area. Apparently their president wants to do one of those 'Southern machine gun shoots,' like the one in Alabama and Kentucky. Sold a lot of 'em to those clubs."

"Nicco, keep an eye on them. If you suspect anything, call Spider. She knows all the cops there. This wouldn't be a sale for her anyway— she doesn't sell legal guns. How are we doing on her replacement shipment?" Tony Evola asked.

"It's set to ship. They're driving their UPS truck down here, and we'll load them out probably this weekend. By Monday or Tuesday of next week, Spider will have the new concrete storage room to hold this shipment, and I suspect many more. Mama's Automatics on the net has orders for more than we're shipping. Angel says, 'Let their asses stew a while, it runs the prices up,' and she's right," Nicco said.

"Son, that goddamned dark net is the creepiest fucking place I've even seen. It has hit men, child porn sites, drugs, slave trading—if there's an evil that exists, it can be found there. It's much like taking the devil's hand and walking through hell. We use it to sell guns, but

I don't even like to click on the computer to pick up our orders. If the cops ever figure out how to get through the encryption, then we're out of business and our asses will be planted in jail."

"Pops, I agree. It scares the shit out of me, too!"

"We'll use it only when needed. You know every FBI and NSA agent in the country is trying to break through the encryptions. Someday they will. Hopefully, we change it often enough to stay ahead of them. The real question is, who has the best computer geeks?" Tony said.

* * *

"Lester, tell me your brain is still working," Jim Webb said, calling on his cell.

"Jim, good to hear from you! Yeah, it's hungry for anything that can sneak in and stick to the brain walls. I've had this teacher working with me for about a week, and she thinks I might pass first grade with a C average," Lester laughed.

"Is Debi back from California?"

"She came back a couple days ago—Thursday, I believe. Her brother is much better. She's at work today doing make-up calls on a Saturday."

"Good! Good! I wanted to let you know where we are with Spider and the gang. The gunroom for the bait shop is functional, and the final trim work should be complete by Monday. I expect the shipment sometime around the first of the week since one of their UPS trucks left out today from S&G. We have remote cameras everywhere," Jim said.

"You guys are going down next Friday and plan to shoot your new automatic on Saturday. Here's what I need: I'm going to drop off some new NSA combo video and sound devices for you to plant in the back of Tony's store. ATF thinks they hide the illegal machine guns and crap somewhere at the back of the place near the shooting range. They will then be nearby with closed circuit receivers to monitor after you leave. You will also have cash for the transaction furnished by our friends at the ATF. We have given you a special identity as a lawyer representing Garland County for the sale of weapons found in the home of Quincy Jackson. New driver's license, business cards, etc. Your name is Hamilton Richardson and your background information will be a part of the package. We have a dedicated line for the number on your card with an answering service recording. Even have a fake office in Little Rock. Think you can learn to be a lawyer in a week?"

"From the ones I've met, it may not take that long," Lester said, chuckling.

"A bid sheet listing the legal automatic weapons that the county wants to sell will be sent to Tony Evola on Monday, and he'll be told it'll be sent to all class three gun dealers in the area. It won't, of course. He'll be pissed because he'll be bidding to buy his own goddamned guns back, but you're going to have a hell of a deal for him. Not only do you represent Garland County, but you also represent the Valley of the Vapors Sportsman's Club for the purchase of the same guns. They want to have a big machine gun shoot twice a year and machine gun rentals almost every day. Tell him they have a shit pot full of money because they sold forty acres of land near the main road into the range. Explain to them they rent machine guns for sixty-five dollars an hour—tell them the gun club will make their money back in the first few months.

"You'll call him on Thursday before you leave to see if he'll meet with you on Saturday since you are going to be there anyway with your girlfriend to watch your buddy Rich shoot. The discussion will be to purchase all the legal automatics by the gun club at the same time the county sells what they have confiscated. Paperwork will have to be made for the transfers, but it leaves a nice profit for Tony, gives the county money it never had, and lets the gun club grab a bunch of automatics at hopefully below-wholesale prices. All legal transactions, if Tony files all the right forms for the government. All this takes quite a while for the sales to take place on both sides of the transaction unless he gets greedy and takes a crooked shortcut that will nail him. We hope to arrest him on several other charges before all this paperwork gets done, but entrapment is something we must avoid at all costs. We really need to snag him on something totally unrelated to this deal. This deal is just to position him to screw up or let us plant bugs to catch him," Jim said.

Lester was impressed at the elaborate plan that was put together between the FBI and ATF. This was going to take time and a hell of a lot of police to arrest Tony and his boys, Stick, Angel, and all her employees at almost exactly the same time. New Orleans police and their ATF people would also be involved.

"Do you want Captain Campanella informed?" Lester asked.

"The Captain would know they'd be in town but would be asked to stand down unless needed," Jim said. "He'd be told about your alias, however.

"The guns that were illegal for all sales were back in Hot Springs. Those automatic weapons primarily manufactured after 1986 will be the ATF's problem. Most likely some will be turned over to the Louisiana Army Reserve unit where a theft took place," Jim said.

"Jesus, what a plan. Do you think Tony will buy the idea?"

"Bottom line, this guy is a business man, and he will be dealing with a slimy lawyer—you. The lawyer will have paperwork to sell the weapons back to the gun club, or if you will, 'us' in real life, with the price to be negotiated and left blank for you and Tony to fill in. The ATF pretty much knows what these automatics are sold for at market price, and you'll have those numbers. You, of course, will lowball him. Tony will come back until you guys agree on a price. We'll ship them, he can pick them up, or if he wants, we can personally deliver them to his store. They must go back to the gun store so Tony has them physically in his possession, according to the government laws, before they're sold and approved. If the paperwork fails, Tony keeps the guns until they're cleared because he's a certified class three dealer. Remember this transaction is very legal if he takes no shortcuts on the paperwork, and I doubt if he will since he knows you also represent Garland County, Arkansas as well as the sheriff's office," Jim said.

"Jim, the story of the club wanting the machine guns to rent may not be true, but Jesus, it sounds so damn believable," Lester said.

"Gun clubs all over the South do this because they know how to do the paperwork. They set up old cars and refrigerators and blow them all to hell. Women, teenagers, little fucking kids—all shooting machine guns. Redneck heaven! I researched it, and most do charge about sixty-five an hour for that kind of shoot. Imagine, ten people lined up—six hundred fifty dollars an hour plus the profit on ammo sales. Shit, I might open a range! Also, they do jungle walks where you go down a trail and shoot full automatic with AK-47s at pop-up targets. The Hot Springs club doesn't do it, probably because they don't know how to get started. They'd be crazy not to do it. Oh, another thing: most of the clubs buy their machine guns from Tony—he's the biggest buyer and seller of fully automatic weapons in the United States. He really doesn't need to sell the illegal stuff, but the 'families' have a need, and he is family," Jim explained.

"Jim, do me a favor."

"What's that, Lester?"

"Put a call in to the club president Monte Hart at American Guns, and tell him if anyone calls about a deal to buy automatic weapons for the club that his attorney for the club is working on it and he didn't know the particulars. Give him my lawyer's name and number. That way if Tony or his sons do their due diligence, our ass will be covered," Lester said.

"Great idea. I'll do that and call you back," Jim said and hung up.

In about ten minutes Jim called back.

"Lester, Monte is fine to play the part and loves the FBI, so it will be okay," he said. "Funny thing—they've talked in their club meetings for the last two years about getting a machine gun owned by the club. Their insurance company wanted to go up on their rates for liability if they did. I explained that at sixty-five an hour they might easily pay for the extra premium. I can't believe I'm trying to sell this guy on getting machine guns. I had to apologize for not staying on task as an FBI guy. Mr. Hart was cool and glad we put him in the loop so he didn't get blindsided."

"Call me if you need anything else, Jim. It might be a good idea to give me a little stick-on listening device for my meeting with Tony. I might get a chance to place it if he is distracted. And I'm going to assume you guys have cleared, or will clear, all these devices with a warrant at some court or judge in New Orleans. One I hope and pray isn't paid off by all the organized crime families in Louisiana. Where the slip up comes isn't from the judges, but from the clerks that type them and make copies and mail them and file them. You know, those ten-dollar-an-hour clerks who are given an extra thousand each year by the mob to report every search warrant that goes through their court. A thousand a year for every judge in the state shared by the families ain't a bad investment. All I'm saying, Jim, is to go directly to the judge with the warrant—get it signed by him—no copies— no clerks. I don't want us floating in a swamp to be a meal for some friggin' alligators," Lester said.

"Got ya! Probably use a federal judge in an adjoining state. Don't worry; we'll take care of it. Glad you're doing okay. Talk to you soon."

Lester didn't feel all that assured but knew it was something he couldn't control. What he could control was learning everything he could about laws concerning automatic weapons .His limited audio tapes didn't cover much, but among the skills being taught by the second grade teacher was also how to access information by asking the computer verbally. It was a new program to activate the Google search engine, verbally reading out loud the results of the search merely by him highlighting the printed results. The lady would be there in an hour for the lesson and then Debi would be home a couple hours later. He had some time so he sat down in front of the computer with a bowl of tuna salad and a big glass of water. He clicked on the Google search page which displayed a beautiful Russian girl in a tiny swimsuit in the background. Debi hated the background image, but refused to pose in the nude to replace it.

"Requirements for owning a machine gun," Lester spoke to the computer.

Several short sentences came up on the screen and he highlighted them and pushed the speak button.

"Federal gun laws for fully automatic weapons dating before 1986" the computer stated with a voice that had no region or accent.

Lester clicked on that one and found several pages of regulations and requirements. Again he highlighted the text and listened to the man from nowhere.

He had found what he wanted and would continue until he knew what the computer knew. He would not be embarrassed in his new role as a slimy lawyer. Becoming a lawyer was really something he wanted to do, now that he could potentially learn anything. Not really a slimy lawyer, but one of the best lawyers anywhere. This game, or acting job, turned something on in his brain that had been latent. The fire was lit. Goals were being set, wheels turning, plans cooking, and nothing would be stopping him.

Chapter Nineteen

Tammy Fortis couldn't believe what she was hearing. Lester was reading a grade-school level book as fast as he could talk. It wasn't this week's assignment—it was next week's homework. He was really reading, and though large words were a stumbling block at times, once he mastered them, he didn't forget the next time they came up. Tammy went to her car and gave Lester assignments she had laid out for three months from now. He wanted to take material to New Orleans later in the week, even though Tammy would return each day until they left on Friday.

When Debi came home later, Lester was typing an outline for his studies for the next week. It included more legal studies, reading assignment for the next few months, which he knew would be done before the trip to New Orleans was over, spelling tests he would give himself if Debi would read the words, and several writing assignments. She couldn't believe it.

Tammy had already called her to say he was like a human computer that just downloaded everything plugged into it. She knew her services wouldn't be needed long.

Debi walked over and sat in Lester's lap, wedging in between him and the laptop computer, as would a family cat wanting attention. He responded and stopped his work to kiss her. She frowned.

"Lester, I'm worried."

"Why?"

"Have you ever known anyone who was a true intellectual? The kind of person who would interject references to obscure literature in sentences as a direct question while they looked at your glazed-over eyes and waited for an answer they knew would never come? The answer would never come because you had no frigging idea what they were talking about. Are you going to be that kind of an intellectual after you learn all this stuff?" Debi asked as she gently bit down on his bottom lip and stretched it out a little before she slowly let go of it and then smiled.

"Yes. Yes, I will! Then I will give you the reference number for the book in question and make you read it before I speak to you again."

"You will always be an asshole. I can be comforted by that," Debi said.

"Why would I ever do anything to cause me to make someone I care about very deeply uncomfortable? Also, I don't like obscure literature."

"I really mean—I guess I mean, will there be any changes? I like you the way you are—the way you are good to me. Can you *not* unlearn that?" Debi asked, feeling a little insecure about this new person emerging.

Lester turned her more in his lap where she would be facing him. He kissed her lightly and locked his blue eyes squarely on her soft brown eyes and spoke softly but sternly.

"Damn it, Debi—I am doing all of this for you. The operation, the study, the tutor, and anything else I do to learn is so I can be normal like you—not superior. I will never be your superior and don't want to be. Just an equal. Sunday mornings—you next to me as I read the newspaper. Can't do that now. Discuss a menu item when we go out to eat. Can't do that now. Take a college entrance exam like you did. Can't do that now. So many things that I want to learn so I won't be a freak. I know I've overcome much of my disability, but I'm still a freak until I can read like a normal human. When you see me studying like crazy it's to be normal first. What comes after that will never be used to belittle anyone, especially you. You—who I love so much!" Lester spoke with every ounce of sincerity in his large body.

Debi seemed satisfied with his long explanation. "I love you, too and don't want you to change. My parents are coming by to check on you tonight, if that's all right."

"Are we cooking them dinner or just drinks and snacks?"

"Drinks and a few nuts and cheese. Mother drinks wine and Dad will but would rather have a good single malt scotch," Debi said as she walked over to Lester's small wine cooler and looked in. "You've got a lot of reds—mostly reds—mostly cabs."

"Mostly because that's what I like—duh."

"I'd better go to the liquor store. I'll get everything we need. They said around sevenish," Debi said.

"Here's my credit card. Get them the good stuff. I'll clean up here and slice some cheese and bust open a can of nuts."

The Greens left around 8:30 and were pleased with Lester's progress. He showed Susan his ambitious study guides and goals for learning. Tom was more interested in when Lester's dad could take them striper fishing. Lester thanked Debi's dad for recommending Dr. Arrison.

After they left, Lester asked if he could get in an hour or two of studying before bed. Debi had a better idea. They would go to bed first and Lester could get up and study as much as he wanted afterwards. This worked out well for both of them. Lester, however, studied much later than he planned, trying to operate with the volume down as the computer spoke. He let it soak in and now listened to everything available on gun laws in the U.S. He looked up actual cases and studied them as they applied to certain state, circuit, and federal ruling. It was fascinating how he memorized the case numbers. He would see the numbers like a picture in his mind. The blood clot on his brain had been like a plug in a sink. Now that it was removed, everything he learned rushed into his brain. Some things came in he didn't want there. If he looked at a serial number on his computer or a bar code on a bottle of wine—there it was stamped on the wall of his brain. Now he avoided looking at numbers because he couldn't stop memorizing them. Before there was a filter—now he had to develop his own filter.

* * *

A tentative peace had been in place in New Orleans after Richie Gambini had been killed. The word was given for no retaliation since Richie had stepped into another family's territory and got what aggressive action brings—aggressive action returned. Below the surface though, the Gambini family was just looking for a chance to catch a member of the Matranga family in a misdeed. It happened about mid-September when ten ladies from the St. Peter Street massage parlor owned by Richie's brother Frank Gambini were given huge bonuses to move to a rival massage parlor owned by the Matrangas. The loss of that many girls meant the St. Peter Street business was liable to find itself at the pearly gates. It could easily go out of business.

A few days later, five members of the Matranga family were having a late evening meal at The Oyster Palace Restaurant in Metairie. Two were uncles of Spider, one was a cousin, and the others were related to her by marriage. They were in the rear next to a wall when someone came from the kitchen, uncovered a Tec-9mm machine pistol from a red cloth napkin draped across his arm and emptied a full thirty-round magazine of Parabellums into the five guys. Unbelievable as it might seem, three of the men were able to get shots off before they died. Some hit other patrons as they gobbled down grilled oysters, but two bullets struck the Gambini family shooter, a hired gun, making the hit a little bit harder to trace. One bullet went through his neck and severed an artery while the other went right into his brain blowing pieces of gray matter into a freshly made crème brûlée back in the kitchen. The evening was ruined for many of the patrons.

Captain Campanella was not the lead on this investigation, but was called in as an advisor because he was Orleans Parish's expert on organized crime. This was Jefferson Parish and popular for great restaurants and a little quieter party scene than New Orleans. It had been called Fat City as far back as anyone could remember. Some give credit to a snowball stand near the Lakeside Shopping Center named Fat City Snowballs, but it wasn't official until the city fathers changed 18th street to Fat City Boulevard in 1973. Most people didn't care.

The Oyster Palace was an upscale eatery which appealed more to people who were willing to spend a little more to get a great culinary experience. It was the least likely place that one would expect a mob hit. Had it been Mosca's or Salvatori's, nobody would have been too surprised, but a classy place like The Oyster Palace raised some eyebrows. "Six People Dead and Four Customers Wounded" blasted the headlines of the *Times-Picayune* and on the news, local and national.

After gathering as much crime scene information as possible, the captain realized the investigation just went backwards from this scene. *Why was the hit ordered? What did the Matranga family do to piss off another crime family? Who was the other family?* The first suspects had to be the Gambini family since Richie was killed by the crime family currently bleeding all over the restaurant floor. It was first hypothesized Richie's killing was set up by Angel Gambini because of an affair Richie had with one of the Asian massage girls. *If these crime families got murdered because of their sexual escapades they all would be dead,* Campanella thought.

It would help to find out about the Tec-9. He asked permission from the Jefferson Parish authorities to check out the gun's bloodlines. He took it back to police headquarters in New Orleans for his people to work on.

Captain Hank Campanella's staff consisted of ten people, which was a very small number of officers for a captain to supervise in a twelve-hundred man police force in a large crime-infested city. Hank's team consisted of experts in intrastate and interstate crime. They had charts on the wall that had interconnected boxes of crime families all over the world. Interpol gave them information and visa-versa. They had hot lines into the FBI and NSA, and sometimes certain CIA operatives were listed under the table. The FBI in Little Rock had increased the boxes on their wall and they knew Lester was working the spread of Spider's kingdom in Hot Springs. Also part of the group was a computer expert that worked full time trying to break the encryption to dark net operations in Louisiana—one in particular was the Louisiana Sportsman's Super Store.

The serial number for the Tec-9 was put in the computer. It came up a Tec-DC9, a model that was made after the assault rifle ban. DC was added and meant "Don't Sell" in California. The only thing changed were the sling hooks placement on the stock and barrel, a joke to everyone in the industry. This particular gun was purchased by Tony Evola's operation but was reported stolen off a UPS truck. He reported it, took the loss off his income tax return, yet he was still the registered owner of this newly-surfaced weapon.

"I might have to give this machine pistol back to Tony Evola after it killed a dinner party of four," Hank said to his officer who was researching the weapon.

Hank stared at the computer screen. "Here's what really happened." He looked to see who was paying attention. "He sold this weapon for about twice what it's worth. Let's say around ten grand."

The captain walked over to the window and looked down from his third floor window at the traffic below as though he were seeing the crime happen.

"He would tell his client the day it was going to be on the UPS truck heading for Chalmette. The package would be a bright color like Day-Glo orange and packed fairly large but not heavy. At a stop where the driver had to go into a business, there would be questions about a delivery—some sort of delay—the truck would be vulnerable with the doors open to God and everybody. The customer would take delivery by snatching the colorful box rather quickly and head out in his vehicle before Mr. UPS got back to his truck."

Captain Campanella turned away from the window, walked to his desk, and put his hand on his desk phone.

"On reaching his call on the big sporting goods store or maybe before, he notices that his big orange box is missing. Calls are made, people are pissed, the driver gets his ass chewed or fired, and the criminal has a machine gun that ain't registered no-fucking-where— just the way he wants it. That gun is golden. Not traceable and could be sold many times at will."

Hank Campanella paced the room and decided he would make a call to a number his staff had provided for him, even though it was late.

"Lester, this is Hank Campanella from New Orleans. How're you doing?"

"Good to hear from you, Captain. I had my brain dusted and

cleaned last week and might be able to read the newspaper before long. Can I help you on the big shooting in Metairie—not your jurisdiction, though. It's all over the news here."

"Consulting—kinda like you do. How do you keep up with which parishes we work in all the way from Arkansas?"

"Hank, it's a sickness. I'll be in New Orleans on Friday, but I'll be using an alias because we're meeting with Tony at the sporting goods store. They said you were to stand down on this one, but I don't agree with them. You know more about these goons that anybody in the state."

"Yeah, I talked to Jim Webb in Little Rock—said you and ATF were going to see if you could catch Tony fucking up. Probably best I'm not in the vicinity since they all know me. They used a Tec-DC9 on this hit. Stolen off a UPS truck in broad daylight just like it was supposed to. So many ways to get away with a machine gun."

"Look, Hank, you can cause Tony a lot of heat over this weapon. Possibly cause him to lose his class three license," Lester said excitedly.

"What do you mean? He never actually received the gun," Hank said, confused.

"The DC model was banned in California as a semi-automatic with the law passed in 1994, and that expired with a sunset provision in 2004," Lester said. "The law for automatics passed in 1986 and never changed. These weapons with the 'DC' in their model number that were modified for fully automatic were banned for resale, even with class three dealers since they were manufactured after 1986. The old Tec-9s made before '86 were good for resale, but if the paperwork showed it as a Tec-DC9 automatic, then you have him by the balls— never meant to be an automatic. He had to have a contract with the person who shipped it on that UPS truck, and they wouldn't have gone to all the trouble to set up the theft if it were the semi-automatic since anybody can buy that stupid gun. Mr. Evola made a contract to buy an unauthorized and banned weapon. Clearly a violation of his license." Lester had put some of the information he found online to good use.

"Lester, this is amazing, if it's accurate."

"Get one of your computer geeks to pull up Firearms Owners

Protection Act of 1986 on Google and start there. Next, take that information to your attorney general's office. Don't let any of it leak or he'll destroy his records, then return the weapon to him since he's the rightful owner and make him produce the paperwork," Lester said. "Hopefully, we'll help you nail him when we come down on Friday. We're making a deal for him to buy back the legal guns we found in Arkansas. One of them is also an illegal, so we might catch him there. Mainly, we're looking for where he keeps the really bad-ass guns, rocket launchers, and tanks." Lester laughed.

"I see why police departments hire you, Lester. I just called to see how the operation went. Jim told me about it."

"Hey, I said I would help you for free when I came down. I was going to The Oyster Palace to eat, but now I don't know."

"There's another one in the Hilton downtown."

"See, you've already saved my trip. I hope when all this is over we can go out for a drink."

"Lester, you just keep on getting better, and stay safe when you come down. Thanks again," Hank said and hung up.

The door opened to the bedroom and Debi stuck her head out. "Who in the hell was that calling this late?" she asked.

"It was the police Captain in New Orleans that you wanted to sleep with. He can't wait until you get there. I've never seen a man so excited!" Lester was laughing as he turned off his computer.

Chapter Twenty

Lester had stopped by the Sheriff's office on Thursday and picked up all the materials left by Jim Webb, including the cash for the MAC-11. There was a note separate from the inventory of guns for Tony Evola's bid. The note indicated that among the automatic weapons listed was a MAC-11/9. This gun was manufactured to be a semi-automatic weapon because of the laws that went into force in 1994. They were difficult to convert to fully automatic since metal pieces were welded inside the weapon to block the conversion. Gunsmiths merely removed the metal and went about their transformation from select fire to full auto. These guns that are converted to fully automatic are illegal because they were manufactured or converted after 1986, but are so similar to the MAC-11s it's hard for even dealers to tell them apart. No doubt Tony knew since he was an expert at identifying guns. Now there was a MAC-11/9 automatic listed on the bid sheet, a part of the cache of weapons found by Lester.

This addition meant there were two illegal conversions for Tony Evola to deal with—the Tec-DC9 recovered from the Oyster Palace shooting and the MAC-11/9. If both of them ended up in his hands or there was proof of ownership, there would be multiple infractions of the law. He might be fined or lose his license over these transactions, but probably wouldn't do any time. They needed to catch him doing something big and bad.

The ATF had been kind enough to create a credit card for Lester under the name Hamilton Richardson, but he was sure the credit line wasn't high enough for him and Debi to skip out of the country. Both were planning to test the alias and the brand new credit card after Debi got off work and when Tammy had finished his reading lesson. Their plans for later that day were to try out a new restaurant in Bonnerdale, which was only about twenty minutes out of Hot Springs. Friends had described it as a big log cabin-style place called Bubba's, located barely inside the Garland County line, just a few yards away from Montgomery County, one of thirty-five dry counties in the state. Blue laws and dry counties always perplex visitors from out of state who are shocked when they are required to remove their beer and wine from their shopping carts on Sundays. However, if they can find a cafe, restaurant, or sports grill open in Garland County, they can drink all they want on Sunday—just can't take it home with them.

Lester had called Tony earlier in the day and set up an appointment for Saturday to discuss the sale of the captured weapons. He had given his name as Hamilton Richardson. He also told Tony to call him Ham and to look for a copy of the bid sheet being faxed to him. They had the meeting set for 1:30, and Rich, Becca, and Debi would be shooting starting at 1:00 for one hour in the indoor range. Special care would be taken to place the video and sound transmitters. The girls would have them in their underwear in case they were searched by any of the Evola family. If the cameras were activated early, while still hidden, there was a chance the panty cams would give the guys on the monitors a thrill.

Debi came home a little early, and Lester was still working with Tammy.

"Okay, Lester, read for me the article called 'Massacre in Africa' on the second page of the paper," Tammy said. Lester blasted through the newspaper account of villagers being hacked to death and only stumbled when he came to African tribal names. Debi just stood there with her mouth open, then looked at Tammy who was smiling, then at Lester who was wearing a smirk.

"Wow, how is this possible?" asked Debi.

"Once he broke through the barrier of phonetically sounding words, there was no stopping him. You may not realize that he has been putting in six or eight hours of study after you go to bed. Remarkably, he retains everything—even barcode numbers on wine bottles. After a little research, I found that Lester now has what is referred to as 'Eidetic' memory. He can recall images, numbers, text, and just about anything he sees accurately for long periods of time—how long we don't know," Tammy explained.

"I expect to enter the Trivial Pursuit championships real soon," Lester said with a laugh.

"I can take you to Vegas and you can do card counting like the *Rain Man* guy," Debi said, and then quickly wondered if she had hurt his feelings comparing him to someone who clearly was mentally challenged. "Honey, I'm sorry. I didn't mean to compare you to someone who was autistic."

"Hey, I like being a new kind of freak, compared to the old one. And, I don't have to watch Judge Wapner every day or go nuts," Lester said, referring to the Raymond Babbitt character played by Dustin Hoffman who had to stop whatever he was doing to watch the TV program or he would have an frantic episode.

"You going to be ready for Bubba's in a few minutes?" Debi asked. "It looks like you haven't packed yet either."

"Won't take me but a minute. Taking all casual pants and shorts. I'm not going to dress up just because I'm a lawyer now," Lester said. "Or do you think I should take some slacks and a polo shirt for my meeting with Tony?

"Yes."

"Okay," Lester said and went back to work with Tammy for a few minutes before it was time to end her session. She gave him a large reading assignment for the trip to New Orleans and part of the weekend and left until their session the next Monday.

Debi convinced Lester to pack before they left for dinner. On the way to Bubba's, Lester started playing the part of Hamilton Richardson.

He acted out discussing buying machine guns and hand grenades from Tony. Debi then quizzed him about his background. She asked where he went to law school, about his parents, brothers or sisters, and his law firm. Everything she asked he had to fabricate quickly or use the limited write-up the FBI had given him. He memorized the special phone number and office address set up to make his business seem authentic. Tomorrow on the way to New Orleans, he would have Becca and Rich try to trip him up with their line of questions.

"I just hope Tony and his boys haven't seen your picture somewhere," Debi said.

They had to search a while to find a parking spot at the huge log cabin-style bar and grill. Entering from the front door, they were amazed at the cavernous size of the interior. No sooner had they entered the first big room, people they knew started greeting them. Between the two of them, it seemed they knew everyone there. As they passed through the middle section they noticed three pool tables. At the one nearest them a man stood chalking the tip of his cue stick.

"Hello, Dad. You winning?"

"Yeah, Son, but just playing for fun," Adrian said. "Hi, Debi." He walked over and hugged her and kissed her on the cheek.

"Would you like to join us for dinner?" Debi asked.

"Thanks, but I just had a big plate of frog legs. I'll have a drink with you guys after I finish this game."

Lester pulled out a chair from a table that provided a view of his dad's pool table and a huge projection TV screen in the back room. A waiter quickly came to their table.

"Lester, what can I get you guys?" he said.

"Uh…it's Jeremy, idn't it?" Lester asked.

"That's right. I worked at the Colorado Grill not far from your office. Lots of people from Hot Springs work here. This place is rockin' every night," he said.

Debi ordered salmon, and Lester found a fried chicken salad on the menu. Both had to try one of their locally-brewed beers.

"Well, no chance of using my phony name or my new credit card here. It's interesting that the people of Hot Springs will try out any new eatery that pops up even if they have to drive twenty miles. I imagine this place pulls in all the thirsty people west of here that live in dry counties," Lester said.

After their food arrived, Adrian came over for a while and had a beer. He checked on Lester's health status and wished them luck in New Orleans. He excused himself when he spotted one of his girlfriends at the front door. She was tall, pretty, with large breasts and bleached blond hair. He didn't bring her by to meet Debi, so she must have been one of the Boot Scooter girls and not a selection from the upscale Electric Cowboy. Shortly afterwards, Debi and Lester left and went home to finish preparing for the trip.

Later at his apartment while Lester was sipping on a glass of Cabernet, reading an eighth grade assignment, his cell phone buzzed.

"Lester, Jim here. Let me give ya an update. The delivery of guns from Tony's was made at the bait store. But—not all of it. Some of the load went to S&G. It's like they're arming the whole group. If that's the case, we may have a hell of a battle on our hands when we move in. Also, Stick has moved one of his portable deer stands high into a red oak tree near the fence on the east side of the building. Can pretty much see everything from there. I'm going to guess one of the guns brought in was a sniper rifle. I asked around, checked federal registrations, and found out he owns the marine M40 which is basically a .308 with a big scope—same gun used in Vietnam many years before Afghanistan. Jake told me he used the same weapon back in the early 70's. Did you know Jake was a sniper in Nam?"

"Believe he told me that. He's a hell of a shot. Not sure we could get his chubby old body up a tree without a cherry picker. We need to place him somewhere to counteract Stick if push comes to shove."

"We'll work on that. Good luck on your trip. Did you get all the devices to plant?"

"Talked to Rich, and he and Becca have them all. I'll call you after everything is in place. I'm guessing your boys will be hooked into the ATF forces?"

"Yeah, we'll test them all before you guys leave town. Eat a po'boy for me," Jim said.

"Hey, Jim, any way to make those devices vibrate when the girls stick them in their underwear?"

"No, but I wish there was. We'd never hear the end of it if we did that to 'em. See ya soon," Jim said, laughing.

Lester picked up Tammy's assignment and tried to get back into the reading material but thought about Stick in a tree, picking off

Lester's friends and fellow officers. If he could sneak up there at night, maybe he could rig an explosive to blow him out of the tree. He didn't have the equipment, but he knew Jim could find someone who did. He called Jim back and asked if he could have it done with a remote. He promised to try to find someone to do it.

Debi came by and took Lester's homework from him and laid it in the floor. She slid into his lap and looked up at him, smiling and tracing his lip with her finger.

"I'm wondering how good a hot-shot attorney performs in bed." She then turned face down in his lap and found him starting to get erect. She bit down gently through his shorts, but hard enough to bring him to full readiness. Lester turned her over and kissed her hard and deep.

"You're fun to have around the house. I thought about a dog and then a cat, but now I'm considering a Greek girl about five-foot-eight who has nice boobs and a great ass. Beautiful lips and gorgeous brown eyes that pull you into them. A dog would be cheaper, but I believe I'll take the Greek girl." Lester laughed and picked Debi up and started to carry her to the bedroom.

"No—you can't do that!" Debi jumped down from his arms. "No lifting for thirty days!"

"Forgot. I think the doctor said for you to be on top and do all the active sexual activity, while I lay there and try my best to enjoy it," Lester said as he started to undress Debi, which wasn't difficult since all she was wearing was a robe. He was still amazed at the beauty of her body and always told her so in detail. She helped him undress and pushed him down on the bed, then climbed on him. For whatever reason, on this night Debi was slow and deliberate, stopping numerous times to tell him how much she loved him. Lester wondered if she was acting this way because he was changing. He could now read on his own and didn't need her to translate anymore. Bottom line, he was less dependent on her for those skills—still dependent, however, for other things.

"Debi, I want you to know how much I love you. Because I can now read, we can share books and discuss what we find in the newspaper, and no, I won't need a translator anymore. But don't think for a second that because of this, I don't need you. You are my best friend and guide through all of these changes. I'm going to continue to work. Next is college at night, my LSAT exam for law school, and I have no idea which school to go to." While he was rambling on, his movement was quickening inside of Debi who was listening but rolling her eyes and biting her lower lip as a signal she was about to climax. As she did, her muscles contracted and caused the same response for Lester. She then lay quietly on top of him for a while.

"I'll be your guide for anything you want to do, babe," Debi said, laughing.

They took a shower together and went to bed commando style as they always did. Tomorrow, the trip to New Orleans would be the start of a new adventure.

Chapter Twenty-One

Coffee was ready for Rich and Becca when they knocked on the apartment door at 7 a.m. the next morning. Debi was introduced to Becca for the first time and was taken aback by how sexy she was in shorts and a tank top. She had met Little Richard at the bait store shooting and was interviewed by him later. Becca had stopped and bought a sack of chocolate donut holes for the trip, knowing no cop on earth could resist them. After they loaded out the Yukon, Rich agreed to drive since Lester was not cleared yet.

Lester shared the information that Jim gave him about the gun shipments to both the bait store and the S&G building.

"I smell a shootout in our future. Think we can push all those ATF and FBI guys to the front to take the first line of fire?" asked Rich.

"Did you see the South Park movie?' Lester asked.

"Yes. The movie makes fun of every race, religion, and sexual orientation on earth. At least the black Chef takes lots of girls to bed," Rich said.

Lester wasn't surprised since Little Richard quoted Chef, Eric and other South Park cartoon characters often.

"As you recall, Battalion 5 was made up entirely of African American soldiers who were to go to battle first against Canada. They were called Operation Human Shield. Directly behind them was Battalion 14 made up of all Caucasian soldiers who were part of 'Operation get behind the darkies,' Lester said, and laughed as Debi hit his arm.

"Lester, that is so racist!"

Rich defended Lester. "Debi, you got to know that show makes fun of everybody. Nobody gets left behind," he said. "Chef calls all the white people 'crackers.'"

"I don't watch it because it embarrasses me, and it's so weird to hear those children cussing," Debi said.

"I thought it was just stupid!" Becca said. "But if I was a kid, I guarantee you I would sneak around someplace to watch it."

"Anyway, we got off the subject, but we have S&G to deal with when we get back," Lester said.

"I hope you guys are in the 'get behind all the other forces battalion' when the raid goes down," said Debi, who was in the back seat with Becca, a donut hole in her hand. "Jesus, these things are good."

"Pass those up front. We probably won't stop for breakfast until Pine Bluff," Rich said.

Debi and Becca got along fine the entire trip, but Debi knew that Lester had dated her—slept with her—and didn't know how to bring up the subject or even if she should. She knew at some point they had to discuss it—it couldn't just float in space between them. What would she say? Something like, "So, how was Lester in bed?" didn't seem appropriate. She would work on what to say, or decide if she should just let it alone.

An hour later they stopped for breakfast at a small cafe on the highway leading out of Pine Bluff where cathead biscuits were a popular item on the menu. The biscuits earned the name by being as big as cat heads. Lunch was in Vicksburg, and later that day, they found their way to the Hilton in downtown New Orleans. During most of the trip Lester had either a reading assignment in front of his eyes or a law book that he had checked out of the library that pertained to cases involving guns. Everyone in the car quizzed him on his new identity, and he found lying and making stuff up was great fun. He had a headache from reading so much by the time they unloaded the car at the hotel.

Becca and Little Richard were sharing a room with two beds in case Rich needed to escape from her at times. They had shared a bed a few times in the past so it wasn't a new experience for either of them, but they hadn't been out together in about four months.

Lester and Debi opted for a king-sized bed since neither wanted to get away. They made reservations for 7:30 at the Oyster Palace for the four of them, and decided to explore Bourbon Street before dinner.

Friday night in the French Quarter was a feast of sensations for the four who were used to a considerably more sedate atmosphere in Hot Springs. Street performers, hawkers for strip clubs, and music coming from everywhere. Jazz, Dixieland, rock and roll all fused together causing an excitement that took them to another world. There weren't many places like this. It seemed so permissive. They walked past the St. Peter Street massage parlor and noticed it said "Closed for Renovation."

"What kind of construction is needed for a place housing a few massage tables, a big box of condoms, and some rubbing oil?" Becca said.

Lester then recalled the recent shooting. "This is the place owned by Spider's brother. The Matrangas stole most of the girls, so the Gambinis gunned down a bunch of Matrangas having diner in Metairie."

Lester thought about the darkness below the revelry at many of the clubs and businesses in the French Quarter. Crime families had been a part of the history of New Orleans for about a hundred years and were unlikely to dispose of their holdings anytime soon. If they owned a strip club, it also gave them a place to deal drugs. If they owned a massage parlor, it also gave them a place for prostitution.

As he walked the streets and saw all the colorful and festive activity around him, he wondered who owned certain businesses. *Did most of these businesses have a box on Jim Webb's charts?* Lester wished, if they existed, he could see the boxes for the entire French Quarter. After walking a few blocks he saw it: the Royal Street Asian Massage parlor. It certainly had a prominent box with arrows pointed directly to Hot Springs, Arkansas.

At the Court of Two Sisters, the group stopped and inquired about their jazz brunch and turtle soup. They were told they would need reservations and because their schedule was in doubt for Sunday they opted not to do it. At Pat O'Brien's, they did the tourist thing and grabbed a Hurricane in a plastic container to go. They visited the Voodoo Shop as well as several shops selling t-shirts and beads. Having explored enough they returned to the hotel in time to clean up for dinner. All made it about 7:30, the ladies wearing dresses and the guys in slacks.

"Lester, when do I get to sleep with the police captain?" Debi asked, laughing.

"Why don't I call him?" Lester said and dialed his cell phone before Debi could grab it.

"Captain Campanella? Hey, we're having dinner at the Oyster Palace downtown. Would you care to join us?"

"Thanks, Lester, but we probably shouldn't do that with the way things are stirred up here. But I'll run by just to meet you guys. Be there in 20 minutes."

"Lester, was that really the captain?" asked Little Richard.

"Yes. He wants to sleep with Debi but doesn't have much time," Lester said.

"Whaaat?" Becca asked.

"Private joke, Becca—but if he really looks hot—maybe," Debi said.

They all ordered drinks and were about to order their entrees when Captain Campanella and an attractive blond lieutenant appeared at their table. He was taller than Lester and in his late forties with some grey hair peppered through thick black hair about his temples. He must have set aside time for the gym because he had no gut and looked extremely fit. He was Italian and had a powerful face with dark eyes and a strong chin. Debi looked at Lester and whispered, "Yes! Yes!—can I take him to our room?"

The Captain acted as though he didn't hear Debi and went about his introduction.

"I'm Hank Campanella, and this lady is Holly Foss." Lester and Rich stood up to great them.

They went around the table and introduced themselves. Lester said to the captain that he was Hamilton Richardson. Hank smiled and whispered that he hoped his meeting would be successful tomorrow.

"Are you expecting an all-out mob war here?" Lester asked.

"Unfortunately, Les—Hamilton, that could be the case. One reason I'm working late tonight. The logical next hit would be from the Matrangas and those aligned with them."

"Tony neutral on this—since he supplies all of them?" Lester whispered.

"That and he's kin to both families," Hank said quietly.

"We'll let you enjoy your dinner and hope we can meet again soon where we have more time to visit. Debi, I'm sorry I don't have time to come to your room tonight, but Holly keeps a tight rein on me."

Debi laughed out loud. "Hank, I didn't think you heard me say that. Lest—uhhh —Hamilton has said all along that I would be required to sleep with you when we came down here. One of our private jokes. Then you turned out to be a hunk. And the joke is on us. About 9 o'clock, would that be okay?" She laughed again and blushed.

"You guys have way too much fun up there in Hot Springs—but I hear things might bust loose there as well. I wish you guys well and want to thank you for your information on the item that now has been returned to its rightful owner," he said. He looked directly at Lester and handed him a card that had his cell number printed on it.

Hank and Holly left, and Lester and Rich checked out the rear end of Holly, whose pants were tight in all the right places. Almost in unison the two girls elbowed the two men at the table.

"Is it tattooed in your brains to check out asses on every girl that walks away from you?" Becca asked.

The two men just smiled and signaled the server that they were ready to order. Everyone ordered grilled oysters, but Lester took his out of the shell and placed them on a salad base that was created especially for him. They had Key lime pie for dessert, after-dinner drinks, and coffee which was all placed on the new credit card. Some time was spent discussing plans for going to the Louisiana Sportsman's Super Store in Chalmette the next day. One thing was for sure: a trip to Café Du Monde would take place first thing in the morning where they would have café au lait and a plate full of beignets covered with powdered sugar. The events that would happen after that didn't really seem to matter.

* * *

On Saturdays, the noon alligator feeding always drew a large crowd at the monstrous sporting goods store. Becca particularly wanted to see it and compare it to a feeding at the Hot Springs Alligator Farm. An announcement said they would feed the alligators in ten minutes. She pushed children aside to lead the group to the edge of the enclosure where the sleeping and bored prehistoric creatures were beginning to stir. A young, slender, and agile man with rubber boots and a pith helmet jumped on the feeding platform. Talking to the crowd with the aid of a microphone clipped to his safari shirt, he explained the eating habits of the now agitated alligators just a few feet below his elevated stage. After explaining ad nauseam how gators and crocodiles perform the death roll and how long it took for food to digest in their bodies, a large percentage of the crowd wanted to see it performed on the speaker. Finally he quit talking long enough to start slinging dead chickens at the large scaled beasts.

Becca seemed pleased but remarked how the Hot Springs guy sometimes got in and amongst the gators as they snapped at his legs. Everyone believed he was one-dead-chicken-removed from an ambulance ride to the nearest artificial limb store. This guy didn't take chances and stayed perched on his platform throughout the ordeal.

The group explored the store and took in all the stuffed big game animals and other creatures placed in reproductions of their natural habitat. Most impressive was a pride of lions that had taken down a wildebeest and were devouring him while he looked to be still alive.

Lester wanted to see the guns that were for sale and headed for the assault rifle section. As he looked at wide assortment of new and used large clip and magazine-fed weapons, he noticed a sign that read, "Automatic weapons are available for those discriminating individuals and sporting clubs who have clean police records and are willing to file an application with the federal government. A $200 fee will be assessed and only automatic weapons that were manufactured on or before 1986 will be considered for sale. Because of the limited supply of these weapons, the prices are reflective of that scarcity. Please ask one of our team members for further information."

A case near the sign held an M60 machine gun and a Browning automatic rifle. Neither had a price attached. Lester commented to the others, "If you have to ask the price, then you can't afford it."

Rich noted the time was 12:45 and directed everyone to a door at the rear of the store that led to the indoor firing range. Near the door was a large counter manned by two guys with name tags that read Alonso Evola and Nicco Evola. Rich introduced himself and then the rest of the group, carefully getting Lester's alias correct. Nicco walked to the door, opened it and led them through the back storage area and further through another set of doors marked "Range." As they entered the next large room, they noticed cubicles lined up side by side and a gun range equipped with electric retractable targets at each shooting position. Earmuffs, shooting glasses, and magazines of ammunition were piled up for them. Six other people were using about twenty cubicles. There didn't appear to be a range master so shooters fired at will.

Nicco said he would be back shortly and soon reappeared with a black hard plastic gun case. He smiled and opened it for Rich. Lying in a cutout of foam backing was a shiny black MAC-11.

"Okay. Who wants to shoot first?" Nicco asked.

Chapter Twenty-Two

The "girls get to shoot first" rule went by the wayside as Nicco explained blowback and rapid-fire gun rise to the group. It was decided that Rich, being the biggest and strongest of the group, would fire first. He moved inside the two-sided firing area with his safety glasses and Peltor Range Guard earmuffs with electronic communication plugs with the capability for a range master to plug in and talk to the shooter while giving him sound protection at the same time. He pulled back the lever to load a shell into the firing chamber. Nicco spoke through the muffs and told him to click off the safety. He held the machine pistol with two hands and aimed at the human silhouette target down range about thirty yards. Nicco instructed him to fire short bursts from the 30-round magazine. Rich pulled the trigger and stopped as the weapon began to rise up on him. After four short bursts he emptied the magazine. The gun performed beautifully, and surprisingly, Rich peppered the target several times. Nicco explained that having the proper-fitting magazine was extremely important. He was offering four guaranteed-to-fit magazines with the purchase and a wholesale price on a thousand rounds of ammunition. Rich said he would take the extra mags and the ammo.

It was time for the others to shoot, and Lester, a.k.a., Hamilton, asked to shoot next since he had a meeting with Tony at 1:30. A new target was installed and sent down range. Lester donned all the protection and aimed with both hands. His first trigger pull was very short, and he observed the placement of the rounds in the target. Making an adjustment, he shot a longer stream of bullets. Checking those placements, he emptied the magazine into the target. As Nicco pulled in the electronic paper silhouette, they saw the heart area of the target man was cut almost completely out. Nicco stuck his hand through it, and said he had never seen a first time shooter do that. Lester apologized to Debi and Becca for not getting to see them shoot, and left, asking Nicco directions to Tony's office. The directions led him upstairs to an array of offices; the largest looked out over the sales floor of Tony Evola's empire. Lester knocked on the inside of an open door with "General Manager" stenciled on the glass. Tony waved him in.

Tony stood up and introduced himself and an older, distinguished grey-headed man named Simon Ferrari. He shook hands with Lester and explained that he was the operations attorney. As Lester sat down adjacent to Ferrari, he passed out cards as he assumed the part of Hamilton Richardson.

"Tony, I'm totally impressed with the operation you've built here. I know you must be really proud," Lester said. "I'm going to guess you're the largest independently-owned store in the country."

"You'd be right about that, Hamilton, and yes, it's been a lot of work—especially after Katrina," Tony said.

"Just call me Ham. Yes, I heard you loaded everything on trucks and sold the inventory to Cabela's in Texas. Worked out for both of you."

"You know, another big store called me to see if it would help either of us to expand into Louisiana. Sometimes it actually helps to have competition so gun shoppers have lots of stores to pick from. Right now they're looking at Shreveport or Monroe, but it's unlikely that the population base would support it. We already have a Cabela's and a Bass Pro Shop in Louisiana, and it cost a lot to build those huge stores. They are a marvelous operations."

"Mr. Richardson, we've prepared a bid list for the guns your sheriff's office confiscated in Garland County," Simon Ferrari said. "Do you have the authority to work with us on this?"

"Yes, I have that authority, but I'm going to guess you guys know prices and market values as good as anyone in the country. You see these same automatic weapons over and over again. To be legal, each sale has to come back through a class three dealer, and there aren't many of those around," Lester said as the bid sheet was handed to him. Along with the paper came a question for Lester that he could only assume was to test his credibility and gun knowledge.

"Mr. Richardson, what can you tell us about MAC-12s?" asked Ferrari.

"You know, I'm not a real expert on guns like Tony, but from what I've read, there is no such thing as a MAC-12. Even though you may see them listed on the internet, they are just a modified MAC-11. MAC-12 became a popular nickname."

Ferrari smiled. Satisfied with Hamilton Richardson's answer, the two gun masters relaxed.

The bid was done with market prices stated in ranges according to past sales and most recent sales. The sheet reminded Lester of a residential housing and listing summary. Their offers for the weapons were on the lower side of the market and recent sale prices but not unreasonably so.

"We'll accept the bid sheet with these changes: the M60s have become more and more scarce, so if you would adjust that sale by one thousand. And, I realize that you have to make a profit with a mark-up from your bid. However, the BAR on the list will bring over twice what you have offered. Increase that amount twenty-five percent plus the adjustment on the M60 and we have a deal."

"Eight hundred adjustment on the M60 and twenty percent increase on the BAR and we'll pour a drink," Ferrari said.

"I believe we can live with that—you've got a deal," Lester said with a smile.

They all shook hands and settled back in their chairs. Lester was handed the agreement and signed it for Garland County, then dropped his pen, letting it roll under Tony's desk. He got down on his knees and reached under the desk for the pen and stuck a listening device underneath while his body shielded his actions from Mr. Ferrari.

As Lester got a hold of the runaway pen and returned to his chair, Tony was readying a drink for him.

"Ham, we have single malt, Jack Daniels, Crown, or whatever," Tony offered.

"Crown—on the rocks with a splash of Louisiana swamp water."

"Have you been following any of the new gun control laws that are pending, Mr. Richardson?" asked Ferrari, who was drinking a single-malt straight up.

"Some, but I'm just a small town lawyer who happens to have the county as a client. I read the proposed 'stand your ground' laws and 'open carry' discussions. I see what Bloomberg is trying to do in New York. I know something about the law passed in 1994, and I'm of course schooled somewhat on weapons manufactured in 1986 and before. Any new proposed laws probably will fall short with a Republican Congress. But I'm guessing, being in the business, you guys stay on top of all that and even throw some money at lobbyists in DC."

"We do, and help the NRA as best we can. California tried to scare us all back in 1994, but the law faded away in ten years and had little effect—actually increased sales and raised the prices for assault guns for fear they were going away. All this Muslim shit sells us guns every day. If I yelled on the loud speakers 'Muslims are going to get your ass,' we would have to put on extra cashiers." Tony laughed, and so did his lawyer.

"Listen, I have another proposal for you guys if you're interested. I also represent the Valley of the Vapors Sports Club in Hot Springs. I've talked to their president, Monte Hart, and he wants me to make you an offer for these guns. They've seen how much money they can make renting these things by the hour and having the big machine gun shoots like they have in Kentucky and Alabama. Would you entertain an offer? The gun club just sold some highway frontage property, so they have some cash. We understand that you'll have to take possession of the guns and then ship them back out to us because of the class three rules," Lester said.

Tony and Simon looked at each other and raised their eyebrows because an obscene profit was about to land on Tony's desk without any effort. A legal sale of several weapons all wrapped up and done without a crime family threatening to cut off his balls unless he reduced the prices on the guns. He had no plans to cut Spider in on this deal, even though half the guns were hers.

Lester reached in his pocket, pulled out some paperwork, made a slight adjustment in his offer, then handed it to Tony. The bid to buy the guns from the county was $43,200, and it had been accepted by Hamilton and represented the wholesale price for a retailer. The cost to buy them back was $58,000. It was almost a $15,000 profit that only required shipping to Chalmette and then turning around without unpacking the boxes and shipping them back to Hot Springs after recording and relabeling. Tony and Simon spoke to each other as though Lester weren't in the room. He waited patiently for them to come to a conclusion.

Finally, Tony spoke. "Ham, you realize that we could sell them here individually and make a lot more money. But time is money. I will see these guns again when the club sells some of them and buys others. I buy and sell with those clubs you talked about and two others in Mississippi. What I really want is a big client in Arkansas. So the answer is yes. I will send a check for the county, and if you would be so kind as to have Monte send me a check. This will be done quickly as club paperwork for automatics is almost automatic." He laughed at his little joke. "I'll send Monte the forms. He'll have to pay two hundred dollars per weapon for the federal fee."

"Mr. Richardson, can we take your group out to eat tonight?" Tony asked.

"Thanks, but they have someplace picked out already. They're downstairs now with your son, shooting themselves goofy. I got to shoot the MAC 11 before I came up here. What kick-ass fun! I see why the gun clubs can charge sixty-five an hour for them," Lester said and handed Tony the offer with all the club information listed on it. A copy would be signed and mailed or faxed to Monte Hart in a few days.

Lester found his group packing up at the range. Nicco had left them a few times during the shoot, so the girls were able to pull the video devices out to film down range and to the left and right. Both took trips to the bathroom and found places in the hallways to leave surveillance cameras. They stuck them under the edge of the firing enclosures facing down range. The little cameras were so small they were almost undetectable, yet had a closed circuit range of almost a mile. As soon as they left, they made contact with the ATF unit using a number Jim Webb had given them. They had already started to pick up the signals. The group had done well.

They pulled onto the highway leading to New Orleans from Chalmette. The group talked excitedly about how much fun it was to shoot the machine pistol. They didn't notice a black Cadillac Escalade pulling out behind them. They also didn't see it following them to their hotel, always staying a couple of cars back so as not to be obvious. It parked across the street for quite a while, then pulled into the hotel parking garage and parked close to Lester's red SUV. Four men got out and took turns watching the movements of the Hot Springs visitors. These four men in suits had been sitting at a table some distance across the restaurant from Lester's group on Friday night when Captain Campanella stopped by their table to say hello. Four visitors from out-of-state spending time at Tony Evola's and talking with the cops piqued their interest. Captain Campanella's visit, while only brief, had been a foolish risk.

Chapter Twenty-Three

Dinner was enjoyed at Commander's Palace and then back to the French Quarter for drinks. Becca was really excited since she had booked a short swamp adventure for them the next morning at nine. She wanted to see a real wild alligator living in a primeval setting, but mainly, it was the airboat ride that was on her bucket list. No one understood her fondness for alligators and swamps. Rich worried about snakes but agreed to go along. The trip was only about an hour long and they would leave from there to go back home.

Lester charged it on the Hamilton Richardson credit card and figured they would bounce that expense back to him when they saw the price. Becca had the directions and acted as navigator for Rich, who was driving. Lester happened to glance behind them a few times and noticed a black Escalade hanging back a few cars behind them. If it was really following them, they would know soon enough.

Their destination was Paradis, Louisiana on the banks of extensive swampland and bayous. It was a small town of around 1,200 people in St. Charles Parish. Lester guessed Paradis was French for Paradise, but that was pretty obvious. Lately, he would spit out other information from some hidden crevice in his brain. The landing where they were meeting the boat was off a rural road, and it was unlikely other cars would be crowding the two-lane roadway. However, the black Escalade was there—several hundred yards back. It was definitely tailing them.

Lester told everyone to bring their weapons just in case. Little Richard began to walk to the dock with his pistol stuck under his belt at his rear, but Lester called him back.

"Rich, let's bring along the MAC-11 and all the magazines in the gym bag. I don't like the looks of those guys," Lester said as he pulled out the bags and gave them to Rich.

"Jesus H. Christ, Lester! My mother told you to keep me out of gunfights. It looks like you're planning one," Debi said as she headed for the waiting boat nevertheless.

"Don't want one, and I'm hoping I'm wrong. Like a good Boy Scout, I'll be prepared. Can't leave you here alone."

At the dock Manny Broussard was talking it up with Becca, who got checked out thoroughly by the old Cajun. She was in full flirt mode with him, which resulted in a large reduction in price since the group wanted a one-hour, instead of the normal four-hour, tour. Next to Manny's boat, the Bayou Flyer, were two more airboats. One was manned by Billy Thibodeaux, and Manny introduced him. He waved a hello to the group. The four found their way into very comfortable seats which featured a second row much higher than the rest. The front of the aluminum craft had a lip that pointed upward at an angle and was used to drop down much like a small landing craft so passengers could go ashore and chase alligators and snakes.

Manny cranked the big engine, and the props in the wired cage began to turn at a high speed.

"Dis babe go mostly fifty miles your hour so I ax y'all ta hold on good," Manny yelled above the noise. The group had to strain to hear him and then translate his heavy accent.

Lester looked back and saw that four men in slacks and dress shirts were loading into Billy Thibodeaux's airboat. He took out his cell phone, checked his signal, and called Hank. After a couple of rings he came on line.

"Are you guys causing trouble?"

"As we speak, we're being followed in the swamp by Billy Thibodeaux's airboat loaded with four men in dress slacks and shirts. They tailed us here in a black Escalade. We're in Manny Broussard's boat out from Paradis landing. I don't believe he knows what's about to happen. Ya'll got some local people to help us? We have our pistols and that little MAC-11 with us. I see Manny has something that looks like a .22 rifle. What do you recommend we do?" Lester asked rather calmly, but Debi was tuned in to every word.

"You calling in for the National Guard, honey?" Debi asked sarcastically.

Lester looked at her and smiled, then turned back to Hank on the phone. He had gone strangely silent for a few seconds.

"Closest Sheriff's department is Boutte two miles away, but I'll alert all of St. Charles Parish. Plenty of help if you weren't in the middle of one of the biggest ass swamps in the world. Tell Manny not to stop to let you hold the baby alligators—haul ass—see if he can lose Billy. Those two happen to be the best airboat captains in Louisiana, so hide-and–seek will be a joke. I think I know who those assholes are. The first time they shoot at you give them everything you've got— maybe they'll back off. Don't let them board you. Swim with the water moccasins before you let them on board. They will smile—kill you all dead. Good luck!"

Lester approached the boat captain. "Manny, I just talked to a police captain in New Orleans. He thinks the four guys that got into Billy's boat are killers and they're after us. You have to outrun Billy— hide us in this swamp or put us where we can take them out. We may need all the weapons we have on us. Is that a .22 you have?"

"What de fok, man? You shitting to me—no? Who you guys are?" Manny was shaken but did speed up his boat and erased any smile that was there just a few seconds before. "Ya, it's a .22 long rifle single shot. For gators."

Lester went around to each of the three and told them to get down below the raised landing platform. Everyone had weapons drawn and since Lester had the best results on the range with the MAC-11, he would use it. Manny told Lester to go ahead and take the .22 and a box of ammunition he pulled from a tackle box next to him. Manny handed the shells over and moved down to the limited cover behind the chairs and a small floor space behind the raised platform for the second row of chairs. Jammed down on one end of the box of .22 shells was a seven-round magazine; another was already installed in the Marlin bolt action rifle. It was extremely simple to operate, so Lester gave Debi a very quick lesson, and she was set to go. The last time Debi and Lester entered into a gunfight, she got mad instead of scared. The pretty little lady didn't care for being shot at. Lester was hoping for the same great attitude this time.

In the distance, Lester could see the other boat as a dot in the distance. Manny had the airboat flying through the swamp and was watching intently for a bend in the bayou where he would be out of sight from Billy. That happened after about fifteen minutes of hard running. He could go left or right out of sight from his chasers. He chose right since it was a more difficult turn and crossed the water in front of the boat behind him. The channel he took was narrow, and he hoped to hide in it while Billy blasted past. Manny timed it to be way down the chute and turned into the deep swamp when Billy flew through. It worked, as he heard them go by at full speed. He turned his motor off in case they were stopping and listening.

As Manny's boat drifted under the low limbs of a bald cypress tree and up against a palmetto, a large water snake crawled from the top of the palm bush and fell into the boat very near Becca's outstretched leg. Rich put his hand over her mouth so she didn't scream, and Manny walked from his perch next to the big props and picked the snake up by its tail and slung it back into the swamp.

"I worry some," Manny said. "When dat boat moves tru da water, in da swamp, dey is a trail. Goes away afta while—not 'fore Billy sees it."

In the distance the sound of an airboat was getting closer and louder. Then it was quieter and further away—then it was coming back and again it passed the entrance to the chute that Manny had taken. It stopped and entered the chute, then stopped again and was quiet. The factor that favored anyone hiding in the swamp was its hugeness, and all the trails look alike. Inexperienced boaters may get so lost they die before they are ever found. Manny and Billy had spent almost every day of their lives in the swamp for over twenty years. No one in Louisiana knew it any better, yet they were helpless to find people who were lost without some kind of clue. Manny knew Billy could read the boat trails, but maybe he wasn't looking that hard—why help them?

Two gunshots disrupted the quietness of the swamp. Birds squawked and screeched at the ear-splitting noise. The shots seemed close by, but sound carries far over the water, even in the swamp. Maybe they were intended to make Billy stop stalling and find the other boat. What if they had wounded Billy to get him to cooperate?

Now it was very quiet. The swamp was really beautiful and for the first time, the Hot Springs group actually noticed the delicate Spanish moss hanging from the trees and the wild splendor around them. A large alligator surfaced not far from the boat and everyone pointed it out to Becca.

A motor started again, and it was moving away from them—south of them—away from the dock at Paradis, which was north. As the motor faded, Lester spoke to Manny.

"Look, Manny, if we run for it north back to Paradis, they'll chase us—maybe they'll run right into the hands of any help that might be coming. If help is coming. Hank said that there was a sheriff's office in Boutte—only two miles away," Lester said. "It's been about a half hour now—somebody's on their way—must be."

"Lester, dey is a little substation there with fo' deputies a workin' shifts. Maybe dey be two a workin' on Sunday and dem are old timers," Manny said. "Ya'll get better help from Luling or if dey's time, from Metairie. I'll hit and turn to Paradis when we clear dis trail."

Manny cranked the engine and gunned the boat towards the main channel. As soon as he cleared the chute, hit the main trail and made the left turn, they could see Billy's boat in the distance behind them to the south.

Lester noticed the distance between the two boats was narrowing. He moved back to Manny's position at the throttle.

"Manny, they're gaining. Why?"

"If I was a guessing, dey got shed of some weight."

"You mean they let some guys out as snipers in a tree or in the mangroves?" Lester asked.

"Dat, or maybe dem shots—took over a man's boat."

Lester jumped to the head of the boat and told everyone to look for a boat waiting in ambush. He took the automatic pistol and lay flat on the floor with his head just above the ramp. He thought he saw movement about a thousand yards ahead. It was a fishing boat moving rapidly out of a trail and pointing directly at the airboat. One man had an assault rifle pointing from the bow and his partner was operating the outboard motor. He fired a few rounds which hit harmlessly short of the airboat. Debi started firing the .22 and splashes of water erupted near the fishing boat. She didn't have a very powerful weapon, but it would go further than anything else they had in the boat. Shots were coming from behind Manny, but they were not yet in range. It would not be long, however. Gunfire was coming from both directions. Manny was closing in quickly on the fishing boat, and now the rounds from the assault rifle were getting closer. A few had buzzed above their heads, and one had struck the heavy landing ramp but didn't penetrate it.

"Debi, let me borrow your .22, sweetie," Lester said. Debi reluctantly handed it to him with a freshly loaded clip.

"Load me another clip."

"Say please."

"Please, goddamn it," Lester said in a calm but stern voice. He was in his combat zone, and Debi had seen it before.

Lester could feel the rounds from the fishing boat zinging above the boat and hitting the cowling around the propellers. He didn't know what would happen if the props took a few rounds, and he didn't want to think about it. He propped the Marlin over the edge of the landing ramp and found the man in the front of the boat in his sight. The water was smooth, and even though Manny had the airboat at top speed, the roll of the boat was minimal and predictable. His first round hit the man operating the motor in the shoulder, causing the boat to swerve broadside towards the mangroves, giving Lester a better shot. He quickly moved the bolt and sent another long rifle .22 round into the chamber.

Lester remembered the first gun that his dad bought him was a .22 and how much he loved it. There wasn't a squirrel or rabbit in Mountain Pine that was safe if Lester had his .22.

As the man in the front of the boat grabbed the sides of the boat to keep from going overboard, his upper body was exposed. Lester had his range now and took a breath and a strange Zen-like calmness came over him, even as rounds from behind Manny struck the prop housing again. Lester had two shots planned: the first was a head shot for the man in the front of the boat. He gently pulled the trigger and watched a bit of pink mist exit the man's head. He slumped quickly, and then Lester found the wounded man who was scrambling for the assault rifle.

Lester thought about the bolt action feature of the rifle he held—so many people wanted automatics, and then they just shot wildly and hit nothing. A bolt action makes you care about the round in the chamber. You miss, and you have to pull back the bolt, eject the shell, and move the fresh round into the chamber. You pay careful attention to how you aim, how you breathe, how you gently squeeze the trigger.

Lester let the man pick up the weapon and start to point it. This action allowed Lester to line up the shot above the barrel and between his eyes. The round found its mark and the man fell into the boat.

Manny blasted past the now unmanned fishing boat and headed toward Paradis. There were boats ahead, but they were far off and indistinguishable. More rounds were coming in, and Manny was in danger of being hit as he was basically unprotected from the rear.

"Manny, take a chute quickly and get us in firing position," Lester said, and Manny did it without saying a word. He blew through the swamp and found a fairly woody area and pulled the airboat behind two huge cypress trees. The center of the bow of the boat was between the large trees. It was a good defensive position. Behind the boat were also huge trees. They knew it was as good as they could hope for.

"Lester, while you were taking out the two guys in the boat, those guys were shooting automatic weapons—big fucking automatics—7.62 SKSs, I'm guessing. We're out-gunned," Rich said.

"SKSs aren't automatics—semiautomatics," Lester reminded him.

For the first time since the chase began, Lester paused to see if he had a signal. He didn't. Everyone checked and no one had a signal. *Not much demand for cellphone towers in the swamp,* Lester thought. If the sheriff's patrol came by they would never find them.

They heard a loud noise at the entrance to the trail, and saw Billy's airboat moving towards them. It might as well have been a German Tiger Tank. The two men in the front were also hiding behind the loading ramp. As soon as they spotted Manny's boat they opened up with automatics. Both were AK-47 fully automatics and used the same 7.62 rounds as the SKS that Rich had misidentified. These rounds were certainly capable of tearing through the hull of the aluminum boat. The rounds were being sprayed all over the swamp but not connecting to their targets. Slowly, they moved closer and closer as Billy idled the boat towards his friend's airboat. When they were about two hundred yards away, they stopped behind a grove of cypress trees.

Lester believed he had two weapons that were useful. The pistols were not much help. Debi was now holding his .45 automatic, Becca had a 9mm automatic, and Rich used a Glock .40 caliber. All of these were great close-combat weapons but pretty useless at 200 yards. The .22 was accurate at 200 yards but needed to hit something vital or they would just laugh it off. The MAC-11 was just an overgrown pistol but had the capacity to sling a lot of inaccurate lead around in hope of a lucky hit. These thugs didn't know they had an automatic weapon, and it just might make a difference being peppered with live rounds all around them.

Billy's boat was now maneuvered in place and both of the men stood up to fire the AKs in their direction. Before they could fire, there was a rapid buzzing sound and .380 rounds flew all around them, striking one of the men in his upper right shooting arm. Lester had used a 32 round magazine, and it only took two seconds to empty it. He was pleased that the man was wounded but was more concerned that 31 rounds missed altogether. He would try the .22.

All Lester's fears were realized when he lined up the sight on the enemy boat. Standing on the bow of the boat was Billy, his hands bound, and a pistol aimed at his head. The man holding the pistol yelled over to Manny's boat.

"Move your boat over here next to us and we won't shoot him. You won't be harmed. We just want to ask you some questions!" the man shouted.

"Who are you? We haven't done anything to you!" Lester yelled back.

"We saw you with Campanella and with Tony Evola. We know you're investigating the Matranga shootings. We don't know if you are FBI or NSA or what the fuck. Just can't let you out of here," he said.

While he was talking, Lester had the .22 next to the tree and found solidity. He knew this gun and had killed two people with it. A lightweight instrument much like the one he had as a child. No other gun would ever be any better than this little gun. It was a child's first extension of power over other creatures. Lester waited patiently until there was a little separation between the man with the pistol and Billy. The time came when a full silhouette of Billy and the man were separated by a ray of light, and he took the shot. He knew he wouldn't miss. The man holding the pistol never heard the crack of the .22. He fell lifelessly to the deck of the boat. Almost immediately after, a sheriff's police boat pulled up next to Billy's boat. They held a gun on the wounded man until they got him on board. Billy was unharmed but had splattered blood on his cheek and shirt.

Manny's and Billy's airboats followed the sheriff's boat and several other police vessels back to Paradis. The fishing boat was recovered and the search for the bodies of the occupants was in progress. Hank was waiting at the dock.

"Why don't you guys get out of town before I'm put out of a job? Looks like these were the guys that hired the hit on the Matrangas. You guys okay?" Hank asked.

"I got to see an alligator, so I'm going back happy," Becca said.

The laughter relieved some of the tension. The group got into the SUV for the drive back to Hot Springs just as it started to rain, hard and steady, with thunder and consistent lightning. In Lester's mind, he thought maybe it was meant for him as a forgiving and cleansing rain.

Chapter Twenty-Four

It rained constantly until they crossed over into Mississippi, where it stopped almost as soon as they entered the state. Lester saw this as a sign. He didn't know if it meant everything that happened in Louisiana had been cleansed, or if it was just a coincidence.

After a stop in Vicksburg for lunch, they were back on the road with Rich driving and Becca riding in the front seat. It appeared the two had enjoyed each other's company and bed-sharing on the trip. Lester had talked to Hank, who took care of the write-up in the *Times-Picayune* Monday edition regarding the shooting.

"Off-duty Police Officers Attacked by Shooters from the Gambini Crime Family."

The article went on to point out the police officers were from Arkansas and referred to Lester as Hamilton Richardson, an attorney for Garland County, Arkansas and his girlfriend, omitting her name. The purpose of the trip was to sell surplus weapons, taken in a raid in Arkansas, to the Louisiana Sportsman's Super Store in Chalmette. It mentioned that the Arkansas deputies, Rich Roberson and Becca Valdez had been attacked while on an airboat tour in the swamp outside of Paradis, LA. The Arkansas group had represented themselves well in the firefight; they had killed three and wounded one more of the gangsters. Captain Hank Campanella, special organized crime investigator of the New Orleans police department, issued a statement identifying the four attackers as suspects in the hiring of hit men responsible for the Matranga killings at the Oyster Palace in Metairie a few days ago.

Lester relayed what Hank had read to him word-for-word to the rest of the group in the car. He explained that Debi's name was left out of the write-up, and he was still Hamilton Richardson, an attorney for Garland County. This ruse had to continue until ATF could put together enough information to raid Tony's place. The article went on to say that a fisherman had been killed and his boat hijacked by the suspects. He hoped maybe Debi could keep this second shootout secret from her parents, but there was a good chance local reporters would pick it up from the national news. It would be something else that Lester would have to atone for with her parents—especially her mom. He had practically promised her that she wouldn't be a part of a gunfight if he saw it coming. If he had left her by herself back at the dock they might have—no, would have—killed her. Lester was going to tell Susan he couldn't abandon her on the docks and hope she would believe he was trying to protect her.

As the rain had stopped and lunch was behind them, Lester believed it was time to break the story of Spider Gambini to Debi. The plan was Little Richard would start the story, and Lester would pick up the events, including the bathtub scene, which Lester knew would cause him unlimited hardship. He considered all the possible consequences and hoped the protection of two other friends might keep him from being strangled by Debi.

"Uh, Debi, the strangest thing happened when you were gone to California," Rich said.

"What was that, Rich?" Debi asked, suspicious of his opening line.

"Well, I get this phone call from someone who says she is Lester's cousin from Tennessee. Says she is Darlene McFarlin and wants to know how he's doing after the surgery and says everyone in Tennessee wants to know," Rich said. He glanced back in the back seat at Debi to see if she was smiling. Lester, on the other hand was turning increasingly pale.

"Well, I told her I didn't know Lester had cousins in Tennessee—told her he couldn't remember much. I said you were having a nurse come by later in the week. I also told her you were in California looking after your brother who had been in a car wreck." Little Richard was nervous as he related the story.

"My God, Rich—that could have been anyone! I can't believe

you gave out that information with him all by himself and couldn't remember shit!"

Lester took the baton and picked up the story.

"Debi, I didn't remember much, but I did remember you telling me a nurse was coming by sometime. I didn't know when. Well, later that day there was a knock on the door and this lady said she was a nurse that you had ordered. Well, she came in and wrote down some information, said I was supposed to have a bath, and she was there to keep me from falling." Lester's voice was shaky. Debi sensed this elaborate explanation was trouble.

"Hold it. What did this nurse look like?" Debi asked. She was starting to suspect something; the ugly nurse would not have generated such an elaborate story.

"Uhhh—she was about thirty-something—rather attractive," Lester said, trying to be underwhelming regarding Spider's drop-dead gorgeous looks.

"Okay, let's get to the good part of the story!".

"Okay...okay. This lady had me fill up the tub and she helped me get in so I wouldn't fall." Lester stopped at this point He wasn't really sure how to explain the rest as a helpless victim of nurse abuse.

"More—I know there's more!" Debi was breathing hard. Lester hoped the weapons were locked up in the back of the car.

"I was just kidding with her that she should get in with me—I know I shouldn't have, but I didn't know much about our relationship then." Lester watched Debi cross her arms in front of her. Tears were welling up in her eyes. Becca was inching down in her seat and Little Richard's eyes were glued to the road.

"For whatever reason, she got in with me. She soaped me down pretty good in front, but that's all that happened." Lester felt like a young boy whose mother caught him playing with himself.

"Does 'soap me down' mean something like a hand job?"

"Yes—but as it happened, I remembered you and me in the shower together and knew we had a relationship. It all came flooding back. Anyway, she left and didn't come back. Now you have to hear who the woman actually was," Lester said.

"I don't care. You can't be trusted by yourself for a few days, then let the first nurse that comes along whack you off." Debi was crying and cursing fitfully.

"I just had a brain operation and didn't remember shit! Give me a little break here."

"A break might just be what we need!" Debi's face was buried in her hands.

"Debi, if he won't tell you, then I will. The girl was Angel 'Spider' Gambini," Rich said.

"What! You believed a mob boss was a nurse?" Debi was incredulous.

"I didn't know any different. She didn't have her mob outfit on. She looked like a kind of pretty nurse to me." Lester's voice cracked as he began to realize the trouble he was in.

"Why would she impersonate a nurse and trick you into getting in a tub with you?" Debi asked.

"I now remember from the couple times that I met her in the past that she seemed to like me. At the meeting at S.G. Crystals, she put her arm around me to lead me through the door and looked at me in the way women look when they're interested."

"What does she look like?" Debi asked.

"I've only seen her picture," Becca said. "But if she looks anything like her picture, she is one hot bitch!"

"Uh…we did some research on her and she was first runner up in the Miss Louisiana beauty contest about sixteen or seventeen years ago," Rich said.

"I was asking Lester!" Debi blurted. "I want to know what you thought she looked like since you pretty much saw all of her."

Lester expected his answer would be a death trap. If lying or exaggeration ever had justification, then its time had come.

"Middle-aged, former beauty queen, on her way down. I'll tell you this, even in her prime—which I will point out, she isn't there anymore—she couldn't match you on any scale," Lester said. Rich and Becca resisted an ovation for his great line of bullshit.

"Nice recovery, butthole," Debi said calmly, a departure from her earlier violent outbursts.

Chap Harper

179

"What color is her hair?"

"Blond, but probably dyed since she's Italian," Lester said.

"Tall?"

"Fairly so, I'd say," Lester squeezed out the answer.

"Long legs so she could wrap then around you in a bathtub?" Debi said, yelling again.

"Jesus, baby, can we get past this? I didn't have to tell you about it, but think we should always be honest with each other," Lester said. He thought to himself it might have been better to have never told her and just risk her finding out from Spider someday.

Lester decided to take a whack at humor to lighten the mood.

"The big defensive line woman with the mustache came by the next day, but I was pretty spoiled by then so I sent her packing," he said, laughing. Rich and Becca joined in.

Debi turned her head towards the window and suppressed a smile.

Becca changed the subject and talked about a restaurant in Pine Bluff where they could stop for dinner if it was open on Sunday.

As the trip progressed, Debi slowly came back to life. When all seemed in a state of normalcy, Lester looked in Debi's eyes and asked her if she would please forgive him for what happened.

"Yes, Lester, I forgive you, but not the bitch that tricked you. If we are ever in a gun fight and she's on the other side—I get to kill her."

"I hope you aren't a part of that again, but you can take her out if you can live with it," Lester said.

"I'll sleep well…don't you worry."

Chapter Twenty-Five

It was late when they returned to Hot Springs. Becca and Little Richard were going to stay at his place, a small house on the road to Bismarck nestled in the woods way off the main road. Rich had purchased the two-bedroom, one-bath cottage with the help of his parents. The forty acres that accompanied the little house made the property a potentially valuable piece of real estate.

Lester and Debi held hands as they walked from the parking lot to his apartment. They dropped their suitcases by the door and went to the shower. Debi was intense as she stared at him during the process of applying soap all over him. Afterwards they barely dried off before heading to the bed. Debi climbed on top and took a position of dominance as though to say, "*I own you, and no one else had better interfere.*"

Afterwards, they both slept well for a while. It had been a long, eventful, and emotional day. Debi and Lester would go back to work on Monday. Debi would catch up with her growing list of clients, and Lester would catch up with Jim at the FBI to see about their next move against Spider.

Debi woke up once during the night, gasping for air. Lester took her in his arms and assured her that she was having a bad dream. She kissed him and told him she loved him and went back to sleep. It was harder for Lester to go back to sleep because he had so many decisions to make. Did he want to finish his undergraduate work and just work as a consultant during that time? He would lose his benefits and have to take one of the college health plans which were limited in coverage. Insurance was important because he didn't know if he might need further surgery. Debi was under twenty-six so she was still on her parents' health coverage. He hated thinking about insurance.

Time was critical, so he was leaning towards an online degree. He believed he could finish enough courses in the next six months. Combined with his blind school credits, he should be ready to enter law school the next fall. A law school in Little Rock featured a lot of courses that could be taken at night and online. Deep down, though, Lester wanted to attend a well-known, preferably East Coast, law school, such as Harvard, Yale, or Georgetown. Maybe Stanford on the West Coast. Everything had opened up for him as a possibility. First, he had to get all of that behind him and take the LSAT entrance exam. He had bought the practice exam and could ace it without a problem. Finally, having solved some of this in his head, he fell asleep.

* * *

Angel Gambini had now heard about both shootings in New Orleans. The first were relatives of hers and the second were members of her deceased husband's family. She wished she could have been there to take them out herself. She was strangely intrigued by the limited report in the local paper. Where was Lester in the newspaper article? Who in the hell was this attorney, Hamilton Richardson? He had a girlfriend, but her name wasn't mentioned. Was she a juvenile and they were protecting her? She smelled a cover up and was sure neither Rich nor Becca could have taken out mobsters with automatic weapons. Only one guy at the sheriff's department could do it and his name wasn't in the paper.

She called information in Little Rock for a listing on the attorney and was given a number. After calling and getting the answering service, she was given the address for an office building on Capitol Street in Little Rock. Since it was about time for her weekly shopping trip to the city, she decided that it was time to visit Mr. Richardson. The next week would be a visit to see her son in New York, so some new clothes would be in order, as well as some gifts for him.

Before hitting the shopping centers in west Little Rock she found a parking spot not far from the building Richardson kept as an office. It was on the third floor of a building that contained mainly government offices and was mostly utilitarian and lacking in charm. She found Suite 326 labeled as Hamilton Richardson. It was locked, but she could see from the window next to the door that there was a reception desk and a huge bookcase filled with law books. Spider knew they were just for show since law was now practiced online or from stored sources on a hard drive. She went to the office next to his and stuck her head in to the federal rural development loan office where she found a young attractive black lady manning a desk.

"Do you happen to know when Mr. Richardson will be back in the office?"

"I don't keep up with dat man. He works out of town most de time. I've only worked here 'bout a month and I ain't never met him. Don't care much for lawyers, so doubt if I missed nuttin," she said, with a thick accent.

Angel decided he might really exist after all since he had an office and a phone number. If he worked primarily with county, state, and federal agencies, then it would make sense to have his office in a federal building. She stopped briefly in the lobby to look at the directory to see who else was in the building.

"Holy shit!" she said loud enough for the security guard at the desk nearby to turn and frown in her direction. Listed with offices in the building were the FBI, ATF, and the DEA. The three circles of hell that would love to lock her up until the next ice age. Was it just a coincidence that this lawyer was surrounded by all this evil? He had to be working with them or for them. Maybe he was ex-military and that's why he was such a good shot. Did they have her in their sights as well?

Spider rushed out of the building. She hurried through her shopping trip and got everything in order to leave in two days for the East Coast. Hot Springs had finally come together with enough inventories to supply product in all her ventures. The meth lab at S.G. Crystals was running full speed along with other drugs sorted and distributed there. A good supply of guns had been delivered to the bait store with more on order. Money was rolling in from the strip clubs, the call girl operation was exploding, and expansion was planned from two states to several others. Rich men paid large sums for beautiful girls delivered to their homes, vacation rentals, or hotels, as long as they looked like they belonged there. Spider taught classes in how to dress like rich bitches and not like whores in line for a John at a brothel.

In a matter of months, Spider had put together a network of businesses easily capable of bringing in a few million a year and would expand exponentially with little work on her part. The drug dealers came to Mt. Ida to pick up the product or it was delivered to them on fake UPS trucks. The dark net was used for most of the large dealer drug sales, the automatic weapons sales, and the call girl payments, which ranged between $1,000 and $10,000. All these transactions were hidden behind encryption so cleverly done the code couldn't be broken and was rewritten weekly.

Spider felt good about her accomplishments, yet loneliness plagued her. Even though her husband cheated, she missed being married. He got himself shot to pieces forcing his crime syndicate into another crime family's territory. When the marriage was good, it was very good. Angel was proud of their son, Frankie. He was a handsome, smart, and athletic young man. There was little doubt he accounted for the total sum of good she had done in her life.

She had recently received a phone call from Nick Martorana, who was her high school boyfriend until she went off to college. The big issue in their relationship was a lack of real family ties between the Matrangas and Martoranas. Nick's dad was an attorney and represented several families in the New Orleans area but didn't have his foot in the crime business. He was clean and so was Nicky, as Angel called him. He married and had a daughter, Gina, who was one year younger than Frankie and attended the same private school. At fourteen she looked much older and was tall and drop-dead gorgeous. Frankie certainly noticed her, but at fifteen he was still a little awkward around girls. Nick's wife passed away from ovarian cancer two years ago. Angel sent him a card as Nicky did for her when Richie was killed. He was going to be in New York while Angel was there for Frankie's birthday and wanted to have dinner with them one night. Now a successful attorney,

Nicky was following in his dad's footsteps. It would be the four of them at Tavern on the Green in the city. Nick knew that Angel came every year for the birthday event and planned ahead to see her. He also had liked being married and missed it as well.

* * *

While Lester was enrolling in online courses during the day, Debi was trying to explain to her mother how Lester couldn't leave her at the dock in Paradis and took her along to protect her. Her mother wasn't happy and kept saying, "Lester promised not to take you on gunfights." It sounded so ridiculous—even funny—for a policeman to promise not to take his girlfriend anywhere gunfire might erupt, but soon Lester would face Susan Green again and groveling was not out of the question. Roses would not do the trick this time. Debi was her only daughter and Susan wanted her protected from bullets buzzing by her head. It had happened twice within a few-week period. Debi told her mom patients were waiting and went back to work.

Lester was back at his desk at the office having enrolled in every course listed in the catalogue in front of him. Also piled on his desk were applications for scholarship and federal Pell grants. Lester had no trouble reading them or filling them out. He was enjoying the process and his new ability to master all forms and applications. While he was in the middle of the paperwork, Mike Adams welcomed him back, then asked if the applications had anything to do with police work.

"Uh, Sheriff, most of these courses are criminal justice-related. Isn't there money available for college courses for members of the department?" Lester asked.

"Yeah, I think so. Ask the clerk. You talked to Jim today?"

"No, but I will soon. Oh, do you mind if I take the sergeant exam this week? I know it's normally given only at certain times, but I'm asking for the special circumstance exception listed on page 2, paragraph 4."

"We'll see. Let me check with the clerk," Mike said and wandered off towards his office. Lester thought Mike might have been a little intimidated by his newfound skills.

"What have you done to Sheriff Adams? He seems a little flustered," Peggy said, standing next to Lester and making sure her hip was pressed against his body.

"Uh—not sure. Maybe he's not used to me reading. It makes it a little harder to bullshit me. Did you find the rules on special exam exceptions?"

"Indeed I did. It clearly states those officers unable to take the exam at normal intervals because of sickness or injury can request make-up exams at any time. Your interview and oral exam was done last time. You passed, and I doubt they will repeat it. A proctor must be present during the entire exam. By the way, Lester, I am an official proctor," Peggy said in a sexy voice.

"Does it mean you and I will be locked in a room together for hours and hours?" Lester asked with a crooked smile. He wondered why he instinctively had to flirt, even when he knew it would get him in trouble.

"Of course, dear. We haven't had fun together in a while. I've missed you. Are you ready?" Peggy wasn't flirting—she was trolling.

"Peggy, we had fun, and I still like you, but it ain't going to happen again. You know I'm involved, and I guess, as pretty as you are, you are, too. I'd appreciate you finding me a space for the exam. Please."

"Come with me, baby." Peggy had Lester follow her to an interrogation room with windows. "You're right, I do have a boyfriend, but we can keep secrets," she said, just stabbing at the air.

She led him to a table and chair.

"You're allowed three hours for the exam."

He had taken it before but basically had sat looking at the exam for three hours since he couldn't read any of it. Neither Sheriff Adams nor the two previous sheriffs would allow it to be given orally. Peggy went to retrieve the exam and asked if he wanted any water. She returned very quickly with the exam, a bottle of water, and a couple sharpened pencils. She placed a digital clock with a timer on the table. She looked at Lester, smiled, and wacked the clock with her hand, starting the three-hour timer. The pretty proctor sat behind a two-way glass mirror and began reading a book, and on occasion she would look at him and blow a kiss.

Lester looked at the second hand on the timer move and started turning pages of the test. He had practiced all the way to New Orleans and back, every night before the trip, and while he was there. He found if he looked the center of the page he could read lines—then pages in seconds. He retained everything he read, even the serial number of the test. In sixteen minutes, Lester hit the button on the clock and stopped. He folded the test and tapped on the window where Peggy was half asleep. Puzzled, she hurried into the room, her eyes wide as she focused on the paper in his hand.

"Did you give up?"

"Nope! I'm finished. Didn't miss any. Whenever Mike will let me, I'll take the lieutenant exam. I'm ready. Do you know if any slots for sergeant are open?"

Peggy rushed the exam to Mike, who graded it with her help. No one had ever aced it, and no one had ever completed it in sixteen minutes. But after the two graders finished, Lester held both records. Mike had no choice but to promote him as of the first of the next month since there was a slot open. He could have asked him to go through the interview part of the exam again, but Lester had always passed that part with flying colors. Mike Adams was happy for Lester, but he realized Lester could be a formidable opponent in the next sheriff's race. The sheriff knew that Lester couldn't take the lieutenant exam until he served as a sergeant for a period of time. Lester didn't care as other goals required his attention. He made a call to Debi.

"Debi, say hi to Sergeant McFarlin." Lester was pleased that this simple challenge had been completed.

"Oh, my God! You did it. It was one of our goals. I'm so happy for you. Was it hard? What did you score?" She was very excited.

"Made a hundred and finished in sixteen minutes," Lester said, bragging a little.

"Holy shit! My god! You're like a machine," Debi said, a little apprehensively.

"No, baby, I'm just me. The same guy you sleep with every night and the same guy who loves you so much he shares his gunfights with you. I've just removed a plug in my brain. Too much info sometimes—

care to know the serial number on the test?" Lester laughed, and Debi joined him.

"Oh, your dad called me and wants all of us to go fishing this weekend," Debi said.

"Yeah, sounds like fun. Think your mother will throw me overboard?"

Chapter Twenty-Six

Immediately after calling Debi, Lester dialed Jim Webb to catch him up.

"Hey, Jim. I guess you heard about the excitement in New Orleans?"

"Lester, you guys are lucky to be alive. But you did some great work. The ATF guys are monitoring everything in Tony's office and the gun range. They haven't opened any secret vault yet, but guys are on it 24/7. You take the exam yet?"

"Yeah, passed it and will be promoted to sergeant first of the month."

"Way to go! What's next for you?"

"Correspondence courses first for a BA and then LSAT test for law school. What's going on with Spider and Stick?" Lester asked.

"We learned from an S.G. informant Spider's leaving in a couple days to visit her son in New York. Guns are moving almost daily from the bait store, picked up by fake UPS trucks. Put two explosives in Stick's tree stand. He found one. Other one looks like a tree branch, still in place. We have the location on ten call girls and will have the rest in a couple of weeks," Jim said.

"What about S.G. Crystals? Are the mikes working?" Lester asked.

"The one you put in the radiation house is working great. They discuss making and shipping the crap. Helps us track everything they do. The one you put under the conveyer belt picks up a little, but the middle of the warehouse is pretty quiet. You do realize, Lester, that everything we get from those devices is illegal, and all records will have to be destroyed. Glad we have them, though," Jim said.

"So the master plan?"

"Once we locate the big vault in New Orleans and see if they have a pattern for opening it, we'll plan our full raid while the illegal weapons are exposed. The bait store, S.G., and the call girls will all happen at once. What we dread is the S.G. raid. Lots of automatic weapons and workers. I'm guessing it will all go down within the next two weeks. Lots of man hours in this, Lester," Jim said, realizing the deputy's tenacity of following up on a domestic shooting had uncovered a sleeping crime giant. Lester snuck around until he found enough evidence to take to his skeptical boss.

"How about Stick? Tailing him?"

"Yes, he goes from the bait store, to the massage parlor, and back to S.G. He's Spider's right-hand man. Spends a lot of time at her condo, but never spends the night. Slam—bam—thank you ma'am," Jim said. "Also, he has these call girls come by every few days at his place, and I bet it's for free, without Spider's knowledge."

"She wouldn't be happy. I'm glad you have a tail on him because I get the impression he follows us on occasion," Lester said.

"He does, but we're behind him or around close by," Jim said. "I think Spider wants to know what you're up to."

"We're going fishing with my dad on Saturday, and I'd appreciate it if you watch him because we'll be in the middle of Lake Ouachita, like sitting ducks."

I don't think he'll be gunning for you, but ya never know. I'll double up on Saturday," Jim said.

"What's Jake been doing in Mount Ida?" Lester asked.

"His crew does some surveillance around S.G. Crystal and even though it's in Garland County, he keeps an eye on the bait store," Jim said. "Oh, I forgot. Sheriff Jake caught one of the employees with drugs on a traffic stop near Pencil Bluff. In exchange for not sending him to jail, he agreed to be an inside informant. He planted a legal video device that covers the whole warehouse floor yesterday. We actually got a warrant directly from a judge who hand-wrote it, so no other employee of the courthouse knows. We've seen the stairs to the underground facility. Also, you were right about the vents covered by tool boxes. Got everything on film. Bad thing—as I said before, they got tons of automatic weapons." Jim then hung up as he had another call.

Lester called Debi and asked if she would like to meet him for dinner. "You pick the place, dear, and don't say you don't care where," Lester said, having been in this scenario before.

"Ok, it's Monday and a lot of places are closed. How about Fisherman's Wharf? It's close to our place." It was really Lester's place, as Debi hadn't stayed in her apartment in weeks. The apartment was now girlified, with sexy panties and bras in the top drawer of his dresser, his jockey shorts and socks relegated to a lowly bottom drawer.

"That's fine wid me. What time do you want to meet?" Lester asked.

"Five-thirtyish?"

"Otay—Buckwheat be dere," Lester said. He waited for Debi to call him racist, but she didn't.

They arrived at almost the same time and were seated promptly since it wasn't busy. After ordering, they talked about the fishing trip and then Debi's growing business. Lester had a question.

"Debi, if I were to go to law school at say Harvard or Yale, could you start your practice out there? At this time, it's just speculation, but I'm shooting for that possibility."

"Of course I could, but most likely I'd partner with an existing clinic. When do we go, sweetie?" Debi said, laughing.

"Hopefully, next fall semester. You see, all I need is to complete two years of college in six months, take the LSAT and get accepted to an Ivy League college. Oh, and find a shit pot of money. Should be a breeze. I want you with me wherever I go. Just asking if you're flexible. I mean—I know you are flexible in bed—but concerning your profession?" Lester said, smiling.

"I am Miss Flexible! Any way you want to flex me!"

"Good. I can quit worrying about going to law school for three or four years by myself."

"Four years? Are you considering a Master's in taxation or something?"

"Probably criminal law. Don't know where, though. Yale is rated the best, Harvard second, and Stanford is the third-ranked school and the best for climate. Debi, we're southern people and Connecticut and Cambridge would have us both cussing the winters. A scholarship is a must at all of these since they all cost about fifty thousand a year. Of course, a small house in Palo Alto would be close to a million. Your brother in Walnut Creek maybe could rent us out a bedroom?" Lester was rambling, but Debi understood that he wanted to build his life around her.

"He's out of the hospital and going through rehab now. Slated to go back to work in a week or so. I'm sure Ray and Sasha would love to have built-in babysitters, but that's a tough commute across the bay from Walnut Creek. If your classes were in off-peak hours, then maybe it wouldn't be that bad. Maybe we could get Dad to buy a fixer-upper for an investment. He has about ten rent houses now. His parents always had them," Debi said.

"I'm guessing he would have to sell all ten of them to get a shack on the peninsula in the bay area, but we'll deal with that later. Let's talk about the fishing trip. Dad wants to meet us for breakfast at Mountain Harbor at seven and then head out. He will go catch some shad for bait before he meets with us. He'll do everything for them on the trip— from baiting their hooks to cleaning the fish. He asked me to take care of the drinks and snacks. Maybe we can go shopping together on Friday and get everything we need?"

"So, are we picking up my parents a little before six Saturday morning?"

"Yes. That will give your mother plenty of time to chew my ass out all the way to the boat dock."

"She will be swift and deadly. I'll try to protect you, but there's only so much I can do."

"Thanks, but at least say you'll attend my graveside services."

"If the weather is nice."

Their food arrived, and Lester immediately became quiet in thought. He took a sweet potato fry and doused it with powdered sugar from a plastic container on his plate. Maybe he would go on the offense with Susan Green, act tough and say he had to keep Debi close.

Maybe he would just take his ass-chewing like a man or bring up law school. Law school could be his savior.

* * *

Sam Reed sat in his Chalmette Cleaning Service van at a small strip shopping center a block from the Louisiana Sportsman's Super Store. At two in the morning, he was alone serving a shift for the Alcohol, Tobacco and Firearms Agency. He attacked the boredom as he played a game of Plants vs. Zombies on his iPad. Surrounded by spying equipment, he sat by himself behind blacked-out windows, primed and ready for anything transmitted from the store. Lester and his confederates had done a great job planting the tiny spy cameras. This wasn't his first night on duty, so loneliness and tedium were the only things he expected.

He was about to take a sip of coffee when he noticed lights and people walking down the center of the practice range at the rear of the store. He was fairly sure Tony and Nicco were leading the assembly of employees moving toward the back of the gun range. Somewhere behind the stacks of sandbags, Nicco reached over and pulled open a panel door, exposing a bright green keyless entry board. He placed his open hand against the emerald-colored light, and huge concrete doors began to open inward; fluorescent bulbs flickered and lit the interior. Sam had seen enough.

"Captain Campanella, sorry to wake you, but you're the coordinator for this operation. This is Sam Reed in the surveillance van; they just opened the secret door!" Sam said, excitedly.

"No problem, Sam. Just tape everything as I'm sure you're doing. What you'll probably see next will be the weapons pulled out and packed for shipment. A UPS truck will appear at the back dock. It'll be fake—with a fake driver. The door will close and legitimacy will reign again for Tony and his sons. Note the time the doors open and close. What I think is, they use the same time every week so that employees don't have to be paid overtime every few days. Great work. I'll notify the whole team." Hank was now wide awake and plotting to possibly take this whole thing down in both states at the same time next week. He knew Spider would be out of town for a few days but would be back on Sunday, if his sources from Jim were correct. Jim Webb would supervise the Arkansas raids. The New Orleans officers would need to know the location of all the fake UPS trucks to take them down. He wouldn't wake Jim or Lester now. There would be plenty of time later in the day to start planning from the top down without letting anything leak out. Most didn't have a need to know—yet.

Chapter Twenty-Seven

Stick gathered up his camouflage carrying case and loaded it into his new Ford 250 XL truck. He paid over $50,000 for it as he required a diesel power plant, crew cab, and four wheel drive. If there was an option available, he bought it or ordered it. He was headed towards Lake Ouachita and had no idea he was being followed. The tail was a professional one, consisting of three cars that pulled over as new tails pulled out. Some of the tails would pass him only to pull out again later. Stick was listening to a country station on satellite radio, oblivious to the elaborate spying being played out around him. He stopped at a grocery store near Mountain Harbor, grabbed a sausage biscuit, drove several miles, and turned onto the road leading to Ouachita Shores Marina. It was around seven in the morning, and he believed there was plenty of time.

At precisely the same time, Lester pulled up to the Mountain Harbor Cafe and helped Susan from the rear seat of the Yukon. She had expressed her concern for the danger that Debi had been in during the airboat ride in New Orleans. Lester apologized and explained that after a few weeks, things should return to normal, once all these people were arrested. He told her that he was trying to get into law school the next year, and hopefully that would be a safe environment. As he exited the car, Adrian was waiting at the door for them. Debi introduced her dad to Adrian and then was intercepted by her mom who had moved in front of her to shake his hand.

"My God, Adrian, you're a John Wayne version of Lester. Debi said you were handsome, but you're just not playing fair," Susan said.

"Ma'am, you're awfully sweet to say that, but I see why Debi is one of the most beautiful young ladies I've ever seen—she looks just like her mother." Adrian said this with a perfect smile.

"You two are so full of shit! Let's have breakfast, so Adrian can tell us about striper fishing," Debi said and pulled her mom inside the cafe.

The cafe smelled like bacon, coffee, and bread baking. Hanging on the wall were several large trophy fish, including a striper that may have weighed thirty pounds. Outside the windows at the side of cafe they could see the resort's swimming pool, and beyond was the marina and the lake. Lake Ouachita sparkled in the morning sunlight. It wound in and out of coves, creeks, and rivers along a shoreline that was over 900 miles long. They found a table near a window and started fumbling through the large plastic menus.

"Coffee for everyone? How 'bout some orange juice?" the waitress with "Georgia" on her name tag asked.

Everyone ordered their breakfast and drinks. Tom said he was paying for the meal, and everyone thanked him. Adrian then explained the adventure.

"Okay, can't guarantee nothing but the shad are running pretty good. I didn't have much trouble netting a bunch of them. Lake's turning over a little as the thermocline is moving more towards the bottom and driving the fish to shallow water. We'll be fishing mainly close to the surface and I'll rig everything. Lester, you brought beer, wine, and snack stuff?"

"Yes, sir! Your brand of beer, too!" Lester was almost embarrassed that long neck Budweiser bottles were all that his dad drank. No fancy crap for him.

Their shopping trip on Friday produced different drinks for everyone. Three kinds of beer and two bottles of wine: one red and the other white. All sorts of cheese, nuts, and chips. Debi thought it was enough food stuff to stock a second Gilligan's Island.

"Adrian, do you have clients every weekend this time of year?" Tom asked.

"It's a beautiful time of the year to fish, so yeah, I stay busy most weekends. Dr. Woodward and Dr. Wright were out last weekend. I think you know them. I told them my son was dating your daughter.

They said they both had worked with you. Even said nice things about you," Adrian said, getting a laugh out of Tom.

* * *

Stick carried his case to a hill near an area called Denby Point where there were no houses. He settled down in a cleared area and got down into a prone position and made what a sniper called his hide. Then he unzipped the case and slid a long Leupold spotting scope out and folded down the tripod attached to it. At that moment, without him having a clue, the cross hairs of three sniper rifles were aimed and focused on him. However, he never produced a weapon, merely a single-lensed and very powerful scope. He was familiar with where Adrian normally fished as he had asked the other striper guides. The three FBI guys kept observing but took no further action. One of them decided to call Lester.

"Lester, this Larry Slater with the FBI. We followed Stick to a point where he has eyes on you with a spotter scope. Doesn't seem to have a weapon, and we have three rifles on him if he tries anything. Just thought you might like to know you were being spied on."

"Hey, I appreciate you guys tracking him. He knows something is up since he found an explosive device in his hide by the warehouse. Thanks again," Lester said.

Lester was standing in the back of the boat while his dad was helping Tom and Susan fish the front of the boat. Debi got up from her seat and stood next to Lester as he placed his phone back in his pocket.

"Debi, look over past the shore and up on the hill. Follow my lead."

Lester looked directly at the hill and raised a middle finger in the air. Debbie did the same. Next, he turned his rear towards the hill and dropped his pants and mooned in the same direction. Debi followed suit. As both of them pulled up their pants there was a yell from the front of the boat in Susan's direction. "Fish on!" Adrian said and immediately started assisting a smiling Susan Green. No one had seen the mooning in the back of the boat.

Shock was the first emotion Stick felt. Abruptly, he looked around but couldn't see anyone. He knew instantly he had been followed and observed. Lester had been tipped off that he was spying on him. Jamming the scope back in its case, he walked back to his truck and blasted down the road and back to highway 270. First, it had been the explosive planted in his hide near S.G., and now this. He wouldn't bother Spider about this since she was in New York, but as soon as she got back they had to beef up security. As he drove back to town, one thing stuck out in his mind—he had seen Debi Green's beautiful ass. Every time the picture of her dropping her pants flashed from his memory, he smiled.

After the fishing trip, Susan and Tom couldn't thank Adrian more. They invited him to dinner sometime soon where he could eat some of their catch. He had cleaned and packaged the stripers for them. They all had a good time, drank a lot, and everyone on board caught several fish. Debi had never caught a big fish, but on this day she had landed, mainly by herself, a twenty-eight pound striper, the biggest of the day. She had hoped her parents would have fun but never thought a fishing trip could be so exciting.

Lester dropped Debi's parents at their house. It was obvious that Susan had at least temporarily forgotten her daughter was almost killed in a swamp a few days before.

Lester and Debi showered together when they got back to the apartment. She was talking non-stop, so excited about the fish. She had even talked about having it mounted for a while until her mother told her it would be expensive and thrown away quickly because she would get tired of it on the wall. Tom had had some ducks stuffed, and they didn't last long around their house. Debi suspected it wasn't her dad that got tired of them.

When they got in bed and snuggled up close, Lester said, "Do you know what Stick is thinking about as he goes to bed tonight?"

"No, what?"

"Your beautiful ass he saw through the scope. It was something he will never forget."

"My little ass?"

"Your beautiful little ass!" Lester reached behind her and pinched her lightly on a cheek. She laughed and snuggled up tightly.

* * *

Stick was on the phone all the way back from his surveillance mission until he found one of the girls who was free to come by and service her boss. It was Saturday, and all the girls were booked at the massage parlor, and no one was free at the two strip clubs. He had all the call girls' numbers and started dialing. He found one available in Little Rock and he booked her, but not for free. He negotiated but got nothing off the standard price. He would write off the money that went to the house and pay her for a normal call but would try to make her spend the night. He would pay for a hotel for the driver.

The sight of Debi's exposed rear had him crazy with horniness. He had to have someone and all night. An hour later, the limo parked in front of his apartment. He had been drinking beer heavily during the wait, which sparked his temper. All his trouble with the law in the past had come from his drinking and smoking pot. The girl came to the door and introduced herself as Roxie Chang. She was a pretty Asian girl with a green dragon tattooed on the back of her hand. He brought her in and went out and paid the limo driver for a hotel room. He refused and said he would wait. Stick argued but got nowhere and angrily turned and headed inside.

"What's your charge without the fee for the house?" Stick asked, even though he knew the answer.

"You know it's five hundred dollars paid upfront. You'll have to explain the other half to Spider. You know damn well she'll make you pay for it if she finds out," Roxie said.

Stick was quiet, partly because he was drunk, and partly because he was seething inside. He went to a drawer and found his stash of hundred dollar bills and counted out five bills for her. She took the money and began to undress. She found a condom in her purse in the general area where she placed the money. She laid her purse nearby on the bed where she could reach it.

Stick undressed and let her put on the condom. With Roxie on her back, he put her legs together and under his. By doing this he could place his feet on the outside of her lower legs for traction making his thrusts strong and penetrating. Once inside her, he slowly began to push his large erection into her and then he did it harder and harder and faster. Roxie had no control in this position since her legs were trapped under him. The position caused her pain and she felt as if she were being raped. She tried to push him off, but she was only about five feet tall and weighed a little over a hundred pounds. He was over twice her size.

"Stick, you're hurting me—please stop!"

"Shut the fuck up!" he said and slapped her in the face, causing blood to run from her lip and her nose. He had his hand on her throat and didn't realize how much pressure he was applying.

"Please stop…stop…stop!"

With one hand momentarily free, she found her purse, reached in and pressed a small electronic instrument that made a buzzing sound. She sensed a darkness come over her. She was going limp.

"What the fuck was that?" Stick demanded. Within seconds someone was at the door.

"Open up, or I call the police!" the limo driver on the other side of the door said.

"Fuck you! Call anybody you want!" Stick hollered from his bedroom.

Suddenly he heard his flimsy apartment door splinter and fall off its hinges. The limo driver, a black man about six foot three and weighing close to three hundred pounds, made the distance from the front door to the bedroom instantly. He grabbed the nude Stick Hennessey by his neck and hair and tossed him on the floor. Stick looked up to see a chrome Desert Eagle .50 caliber pressed into his forehead.

"Tell you what, Stick. Since you're the straw boss around here, another thousand dollars will make all this go away," the limo driver said.

Stick got up and pulled more bills from his dresser and handed them over. The gun was leveled at Stick again while Roxie was getting dressed. She went into the bathroom and wet a towel to wipe the blood from her face.

"One other thing, Stick. Tell Roxie you're sorry for the way you treated her," the big black guy said as he leveled the pistol that could literally blow Stick's head across the room.

"Sorry I hit you, Roxie—I'm drunk."

"Don't ever call me again, you asshole!" Roxie said as she headed out the door.

Seconds later, the limo raced out of the parking lot.

Stick tried to repair his door but knew it was going to have to be replaced. What had just happened? He could have easily killed Roxie! The black man could have killed him. Roxie could have had a gun in her purse and shot him. All sorts of scenarios and none of them good. He knew when he drank, bad things happened. Stick saw things were coming unglued all around him. People were tailing him and probably his fellow workers. He was tailed today and they knew about his sniper hide. His stand was compromised. Time to rig up a portable one in the woods. He had to get in control. He had to meet with Spider. Stick didn't want to die. He had come close to death this time. As close as he had come to dying since he was wounded in Afghanistan. One thing haunted him: if the limo driver hadn't come in would he have killed Roxie? He really didn't know. Maybe. Probably.

Chapter Twenty-Eight

Hank Campanella started coordinating personnel in two states for the probability that the following Tuesday would be the day for raids. It was Sunday afternoon, and there wasn't much time. He thought about the Chalmette operation first and had the idea of waiting until the UPS truck pulled up to load weapons. The back door would be opened, the truck would be partly loaded with illegal weapons, and the secret door on the vault would still be standing open. But there was a problem. The Arkansas locations wouldn't be open at that hour. If they shut down Tony Evola's huge automatic weapons empire operation suddenly, maybe no one would warn Spider.

Jim Webb had filled Lester in on the vault and the likelihood of a Tuesday morning raid, but details needed to be squared away. On Sunday afternoon, an emergency conference call with Lester, Sheriff Mike Adams, and Sheriff Jake took place. He started with his sniper.

"Jake, see if you can find out where Stick moves his tree stand. The explosives he found will cause him to move. I'm thinking maybe we can rig up a Texas deer stand mounted on the back of a pickup truck or a tall cherry picker. Put some steel around for protection and a huge camo drape. Then move it to the woods on the west side of the warehouse. If we do it early Tuesday morning, we might sneak it in and get set up, but we'll have to take out the night guard at the gate. Your job will be to take out Stick before he takes you out," Jim said, knowing sniper-on-sniper was a deadly game. Jake had a box of medals from Vietnam to match the box of medals Stick earned in Afghanistan.

"My boys and I will work out the stand. Know a construction guy that has a cherry picker and think I can come up with camo and tree limbs. You take care of the guy at the gate. We'll do our part. You guys may need to cut power to the place for a few minutes, so their security cameras don't pick us up. Usually the guard at the gate is the only one there, but other times someone monitors from the inside too. We'll know by the cars parked there," Jake said with the knowledge that he had acquired performing surveillance on S.G. Crystals for a few weeks.

"Who takes the lead on this S.G. Crystals raid?" Lester asked.

"DEA first with backup from everyone else," said Jim. "We'll have them, plus ATF, FBI, state police, and sheriff's department. One ten-man SWAT team with a Lenco Bearcat armored response vehicle, which is close to being a tank. And probably fifty men."

"Against how many?" Mike Adams asked.

"We don't know how many will work tomorrow, but the inside camera gives a count between twenty-two to twenty-nine when Stick and Spider are there. We've counted as many as fifteen automatic weapons. There are three guards who work in shifts and they all have 9mm H&K automatics. The front gate guy is relieved at eight each morning. Usually just waves at the employees as they come through the gate—doesn't even look at them. Mostly has his face in a magazine, security monitors, or TV set. Stick and Spider blow through there and never look at him. At night he leaves several times to go in for coffee or to use the bathroom. He's the key to us getting set up," Jim said.

"Just a thought, Jim: why don't we gas this guy with a drone—we do have drones, don't we?" Lester asked.

"DEA has some. Let me see if we can get one and some kind of gas that would allow us to capture him and take his place. Maybe we can get someone over the fence if we can turn off the power, get the guard, and take him captive. Fence is electrified. Powering off is essential. We need one of our guys to take his place—open the gate and look the other way when employees come to work—should be about the same height and weight. If we have him gassed, we'll need a ladder or two to get over the fence," Jim said.

"Mike, Lester, we need you Garland County officers to get the bait store and the massage parlor. Can you guys do that? Want to warn you, Stick keeps one or two guards sleeping at the bait shop. They stay in the new extension built on in the back. If both are there, you'll see a

Jeep and a Mustang parked in back. Assume they will have automatic weapons since they sell them," Jim said. "Oh, ATF will be there for sure to be the lead."

"We'll see if we can get the Hot Springs police department to take care of the massage parlor and fill them in on the call girls since some of the girls work out of there," Sheriff Adams said. "We'll take down the bait store and load up the guns. If we get done early there, we'll come down the road to help you."

"We'll work on all this tomorrow and then hold tight until we hear from Hank in New Orleans. Look for another conference call tomorrow afternoon. The next one will be early Tuesday with a go or no go. Thanks for being on the call," Jim said.

Lester put down the phone and walked in where Debi was watching TV. She patted the couch so he would sit next to her.

"You guys putting the final part of the plan together?" She tried to sound unaffected by another armed conflict about to take place, but it wasn't working. She started getting upset. "When you go, I want you in the 'Get behind everyone else battalion.' Can't have you dying. I want to see what our kids look like. I want—you alive!" Debi said, tears flowing down her face as the stark reality of the raid was actually materializing.

"Hey! Hey, Debi, I'm not even going to be a part of the big raid on the warehouse. Little Rich, Becca, Mike, and about ten of our other officers are going to take out the bait store. ATF will take the lead there. If we get done in time we might go help with the clean-up," Lester said as he pulled her next to him and hugged her. "Please don't worry about me. I'll be fine."

"Things go wrong—they always do!"

"I'll have on body armor, Kevlar helmet, and metal ballistic inserts. So if I'm hit—less of a problem," Lester said. He ran his hand through her hair and kissed her softly. "Debi, it's my job and you know it."

"I don't have to like it," she said and kissed him back.

"Why don't we go to the movies? I'll even sit through a chick flick for you."

"I guess. Let me go online and check the times. Do you want

to eat first or afterwards?" Debi asked as she opened her laptop and typed in "movies Hot Springs AR," and then hit Enter. They picked a movie for around seven and decided to fix a salad and eat first. She was emotionally calmer but inside was a festering pain. There was no guarantee Lester would make it through the upcoming action. Deep down inside, she questioned whether she could handle living with someone who might not come home someday. Debi understood one reason the divorce rate was so high with policemen. It might not be the life for her and their children. Her feelings and thoughts were not positive.

After the movie and when they went to bed, Lester said he would feel better if he could go to his church on Monday and asked if she wanted to go with him. They planned it for after work on Monday.

* * *

Spider had a great visit with her son Frankie, her old boyfriend Nicky Martorana, and his daughter Gina at dinner on Saturday night. It was a good feeling to be with someone she had really cared for in the past. However, the same problem existed as it did during college. Nicky was clean and legal; Angel wasn't. During dinner, he read into their conversation her businesses were not ones he could condone or be a partner in. His law practice had grown, and like his father, the representation of organized crime figures was still was a part of his practice. But that was as far as he dwelled in criminal activities.

Gina and Frankie got along fine. He overcame his shyness and asked her to an upcoming dance at his school. She accepted and asked about watching him play football when she found out he was on the team. At this point she was a little taller than him, but as they walked together they made an attractive couple. Spider thought to herself, "*These two good looking kids are both clean and could have a life together if it worked out that way.*"

Spider had a lot of money put back in accounts placed carefully in the Cayman Islands. There was a will and trust and an attorney in New Orleans primed to take care of Frankie if she were taken out of the picture. She wanted Nick to handle it. After pulling him to the side as the young couple walked ahead of them in Central Park, Spider confided that if they couldn't get together romantically, she wanted him to handle all her legal issues, which were numerous. And to make sure Frankie was taken care of as well. Nick pulled a notebook from his coat and wrote out a contract while he propped the pad on a rock. Angel signed it and agreed to sign a more formal contract later. She also gave him a card and a check on the off-shore account, which she signed and left the amount blank. This was her ultimate demonstration of faith. Nick accepted it and told her he wished things could be different. She leaned over and kissed him softly and then harder. He looked surprised.

"I have always loved you, Nick, but I am trouble—I wish I wasn't, but I know what will happen in the future—it's inevitable. Please take care of Frankie if anything happens to me," she said, with the first tears that had crept into her eyes since Richie died.

The next day Angel boarded a plane back to Arkansas. She didn't know why but her trip back seemed sad, dark, and foreboding—it was an inexplicable, malevolent feeling. She smiled when she remembered Frankie and Gina together and she pulled out her iPhone. Tapping on the camera setting, she thumbed through her pictures and found one of Frankie and Gina posing next to each other at dinner. Both were so attractive and innocent. She smiled even more and tried to push the bad feeling away. She went back to those pictures many times on the flight.

Chapter Twenty-Nine

It was late when Stick picked up Spider at the airport in Little Rock. There weren't a lot of direct flights to any major cities out of Clinton National Airport, which was called "National" to signal an apology to all would-be passengers that it didn't accommodate international flights. She was in a good mood since she had gotten to visit with Frankie for a while. Stick, on the other hand, wasn't smiling, yet didn't want to dampen his boss's good feelings. He sure as hell wasn't going to tell her about the hooker he slapped and choked, and how he didn't at first pay Spider's cut for the transaction. The part about him being followed needed to be discussed but not now. He let her rattle on about the trip and her old boyfriend and bask in the warmth of her good time.

After a while she wanted to know how everything was going at all her operations. He went over what had happened since she had been gone, which was only a few days. She wanted a report on Lester and the police looking into their operations. Stick finally told her about following them on a fishing trip and believing he had been watched as well. Then he told her about the explosive device near his tree stand. Spider wanted the guards at the warehouse doubled and told him to get another car, a rental, and switch out so he would be harder to follow. She would do the same.

Spider then did the unimaginable. She invited Stick to spend the night. He was shocked but guessed that it had something to do with her visit or her old boyfriend or maybe the feeling that everything was closing in. He accepted, and on this night he saw another side of Angel Gambini. She kissed him and held him tight after they had sex. They slept together in each other's arms. She woke him in the morning, kissing him and wanting to make love. It was all strange to Stick, but he knew it wasn't likely to continue.

Stick had a lot to do that day, including tree stand work. He left for S.G. Crystals without stopping at his apartment, where a door was being installed at his expense. Before he left Spider's place, he had a rental car delivered to a nearby restaurant where he took delivery and gave the man a ride back to his agency. There he told them he wanted a different car and switched to a minivan that was parked to the rear of the Agency Rent-a-Car office. He took back streets and hoped he had shaken off his tail.

At S.G. Crystals, he put people on alert and ordered the guards doubled but found that required hiring one more since the late shift extra guard was on vacation. He put out calls for people to interview for the job and got one of the limo drivers to fill in. The deer stand wasn't hard to move to the tree line right behind the rear fence. Height was important for a sniper so he added a long ladder so he could reach the steps on his stand. After adding some camouflage and tree branches around his "hide," he was confident about the views he could get. It was actually better than the one he abandoned.

Just after he installed it, a call came in that applicants were coming in for the guard position. He called the front guard post and asked for the electricity to be turned off so he could use a gate at the rear of the compound. A red light at the top of the gate turned green. He tentatively grabbed the handle of the gate and walked in front of the car garage and into the warehouse. Flexible hoses hung down from the ceilings and connected to the vents formerly hidden under the tool boxes. The meth operation was going at full capacity this morning. Stick crossed the warehouse floor and entered his office where applications for two individuals in the reception area sat on his desk He was in his element and felt good. Spider had also asked him to spend the night again. It was mysterious, and he liked it.

* * *

Larry and Doug Thacker had only one job, and it was to fill the orders for automatic weapons which came through their small office in the back of the Beer, Bait and Ammo store on Highway 270 in Garland County. Rarely did they work in the bait and liquor store that faced the highway, so there were long periods of time where very little happened. To make matters worse, they lived there as well. Two bored redneck ex-cons in a roomful of automatic weapons was a formula for disaster. There was one weapon among them all they handled—maybe even fondled—every day.

Neither Larry nor Doug was particularly large, but both brothers were strong and had large arms and muscular upper bodies. Even given their strength, it was all they could do to pick up all the required hardware required to fire a General Electric XM214 Minigun. It was introduced on screen in 1987 in the movie *Predator,* starring Jessie Ventura. The real star of the movie was a hand-held electric Gatlin gun nicknamed "Painless." This weapon had an electric-powered rotating set of barrels that allowed for firepower that approached 10,000 rounds a minute. One thousand rounds, and the feeding belt weighed thirty-five pounds. The gun itself was thirty pounds. New lithium batteries weighed another seven pounds, good for one series of thousand-round bursts, then a change of batteries was needed or a wait of three hours to recharge them. This was only part of the problem. The multiple recoil force was so strong that even a very large individual would be spun to the right and could easily spray his own forces with .223 ammo, cutting their bodies into small pieces. The brothers would soon learn a lesson about the recoil issue in real-life.

It was Monday, and they didn't anticipate any orders to be filled since the work orders and invoices usually came a few days ahead of the UPS truck pick up, giving them time to box them for shipment. It was a perfect day to try out the Minigun. The Thacker boys had spent their own money on 2,000 rounds of ammunition so that each would have the pleasure of burning up over $100 each to pull the trigger for a few seconds. They drove the jeep up a dirt road into the nearby Ouachita National Forrest and found a clearing backed by a sloping hill next to the road.

Larry decided he would fire first. He put on the thirty-five pound backpack loaded with coils of ammo, strapped on the battery pack, connected the electric barrel spinner and then picked up the weapon and spun the barrels to see if it was functioning. It whizzed and buzzed as the multiple barrels spun around. The huge belt-fed magazine running out of the backpack was slid into place and the safety clicked off, exposing a red firing dot. Holding the heavy contraption at his waist, he prepared to fire. Several bottles and cans were set up as targets at the bottom of the hill. Larry looked at his brother, smiled, looked back at the target and pulled the trigger. Red tracer fire shot out the barrels and lit up the entire area in front of them. Bullets ripped up the soil at the base of the hill above the targets and immediately started trailing to the right. The torque of the recoil pulled him to his right and downward exactly in the direction of his Jeep—he was unable to stop firing. The hood flew off first as the bullets tore through the body of the Jeep right above the doors and traveled to the rear of the vehicle. For all practical purposes, it was cut in half. The barrels were still spinning and buzzing as the roof of the jeep collapsed onto the bullet-ridden car body. Doug elected not to shoot. They called a tow truck to haul what was left of the Jeep to a wrecking yard. Not a single round out of the thousand came close to any of the targets.

* * *

Debi was waiting outside her office as Lester pulled up. He got out and opened her door. While helping her into his car, he pinched her right butt cheek, but only lightly.

"You must always get a reward for your good deeds," she said, leaning over and kissing him.

"Me get big reward later. Tarzan want Jane in tree house. Boy and Cheetah go play with crocodiles. Tarzan and Jane get naked," Lester said, trying to sound like Johnny Weissmuller, even though he wasn't sure Debi had watched the old films.

"Jane want big screen TV, better tree house, nicer neighborhood, less wild animals, and real name for Boy. Then Jane get naked. Oh, yeah...lose the monkey."

"Jane much trouble!"

"Jane worth it. Jane much fun naked!"

Lester and Debi laughed at their little skit and talked about Lester receiving his first correspondence course in the mail. He had ordered it a few weeks back, even though he wasn't sure of his school funding yet. It was criminal justice studies at a junior level, which now was being paid for by the Sheriff's office. Even though he did his assignments at his desk at work, he was able to complete ten out of thirty chapters, along with the chapter tests. The final required a proctor at a local exam center at National Park College. He would be ready for it in a few days.

"Lester, are we going to your church tonight because you're afraid you might be killed tomorrow?" Debi asked point-blank.

"It might keep me from getting killed. Going there and listening to people handling the broken pieces of their lives and trying to put them back together again helps me. I just need the feeling of humans coming together. They sit at tables around food and refuel with both internal and external energy against a world that might rip them apart. They usually don't realize they are uniting with the people at their tables and near them to fight against everyday problems and sometimes very evil forces. There is love and there is hate. I can feel that energy. I soak it up and it's calming, sort of like taking a tranquilizer."

"If you just took a tranquilizer, it would save you on gas in your big SUV," Debi said.

"It wouldn't be the same. You just listen when we get there and don't talk."

"I'm hungry. Why can't I eat something?" Debi whined.

"I'm not taking you to my church anymore if you are going to be fussy. I'll take you anyplace you want afterwards, so be thinking about who might be open on Monday night."

The cafe in Kirby was crowded for some reason, and it was difficult to find a place to park.

"Looks like a lot of people think they're going to die tomorrow," Debi said sarcastically.

"You're being particularly obnoxious today," Lester said.

They entered the cafe to find every table taken except for Lester's favorite table next to the window. The waitress who waited on them before smiled at Lester and led them to the small table with the checkered tablecloth.

Debi was astonished. "How did they know you needed this table tonight?"

"It's a sign—it's a sign!" Lester said with a grin.

Chapter Thirty

Lester had listened to a couple conversations and was just getting into the spirit of his church visit when his cell phone went off. It was Jim Webb. He knew it would be a long call, so he handed Debi a twenty-dollar bill and asked her to pay for the coffee. He went outside with the call, and when Debi joined him, he handed over the keys. She took the hint and drove them from Kirby back towards Hot Springs. She tried to piece together the conversation by listening to Lester's responses, but a lot was lost in translation.

"What time for the bait store raid? Parameds will be parked where? Helicopters with swat members are landing where? What time in the morning will we know for sure? Okay. Okay. Holy shit! Okay." Lester clicked off his phone to find Debi pulling into Red Lobster in Hot Springs.

"Have I been on the phone that long?"

"Just tell me what the 'Holy Shit' part was about."

"We'll have two ten-man SWAT teams from the state police. Each one has two five-man elements that work different assignments. The Arkansas National Guard will have two helicopters in the area. One is an Apache attack helicopter with a front-mounted 30mm chain gun and Hellfire missiles with thermobaric explosives. The number of people involved now is closer to one hundred. Isn't that worthy of a 'Holy Shit'?"

"My God! You guys will be shooting at each other."

"Friendly fire is always a problem, especially if the teams have never worked together before," Lester said as he opened the restaurant door for Debi.

"Let's eat up tonight. I don't want my baby going off to war on an empty stomach," Debi said.

"Good idea. Tarzan hungry. Jane play with Tarzan later?"

"Jane play with Tarzan long time."

* * *

Over fifty men from several different agencies were in strategic areas around the Louisiana Sportsman's Super Store in Chalmette. No one knew for sure if it would be a go, but the command center was waiting by the TV monitors ready to start an operation that would incorporate hundreds of men in two states. If it happened, people would die—probably on both sides of the law.

"Screen's still dark," the technician said as several senior officers stood up in the van.

The ATF was taking the lead. Hank Campanella was supervising and was in the van waiting to give the word to move out. It had been a long investigation. Long before Lester McFarlin got involved, Hank had tried to catch Tony Evola selling illegal guns and was about to move in on him. He had someone inside the operation, but Katrina and the subsequent flooding stopped the clandestine operation. When the flooding took place, Tony sold most of his legal gun inventory to Cabela's and hid his automatics in a truck in an abandoned warehouse. Hank's informant died in a suspicious drowning incident during the flooding—suspicious since when he was found his hands were tied behind him. One piece of evidence that Hank still held, though, was the identity of the recipients of automatic weapons shipped by Tony Evola to the crime bosses in New Orleans. He hoped this raid would come next. Hank believed he could put away many of the crime bosses for possession of automatic weapons, much like Al Capone's tax evasion conviction in the thirties. It was a long shot, but arresting them for murder, drug smuggling, prostitution and other crimes was close to impossible because of the levels of under-bosses and contract employees. He was sure, though, the gangsters would always have their own personal automatic weapons handy. Many of them were felons, and combining the two offenses would put them away for quite a while.

Hank poured his third cup of coffee and looked at his cell phone where about ten messages were posted, all from those group leaders in the field. Several units were posted at the edge of the swamp directly behind the big store. One message just said, "Good luck, baby." It was from his girlfriend, who was also one of his lieutenants. The relationship was an open secret in the police department. Eventually, one of them would have to go. If this operation went well, Hank might be offered a job with ATF, and maybe it would solve the problem of sleeping with one of his lieutenants. He hoped the relationship would last, but two of his marriages had not survived the police work. It was really tough on marital bliss.

Suddenly there was a flicker on the screen and the inside of the warehouse illuminated, reflecting on people moving around by the firing range. The Second Coming would not have produced greater excitement within the van.

Hank called the men in the field and told them about the golden moment: a time when the UPS truck backed up, opened its doors, and at least six weapons were loaded onto the truck. Behind the opened warehouse doors, the secret vault would be exposed and vulnerable. Hank also had the presence of mind to call Jim Webb in Little Rock and tell him to prepare his officers.

Patiently, Hank watched the multiple screens and listened to Tony in his office until he moved to another area. Nicco opened the vault and supervised which weapons were to be packed and shipped. They were placed on a long table and boxed, taped, labeled, and stacked near the door. Hank counted twelve workers on the floor and two armed guards near the door. He was unsure if more workers were in other parts of the building or in the vault. There was a sound and the two guards moved to the double metal doors and opened them. The UPS driver came in and was handed an invoice or delivery list for the weapons. Hurriedly, the packers started moving the boxes onto the truck. Hank waited until six boxes were on the truck and then he shouted into the microphone.

"Go! Go! Go!" Hank was high on adrenalin and now could only watch as the well-planned raid took place. Twenty ATF agents raced up the loading platform and through the back door. They were immediately met with automatic machine gun fire from AR-15s using .223 rounds that can penetrate normal body armor. The rounds can go between the fabric but not the metal plates inserted in pouches in the vests. Several of the bulletproof vests were compromised, and at least two ATF agents who had not been protected by the metal plates were wounded. All kept fighting, as the wounds were minor. The ATF agents, however, were using something much more powerful. Ten of them were using converted BARs with 91-round top-loading drum magazines designed by the Polish army after World War II. The BARs never lost favor with the ATF, and they loved the modification. With the powerful 30.06 cartridges, the bullets ripped through doors, tables, and human flesh. The rest of the agents had M14s with big 7.62 rounds and 20 round clips. None of the ATF or FBI forces had any of the small round weapons used in Vietnam or Afghanistan. The Alcohol, Tobacco and Fire Arms Agency didn't believe in them. They should know about guns if anybody did.

Tony Evola came down the steps from an upper office with a TEC-9 and opened up on the invading ATF men. Some were hit but returned fire with several of the BARs, almost cutting him in half. The two guards who had fired the AR-15 were lying dead on the floor. From the hallway, behind a pile of hay bales for archery practice, two AK-47s sprayed the area. One of the ATF men was hit on a metal plate, and it partly penetrated and knocked him down. By this time, all the ATF SWAT team had entered the building. The men took cover wherever they could and started returning fire. The overwhelming fire from powerful weapons penetrated the bales of hay and blew both of Tony's guards down the hallway.

Behind them, a MAC-10 opened up and caught them off guard, striking and wounding four of the officers. Some were hit with the small arm fire, and one had a serious head wound. The shooter was Nicco Evola, and he was running to shut the door for the arsenal. The

BARs cut him down, but not before he pushed the button that closed the heavy concrete and steel doors.

Popping sounds were heard at the front of the store as the sheriff's officers and some of the New Orleans police officers crashed through the front door and found a couple of employees willing to engage them. Hank was with them and quickly rushed to the back of the store to assess the situation. Behind him paramedics rushed to the aid of the downed agents. Smoke filled the area from all the rounds fired, and repeated muzzle blasts near the hay bales started a small fire.

Hank smelled freshly fired rounds and blood as he entered the area where the firefight had taken place. Blood from the injured combatants covered the floor. Some of the wounds inflicted on the ATF officers were serious. Thankfully, they were getting immediate medical attention from medics that entered from the back door. The ATF agent with the head wound hadn't been so lucky. He was staring upward, not moving. *"None of this was worth that man's life,"* Hank thought.

Hank saw that Nicco was lying over the sandbags at the end of the shooting range and the doors to the secret vault were closed. He asked a couple of his men to follow him to the area where Nicco lay. He instructed them to carry Nicco's body over to where Hank had opened the lighted control panel. As they moved the body forward, Hank grabbed Nicco's limp right hand and pressed it against the green glowing light. There was a sound from within the mechanism as the doors began to open. The body was then handed over to medics who were now collecting bodies and marking where they fell for the crime scene identification. The three men walked into the vault.

Lights from the ceiling and from the walls generated a warm bright light everywhere. It was apparent that some of the lights remained on all the time to keep the moisture down and retard the formation of rust on the weapons. The rooms were sectioned off by long gun racks, and shelves containing ammo for those weapons were below them. The weapons were staggered from small to large cartridge size. Large was relative, considering that they had cannon shells and equipment to fire them.

"My God! A lot of governments out there can't boast of an arsenal like this," Hank said. "My guess is that some countries buy their weapons here."

As they explored the monstrous collection of guns and artillery, it became clear Tony and Nicco were international arms dealers— organized crime was just a sideline. One room was just for missiles. He recognized Stinger, Sidewinder, Tomahawk, and parts for SAM missiles. Hank had no doubt that Tony probably did supply countries with all their weaponry needs. He was close to a waterway and could ship unnoticed all over the world. Hank then invited the ATF and FBI advisors to inventory the entire storage area. He put in a call to Jim to fill him in on the raid and let him know they were likely to find any kind of weapon during the Arkansas raid.

Jim Webb put down the phone after hearing one of the ATF officers was killed and learning of the possible weapons in Arkansas.

"Jesus H. Christ! he said to himself. *I hope we can do it by the book. We can't make any fucking mistakes."* He started making calls. It was now 4:15 in the morning. He didn't have much time.

Chapter Thirty-One

Lester took the call at somewhere after 4 a.m. in the kitchen where he was already having coffee. Debi was asleep, and there was no reason to wake her. His instruction from Jim was to meet about a mile east of the bait store on a side road out of the view of traffic on highway 270 and wait until everyone assembled. All the Garland County Sheriff's Department personnel were headed out at the same time, equipped with full body armor and automatic weapons.

By this time Lester had heard about the ATF using modified Browning Automatic Rifles and M14s and wished instead for the impotent AR-15s with the small .223 rounds he could surround with the BARS. He and Little Richard were taking along their MAC-11 just to spray some rounds if needed. Everyone would be issued gas masks since they planned to shoot canisters into the bait shop if necessary. Shotguns were already in the patrol cars with plenty of buckshot and slugs on board.

Sheriff Adams had told everyone to meet at the sheriff's office at 5:30 a.m. and pair up. He and Rich would be together. Becca would be with one of the lieutenants, and Mike Adams would partner with the head ATF agent so the forces could be coordinated. A SWAT team from the Hot Springs Police Department was on standby as backup. It seemed to Lester that this was the biggest police action in the history of the state.

After suiting up, he woke Debi and kissed her gently. She panicked when she suddenly realized he had on full body armor.

"Oh, my God! It's on, isn't it?"

"Afraid so. The big raid in Chalmette was a big success, thanks to you girls hiding the cameras. Once we finish this operation, Hot Springs will be a little safer. We'll have overwhelming forces on the ground today, along with a couple helicopters. Don't worry about me; I'll be fine."

"Sure, I should suddenly not care if you live or die," Debi said sarcastically.

"I care and want to come back home to you."

"Then make sure you do." Debi held her crying until Lester left the apartment.

Lester kissed her and drove his SUV to the Sheriff's office where he teamed up with Rich and the rest of the department. There wasn't anyone he would rather be with in a firefight than Rich. The ATF and FBI were already on their way to the staging site. Two ambulances were headed to the meeting places on Crystal Springs Road. Lester couldn't help but be excited about the raid. It was always an adrenalin rush, even though he knew the dangers. But this time, he had no idea about the weaponry that would be aimed at him and his fellow officers.

The bait store opened at 7 a.m. since it sold bait to eager fishermen. They were going to surround the little building with patrol cars at just after 8 a.m. They were coordinating with the big raid at the S.G. Crystals warehouse that would start at the same time. The news agencies in New Orleans had all agreed to not release the story until 8:15 a.m.

There was a chance that Spider could get a call from someone in New Orleans. She was not expected at the raid since she rarely showed up until afternoon. There was a tail on her Hummer, but the agent following suspected she now had a rental. In other words, she had lost her tail. So had Stick, but most assumed he would be at S.G.

As Stick drove to the warehouse in a grey minivan, he saw a Garland County Sheriff's patrol car pull off on Crystal Springs Road. He didn't think anything about it since it was their county and they patrolled the area frequently. As he passed his bait store, he noticed the new Beer, Bait and Ammo neon lights were on and his employee's car was parked out front. Only Doug's Mustang was parked in the back. Stick had gotten a text the day before that Larry's Jeep was in the shop for repairs. The truth was, it was in a wrecking yard waiting on the insurance adjuster to be shocked out of his mind. Never had he seen a car cut in half by a machine gun. Larry wasn't sure his insurance would pay, but it was unlikely the policy had a clause saying, "If your Jeep is cut in half by a Gatlin gun, it won't be covered."

Stick drove on to the road that led to the compound and failed to see Jake's hide covered in camo far up in the trees just west of the electrified fence. His cherry picker lift had been towed in and placed far back in the trees, high enough to see over the whole area. Jake had found Stick's deer stand and estimated the shot would be around two hundred yards. He knew he would have only one shot before Stick was on him.

He was in the cherry picker with large pieces of steel propped in front of him. He watched Stick enter through the gate. Stick pulled up in his rental car and waved at the guard, who had most of his head buried in a *Hustler* magazine. The guard didn't show enough of his face to concern Stick. If his face had been exposed, Stick would have known it wasn't his employee since he had hired them all. He could see another guard in the distance walking the perimeter with his back towards Stick. Other employees were lining up to come through the gate, so the guard just left it open and waved people through.

As Stick entered the building, it started raining, and he could hear thunder in the distance. The day didn't appear to be any different than any other day, and he began to go through the orders and invoices on his desk. There was an order for a M48 machine gun and another for five AK-47s. Immediately, he faxed the order over to the bait store. In a few minutes, he got a call from Doug.

"Boss, we only got three AKs. Do you have some there you might want to trade out for AR-15s or something?" Doug asked.

"We got plenty here to trade out. I'll bring them by about noon. We don't need to ship them until tomorrow. I'll see if Tony has some," Stick said and dialed the Super Store in Chalmette. He got the answering machine so he left the order for ten AK-47s, one of his most popular guns.

Spider was up, showered and dressed for the day. She had enjoyed her night with Stick and was curious what he thought about it. Spider wondered why she did it. Maybe it was to get a little closer to someone since she couldn't have Nicky. As she was about to leave to have breakfast at Hester's, her cell phone rang. It was not a number she recognized, but the prefix was from the New Orleans area. She took a chance and answered it.

"Hello. Who is this?" Spider asked.

"Your cousin, Gino Matranga."

"Gino, I haven't heard your name in a while. What's up?"

"I wanted you to know that Tony's store was raided early this morning. He and Nicco and a couple of his other sons were killed. It was the ATF and FBI and some of the locals. Just wanted to warn you—you're next. I gotta go. Good luck."

"Ahh—thanks, Gino."

The time was 8:20 a.m. She had no idea that both raids were already taking place. She tried to call Stick, but there was no answer. She tried the bait store with the same result. She had the rental car in back of her condo and probably could sneak out without being followed. Where would she go? She had heard that the massage parlor was being watched along with the two strip clubs. What would Frankie think if she was arrested? He knew she did some of the family's business, so it wouldn't be much of a surprise. Going back to New Orleans as a crime family war was about to break out had very little appeal.

She wondered if Debi had left Lester's apartment yet to go to work. She knew her small BMW convertible. Spider ran out the back of her condo and jumped in the rental car, a white Dodge minivan, about as far from her normal choice of transportation as possible. She covered her head in a scarf and blew by the black car parked near the entrance to her condo. It didn't follow her. She pulled up to Lester's apartment as Debi was locking up and walking to her car. Spider pulled in next to her and got out. With her gun pointed at Debi, she took the keys from her hand.

"Sweetie, let's go back inside," Spider said and motioned for her to walk back to the apartment.

"You must be Spider, the lady that takes advantage of men

recovering from brain operations." Debi had a knack for turning fear into anger, and this encounter was no exception.

"He needed a bath and seemed to enjoy the experience. He's a handsome man," Spider said, as she unlocked Lester's apartment and followed Debi inside.

"He said you were pretty. How come you aren't married to some rich dude?" Debi asked as she sat down on the couch. Spider pulled up a dining room chair and sat across from her with the Beretta 9mm aimed in Debi's direction.

"I was. He cheated on me, and even worse, he cheated on one of the other families in town."

"Sorry. I don't guess Lester really cheated on me since he wasn't in his right mind."

"Think what you want, dear, but it isn't hard for me to get guys to do what I want—or should I say, what they want?"

"So, Spider, what are you going to do with me?"

"I'm not sure, but I don't have a lot of options right now. I'm guessing all my places are being raided. The most important lawman in the area is fighting the big war while his sweetheart has a gun pointed at her. Let's just say you're a very important asset to me right now. When Lester finds out he'll do anything to get you back."

Spider got up, went to the kitchen and opened the refrigerator. "Would you like a beer, some wine, or maybe bottled water while we wait?"

"Why don't I fix us a cup of coffee, Spider? It's already hot...just turned off the pot."

"I'll get it. And call me Angel. The Spider part was because everyone thought I had my husband killed. Turns out I didn't."

The two beautiful girls had coffee. Both wondered how they had turned out so different. One became a professional speech therapist and the other a career criminal. Although their backgrounds were of interest to each other, there was little doubt in Debi's mind that the blond, former beauty queen would kill her without batting an eye. It would be a long time before Lester called and neither really knew what would happen after that.

* * *

Lester and Rich met with six other patrol cars and five ATF vehicles and a couple of paramed units on Crystal Springs Road not far from the resort.

"Lester, do you think Mike will approve our office party on one of the houseboat rentals at the marina here?" Rich asked.

"Why not? It's only seven thousand a week for an eighty-foot boat," Lester said.

Mike Adams walked up with Becca and several other officers.

"What're you clowns up to over here?" Mike asked.

"Sheriff, we have our annual picnic each year and as chairman of that committee, I have decided we'll rent a houseboat. It'll be free, of course, since there's still money left in the gun fund, plus the extra money from the sale in New Orleans. Maybe rent it for two or three days since we'll have to party in shifts. I can tell by the look on your face that you really like the idea," Lester said.

"You two are full of shit! Those houseboats probably cost a couple hundred dollars a day. You need to concentrate on the raid about to take place so you don't get your asses blown off," Mike said. He stepped back as the ATF team leader walked in front of him to address the group of police officers.

"Gentlemen, I'm Special Agent Supervisor R.J. Owen with the Bureau of Alcohol, Tobacco, Firearms and Explosives. First, I would like to thank the Garland County Sheriff Department's exemplary work in exposing these suspected violations to our attention. A special thanks to Lester McFarlin for turning an ordinary domestic shooting into a two-state investigation of organized crime. But now the dangerous part takes place right down the road from here. A bait store has built an extension on the rear of the building and shipments of weapons have been going out in the last few weeks. We don't know what's in there, but we'll prepare for the worst. Also, there's a female employee that works in the front of the store, and we believe she's clean and must be protected at all costs. The plan will be to circle our patrol cars end-to-end, surrounding the building as best as possible. The two medic teams will set up their ambulances on each side of the building at least two hundred feet out and remain behind the vehicles for cover. The two elements of the Hot Springs Police SWAT team will stand by the ambulances as backup. Each of my Special Agents and the other police officers will use their wheel wells for maximum protection. If the suspects are using green-tipped, armor-piercing .223 ammunition, you need to know it will penetrate your vest. Use your metal plate inserts to full advantage. When we arrive on site, I will try to talk them out with a speaker. If they fire on us, then you can return fire, but not until then. Good luck and may God be with you."

Lester looked around and saw some of the men whispering prayers. He had never been in combat, but heard it was very common to pray before patrols and firefights. He didn't spend a lot of time at his church but still felt at peace.

In about ten minutes, the officers' cars started jockeying in place to form a circle. Everyone bailed out of their vehicles and quickly moved to the opposite side of the cars.

Special Agent Owen turned on his bullhorn with a screech that made several people cover their ears.

"Those of you in the building need to come out with your hands up where we can see your palms. You are surrounded by federal and local police officers. You will not be harmed."

On the side of the building, directly across from where Lester and Rich were parked was a small window, more like a wooden flap with hinges at the bottom and a catch of some sort on the top. A hand reached out and slipped the sliding clasp out of the holder and let the small wooden door drop down, slamming into the side of the building. Nothing happened at first, then a multi-barreled object was pushed out that window. Lester recognized it immediately.

"It's a Gatlin gun! Take cover now!"

Chapter Thirty-Two

Sherriff Jake Thomas was secure in his camouflaged cherry picker, adjusting the height with his onboard control panel until a downward angle pointed two-hundred yards away directly at Stick's hide. Jake had the best view of the raid at S.G. Crystals.

First, they cut the power. This is common practice for police who enter a residence or building, as it creates problems with security cameras and lighting, and causes overall confusion. However, they only had about 20 seconds of outage when the emergency generators kicked on. Stick was looking at a video screen which showed the gate entrance free of traffic. The screen went black, then flickered back on in a few seconds. Now the screen was filled with men in black body armor and helmets running through an open gate carrying automatic weapons, and Stick's guards were with them.

The generators ran essential electrical items such as lights, office equipment, and communications but didn't power up the electrified fence or the power fans in the meth-cooking area. The people below the warehouse floor began to pour out of the underground operation since the poisoned fumes would kill them without the huge fans pulling the fumes out of the production facility. They didn't surface empty-handed; each carried an automatic weapon. Stick immediately ran through the warehouse, out the rear door and through the fence toward his tree stand. On the way, he instructed his warehouse supervisor to take charge of the workers and prepare to take out the attackers.

The supervisor was Harlan Antoine, a war buddy who had fought in Iraq and Afghanistan. He had been a great soldier before getting hooked on heroin and pain killers after being shot in the back. Stick rarely saw him when he wasn't either stoned or drunk. Usually both. Today Stick didn't care because he knew combat would overcome any of his issues.

Jake could see blurry images of Stick running through the heavy brush and trees toward the stand. He saw glimpses of his tan shirt with a black collar as he climbed up the tree. He let Stick position himself over his rifle and move his scope downwards towards the invaders who were now under fire from the front of the office through windows. He saw one DEA agent fall. Jake took aim at the side of Stick's head. The rain made splotches on his scope and the wind picked up when it came down hard. The old sheriff tried to make his shot between heartbeats with a pull on the trigger that was so slow it surprised him when it went off.

The wind blew across the bullet's path as Jake squeezed off the round and hit Stick's rifle right above the trigger housing on the metal part of the Remington 700. Part of the bullet fragment took off most of his left ear and drove pieces of metal above his right eye. A large fragment took off his middle finger on his left hand. Blood covered his face and hands. Stick quickly ducked down in his hide and pulled off his T-shirt to make a bandage and wipe the blood from his eyes. Pulling the bolt back and checking the rifle, he saw visible damage to the metal receiver and the wood below it, but it still functioned. The rugged Remington 700-.308 caliber had been in worse battles.

Teeming with anger, Stick found an area through a leafy branch he had taken into the blind. Slowly and carefully, he moved the scope and hunted the treetops until he saw the outline of the cherry picker. Then he saw Jake and the burlap rags that covered him and his rifle. *Nice hide,* Stick thought to himself.

Rain continued to pelt the area, and he marveled at the shot the other sniper had made in those conditions. He would just have to adjust, adapt, and compensate. Jake was higher than his tree stand, so Stick's shot was elevated. That meant bullet drop, but not much at two hundred yards. He took a bead on Jake's head right above his scope and between two large pieces of iron propped against the side of the cherry picker cage. As Stick pulled the trigger, Jake fired again, just a millisecond before Stick. This bullet caught Stick in the jaw and exited his neck. He stuck his t-shirt in his mouth to control the bleeding and moved down in the stand.

Jake, too, was hit and thought he was dead, but he woke up after a few seconds. His head was bleeding profusely. Blood dripped into his eyes and made it impossible to see. The bullet had gone a little bit high since Jake had fired at exactly the right time to elevate Stick's round. It hit Jake's helmet and then tore through his head, digging into his skull just above his brain. He wanted to shoot again but couldn't see for the blood. He couldn't be sure if Stick was lining up another shot, so he reached up and touched the big piece of flat iron and pulled himself behind it. Stick couldn't shoot what he couldn't see.

Suddenly a roar filled the air. Jake wiped his eyes enough to see a helicopter edging its way towards Stick's tree stand. There was a shot and a man dropped out of an open door of the helicopter onto the roof of the warehouse. Bright orange and red streaks filled the distance between the hovering Apache helicopter and the deer stand high in a white oak tree. The 30 mm chain gun took down several trees and undulated like the red tornado it is often called. It was certain and instant death for Hunter "Stick" Hennessey.

Chapter Thirty-Three

Red flashing fire shot out the small opening in the wall in a violent stream. A few police officers froze in terror and were shot in the process. The pattern of fire started from the shooter's left and moved to the right in a tremendous downward motion, slicing patrol cars into pieces like a machete slicing a watermelon. The firing stopped abruptly one car past Lester and Rich's patrol car. As Lester tried to shove his entire body into the wheel well of the patrol cruiser, metal, glass and bullets showered him and Rich with pieces of what used to be their car. Rounds also struck the ambulance parked some distance away.

Lester didn't know a lot about the operation of the Minigun, but figured a complicated piece of equipment capable of firing so many rounds might take a while to reload. He took a chance and stood up and fired thirty-two rounds in about two seconds from the MAC-11 into that same window. He heard a scream and curse from inside. Every available officer also started firing into the hole. Rich fired tear gas and flash bang grenades. It must have awakened the men in the building since more machine gun fire came through the window, mainly striking Rich's patrol car and the one next to it where Becca and the lieutenant were hunkered down by their wheel wells and flat tires. Lester could see that the two were bleeding, as were several officers along the row of busted up cars. Rich and Lester were no exception, but their wounds were mostly superficial.

The ATF forces lined up with their backs to the building and lobbed several flashbang and stun grenades through the opening. Tear gas followed, then two BARs with 91 round clips were stuck in the window and fired until they both just clicked. A team of five ATF forces used a battering ram on the back door. They crashed through the door and found Larry lying dead on the floor.

Special agent Owen followed his men through the door.

"Jesus H. Christ! There are rocket launchers and hand-held missiles in here!" Owen said.

Before he could say any more, there was a scream from the front of the bait store. Lester moved behind the circle of dilapidated and smoking patrol cars until he could see the front of the building. Once there, Lester saw Doug with a chrome model 1911 .45 leveled at the earhole of a short redheaded girl who worked in the store.

Sandy Woodward had come to work that day expecting to earn a paycheck to make payments on her car and apartment. The job wasn't that great, especially when she had to count out crickets for fishermen. Once a box of red worms fell off the shelf and she had to pick them up and re-box about a hundred worms. Minnows weren't much better. She did it because she needed a job and it paid more than most jobs in Hot Springs. Larry and Doug flirted with her, but she ignored them and was glad they were in the back most of the time. They told her to buzz them if anybody ever came in to rob the place. A button for the buzzer was placed under the cash register. She had only used it twice: once for a drunk that was falling all over the store, and the two boys tossed him out of the store. The other time was when a large snake was coiled up out front as she opened the front door. They came out and shot it several times.

"Copperhead. Poisonous. Took care of it for ya," they told her.

She worried that some dope addict might try to rob her like Jody was robbed not long before. Having a gun stuck in the side of her head was never a work hazard she had imagined.

Lester noticed her hair was medium length. She was about five-foot-three or four inches tall, and Doug was about five-foot-eight-or-nine inches tall. He watched the rhythm and motion of their bodies as they headed toward the girl's car parked about fifty feet away. Lester walked behind the police cars in perfect syncopation with the boy and the girl. He jerked an AR-15 rifle from the hand of one of the sheriff's officers as he passed him. Instinctively, he watched the difference between the heads bobbing and the flow of her hair as Doug's head moved slightly to the front of hers. They were only inches apart, sometimes fractions of a second where another separation existed. In Lester's mind they were in slow motion.

Lester stopped and rose up above a patrol car. He pulled the trigger—the bullet entered her hair above her neck as it flowed backward and then crossed over between them and entered Doug's brain right behind his ear. Doug collapsed on the gravel driveway; his gun landed beside him. The girl screamed and grabbed the back of her head and touched her singed hair. ATF agents ran and held her as she was shaking and crying. Lester handed the rifle back to the officer and walked over to where the ambulance had pulled up and started a triage to assess the worst cases.

After having his and Little Richard's minor wounds treated, they wanted to go help at the S.G. Crystals warehouse, but someone would have to give them a ride since Rich's patrol car was a pile of smoking metal. Hot Springs SWAT team was heading in that direction and agreed to let them tag along. As they walked over to one of the SWAT vehicles, Sandy, the clerk from the bait shop, ran over and thanked Lester for taking out the guy that was taking her hostage.

They drove toward S.G. thinking that it would all be over when they got there. They would soon find out differently.

Chapter Thirty-Four

Spider placed her heavily-creamed coffee down on Lester's dining table next to her Beretta. Her cell phone was ringing to the tune of background music saying, "Whatcha gonna do when they come for you?" from some cop show on TV. She answered and pointed the gun in Debi's direction.

Debi and Angel Gambini had talked about purses, shoes, manicures, makeup, and boys. If things were different, they may have been friends—but they were from alien worlds. One was a productive member of society, and the other was a cunning and successful criminal. She smiled as she glanced at the name on her phone screen.

"Vander! Are you here yet?" Angel asked.

"Be there in thirty minutes. Go through the private hangar gate at the airport—at the far end by the big white hanger. Ashley will be waiting for you to unlock the gate and let you in. Anybody with you?" Vander Usterhoff asked.

"A girl, but she won't be going with us. She's a catch and release. When you see her you you'll want her to go with us," Angel said.

"Let's bring her."

"She's Lester McFarlin's girlfriend. We don't need the heat."

"He's the reason this whole thing is going down. You know that, don't you, Spider?"

"Only too well. See you there."

"Oh, got your 'go' bag?" Vander asked.

"Yep—passports, money, credit cards, toothpaste and a change of panties."

She hung up the phone and turned to Debi. "Debi, you're going to give me a ride. Let's take my rental since no one has figured out that it belongs to me."

"We're going where?"

"Just drive," Angel said and handed Debi the keys for the minivan. Debi pushed a wrong button and both center sliding doors started to open. Spider took the keys away from her and closed those doors and opened the right ones. Once in the car, Spider put the keys in the ignition and started it for Debi.

"Out to Airport Road."

Debi turned on Central until she came to the bypass and took it to the Airport Road exit. Spider motioned to her to turn right. She kept the gun leveled at Debi the entire trip.

"How did this Vander guy get back in the states? I remember Lester telling me he went to a country without an extradition treaty with the US—Venezuela, maybe?"

"Well, it seems the crack professionals with the FBI and City Police never filed charges against Vander. The call girl never gave him up since he sent money for her defense fund. She told the cops she never met the man she worked for and was told his name was "Sugar Man." Of course, the business had a zero paper trail. He's a model citizen and free to come and go in the US, but he is no longer welcome in Venezuela. You see, they don't allow dual citizenship. When they gave him a deadline to officially denounce his US citizenship in writing, Vander became patriotic. 'Fuck you, and the banana cart you rode in on,' he told them.

"He left the country and brought his girlfriend Tammy back as well. You see, Vander is a Jew, and many of his relatives died in Eastern European Nazi death camps. He loves America, and he loves to run whorehouses. That skill and flying are all that he knows."

"I don't guess you're going to tell me where you guys are flying off to?"

"I doubt if he knows. Unfortunately the countries that don't have extradition treaties with the US are shit holes. Better than Federal prison, but not by much."

"You've got clean panties so you can afford a little time to shop around for a country," Debi said.

Spider smiled and directed her to turn into the Hot Springs Memorial Field. Then she pointed to a gate on the other side of a huge white hangar building, where a pretty blond girl wearing aviation overalls was standing. It was obvious to Debi the body under the loose work clothes was anything but ordinary.

Parking by the curb, Spider took the keys from the ignition and told Debi to follow her inside. The girl in overalls led the way to a private hangar leased by Vander. She explained Vander had gotten her out of some trouble. He let her live in the hangar, look after his belongings, and service his plane. She stopped short of explaining any other duties required of her.

"Vander just called. He'll touch down in about five minutes. I'll have him refueled and out of here in twenty minutes. He'll fly visual flight rules, so I don't have to file his plans," she said.

Debi looked around the hangar and could see a woman's touch. Everything was clean and in place. A small window on a back wall sported bright yellow curtains. It was doubtful Vander had a hand in that project. There were metal stairs leading upstairs where Debi assumed the girl's living quarters were since the stairs were covered by bright yellow carpet. A sound in the distance signaled the approach of Vander's twin engine plane. He set it down with only a small burst of smoke from the tires on landing. He abruptly pulled around and nosed the plane toward the hangar. A fuel truck pulled up next to the plane as soon as it stopped. Vander exited the plane and ran to Ashley and kissed her.

"Angel, this is Ashley. I guess you've met. You must be Lester's girl, Debi?" Vander said as he shook her hand and kissed Spider on the cheek.

Tammy wasn't on the plane. Vander explained she wanted to visit her home in Oklahoma. He didn't know if she would travel with him in the future. He didn't seem concerned.

Debi had expected him to be a grey-haired, pot-bellied man wearing a used car salesman's clothing. He surprised her in every aspect. He was tall with a dark complexion and dark hair that only had a touch of grey around his temples. He had a handsome face with deep, dark eyes and strong features. He was muscular, with broad shoulders and a flat stomach. He wore prep-school-yellow Ralph Lauren slacks, lime green polo shirt, and tassel loafers without socks. His smile was contagious and sincere. Debi realized how this man could recruit pretty women for the call girl business. He was exactly the opposite of what she had pictured.

The driver of the refueling truck handed the ticket to Ashley and drove back to the terminal. Angel grabbed her go bag and walked towards the plane with Vander. Ashley kissed him good-bye, then Angel motioned for Debi to come over to the plane with her. As Debi approached, she handed the keys to Ashley.

"In thirty minutes give the keys to Debi," Spider said and turned to Debi. She smiled and walked over to her.

Angel put her arm around Debi and said, "You take care of Lester. He's one of my favorite people in the world and you are one lucky-ass girl."

"I know…and thanks," Debi said with a smile.

"Give him this for me," Angel pulled Debi in close with her arm around Debi's waist and kissed her on the lips, a very sweet, lingering kiss. She then turned and got on the plane with Vander. For a moment, Debi stood frozen, eyes wide with shock. A strange realization came over Debi that there was some good in Angel—maybe a lot of good. She snapped back when she thought of all the guns and illegal drugs Spider had sold and how many lives had been affected.

When she turned around, Ashley had pulled up a chair for her and was sitting across from her with her purse in her lap—her hand was in her purse. Debi got the picture.

Chapter Thirty-Five

Lester and Rich wore bandages on various parts of their body where pieces of metal and glass had missed their body armor and penetrated their skin. If anyone doubted the effectiveness of the jackets and helmets, they just needed to look at those who had been near the line of fire when the Minigun tore loose. Shards of glass and metal stuck out of the body armor and helmets like a pin cushion, only these had the sharp edges pointing out. Everyone was careful about touching either of these items in fear of being severely cut. As they bounced around in the back of the ATF SUV, the officers who were on the other end of the building and saw no action were amazed by all the crap stuck in their gear.

In about fifteen minutes, the SUV turned onto the dirt and gravel road leading to the S.G. warehouse. In the distance, they could hear gun fire. The single fire seemed closer and the automatic fire appeared to be farther off. Ahead, DEA men in full body armor were lined up at the front of the S.G. Crystal building. They were taking fire from the woods on both sides and inside from the production floor. The ATF vehicle slid to a stop off the gravel road behind several other cars. Two ambulances were parked to the side and paramedics worked on several downed officers. Lester and Rich entered the gate as the DEA guys laid down a huge amount of covering fire into the woods. Once inside the office, they crawled along the inside wall until they came to a double door where officers were positioned on each side.

"Jim Webb, it's nice to see you get out in the field occasionally," Lester said as he took a position across from Jim at the partly-opened double door.

"Lester, you have several holes in you. Did you have trouble ducking?" Jim asked.

"Hard to duck a thousand rounds from a Gatlin gun. I don't think we had Miniguns listed in our catalogue of available weapons," Lester said.

"We've been stalled out here because there are three machine gun nests on that big warehouse floor. A couple of M60s and a BAR with a big magazine. They're behind sandbags and those huge piles of ore. Got any ideas?"

"Can you get that Apache I saw parked on the way in back in the air?" Lester asked.

"No problem. They sat down to reload the chain gun. Took out Stick Hennessey in his deer stand."

"My God! Is Jake okay?"

"Yeah, he has a crease in the center of his skull, but he's going to be fine. Word is, he and Stick had a hell of a shootout. Old man held his own," Jim said.

"Okay, here's the plan," Lester said. "Have one of your men count the metal ribs on the west side of the building and tell me exactly where the machine guns are in relation to those. Next, is the third machine gun in a nest?"

"No. He's mobile and I've been told he's one of Stick's war buddies. Right now he's at the other side of that little house. They did the count and two ribs for the first one and six and a half ribs for the second one."

"Get the Apache in the air and have it rake the woods with that chain gun when they see me go around the side of the building. As soon as I take out the machine guns, have your guys pitch a grenade behind the house and flush him out. Have the copter rake the other side of the woods afterwards. Got it?"

Jim nodded.

"I'll wait to go until I see the Apache blasting away. And get me that count."

"You know the whole place might go up because of meth fumes, Lester," Jim said.

"Then clear them out before you throw it."

Lester and Rich crawled along the wall and then exited the building. An ATF officer outside the door traded Lester the BAR with the big capacity Polish drum magazine for the small round MAC-11. Rich and Lester hugged the front wall of the building until they came to the corner. When Lester turned to ask Little Richard to cover him, he noticed a BAR in his hand. He must have made a trade as well.

"We've got to get some of those babies. Best big bullet hand-held ever made," Lester said.

A roaring sound above them suggested the Apache was about to rain fire down on the forest.

Again the twisting tunnel of red-orange fire snaked through the woods, knocking down trees and catching brush on fire. Lester ran with his face toward the metal on the side of the building. Rich watched the woods for any movements but saw nothing but trees falling over from the chain gun. Lester suddenly stopped about thirty feet from the end of the building and stepped back a few feet, adjusting the muzzle of his big automatic rifle. Once he was satisfied he had the right angle, he discharged about fifty rounds into the side of the building, above the second rib.

Inside, the two men working the machine gun nest near the back of the warehouse stood up as the first few rounds came through on their position. Then several large 30.06 bullets tore into them.

At the second machine gun bunker about thirty feet away, three men working behind sandbags started to move out but were cut down by Lester through the side of the building. His count on the metal ribs of the building had been accurate at six and a half, deadly for the men on the machine guns. Insulation and drywall floated in the air above both of the machine gun placements. Almost immediately after Lester stopped shooting, a grenade went off in the warehouse. Harland Antoine, who had set up his BAR as a bunker weapon, dove for cover when he saw the grenade roll in. When it exploded, his eardrums burst. He was still alive and was holding his weapon when the DEA and FBI rushed in, firing at everything they saw. Harland remained hidden in the corner behind a few sheets of plywood. Lester checked his weapon to see if he had some rounds left and entered the warehouse from the rear.

Five rounds left—should be fine.

He came around the corner with Rich behind him and observed the chaotic activity in the warehouse. The gunfire had subsided and the employees that weren't killed or wounded had their hands up. He walked to the center of the warehouse and watched as Jim supervised the crime scene investigation. It appeared that it would just be paperwork now. Jim spotted Lester across the large warehouse floor and waved him over. Lester was preoccupied. Something didn't seem right.

"Rich, where is that third machine gun guy? He had a BAR. I recognized the distinctive sound it made."

"Jim said he was behind that house up there. Wow! Half of it's blown away," Rich said. Lester kept trying to figure out what was out of order. Just as Jim Webb started walking toward Lester, both Lester and Rich saw movement in the front corner of the warehouse behind some plywood.

"Jim, get down!" Lester screamed and watched Jim drop face down to the concrete floor.

Harlan emerged from behind the plywood with fire coming out the end of his BAR on fully automatic and a callous "don't care if I die" look on his face. Rich caught a bullet in his shoulder. One went through Lester's calf, causing him to pull his first round slightly to the right. Remarkably, the round caught Harlan in the chest. The audible "clunk" from the metal plate insert knocked Harland to the floor. He recovered, only to be sprayed by Rich's BAR. Most of the shots were to his body armor and non-lethal areas of his body. He went down again, and this time when he got up, he had the big BAR aimed in Lester's direction. He hesitated a fraction of a second too long, and Lester hit him on the bridge of the nose, misting his brain on the big round's exit out the rear. It was truly over.

Medics were all over Rich and Lester to stop the bleeding and clean the wounds.

"Hey, Lester. I owe you lunch for saving my ass," said Jim Webb.

"No, Jim, you owe Debi and me dinner in Little Rock. Say, Sonny's Steak House," Lester said.

He suddenly realized Debi was probably worried and wondering why she hadn't heard from him.

Lester dialed her cell. Her phone rang several times but no answer. Before he had stuck it back in his pocket he got a call. It was Debi.

"Hi, Baby. I'm still alive and it's all over," Lester said.

"That's great! Are you hurt?"

"A few scratches, but all of our people survived."

"Does that mean you had your dick blown off and you have no arms and legs?" Debi asked, knowing it was always more serious than he let on.

"Oh, by the way, do you remember that cute crime boss you were looking for?"

"Spider?"

"Well, she kidnapped me today. Took me to the airport and flew off with that Vander guy."

"What the fuck! Are you okay? Where is she now?"

"Riding a frigging cloud, I would say. Going to some country that doesn't have extradition."

"Holy shit! Jim, get over here." Jim had only taken a few steps and turned to see what he wanted. "Spider skipped town with Vander in his plane. We need to call the FAA or whoever to try to catch her ass," Lester said. He couldn't believe they had let the principal criminal slip out of their hands.

"Don't really have enough to convict her on anything. Everything was in Stick's name. The massage parlor, strip clubs, bait store, S.G. Crystals, and all the gun sales, and even Spider's condo—all in Stick's name. We have a lot of circumstantial evidence, and maybe we could find an employee stupid enough to testify against her. Other than that, we got nothing. Keep in mind we have just taken on one of the biggest crime operations in the US and brought them down."

Lester and Rich looked at each other and shook their heads. Apparently, crime did pay, and pretty well, if you kept your name off the deeds and contracts.

Mike Adams walked up as the medics worked on the two.

"Big fucking mess you made here, boys. Glad we don't have to clean it up." He shook hands with both of them. "You guys did good today," Mike said.

After bumming rides, Lester and Rich found their way back to the sheriff's office, where they picked up their cars. Lester was happy to see his red Yukon and was so glad he didn't work out of it on this day.

All the familiar places seemed so special today. As he passed the racetrack, he admired the new addition to the casino. He passed by Stubby's and smiled as he thought about their ribs. When he drove by the mall, he tried to read the titles of all the movies that were playing at the theater.

Pulling up to his apartment, he saw Debi running out to meet him. She had tears in her eyes. Lester got out of his car and hobbled toward her. She immediately assessed his bandaged areas, counted his body parts, and put her arms around him.

"I have something for you, Lester." She kissed him with about the same intensity as Spider had kissed her. "That kiss was from Spider. She wants me to take care of you."

"Spider kissed you on the lips?"

"Yes, and it was nice. Maybe I'm part lesbian?"

"So, every time I kiss you—I'll be kissing two pretty women at the same time?"

"Yes—I guess so."

"Well, let's get started."

The End

Epilogue

Two weeks later

Sheriff Jake, Lester and Debi sat in a booth at the Mt. Ida Cafe. It was a beautiful fall day, and to make the day more interesting, a Razorback game in Fayetteville was on Lester and Debi's schedule for later in the afternoon. They had stopped at the cafe to buy Jake's lunch before traveling up the road to Y City and then up to Fort Smith where they would take the four-lane highway that rose up and cut into the Boston Mountains and then went through Arkansas's only road tunnel on the way to Razorback stadium.

"Looks like the head wound is healing, Jake, but it's going to be a battle scar," Lester said.

"Hell, it don't even show if I wear a hat. Kind of proud of it if you want the truth. Old Stick woulda killed me if I hadn't pulled the trigger a fraction of a second before he did."

"Are things boring for you now?" Debi asked.

"Plenty to do with meth labs popping up all over the place, and there's always domestic fights. Usually there's drugs or alcohol to blame. Hope we never have a big deal like Lester uncovered—made the national news, it did."

A bone-weary waitress laid a tray on the table next to their booth. The first Cafe sandwich was set in front of Jake. Next they were placed in front of Debi and Lester. Debi gasped, "Holy mother of God."

The sandwiches before them were beyond belief. Yes, there was a hamburger bun involved, but between the bottom one and the top were at least three huge beef patties, cheese on several layers, one fried egg, onion rings, lettuce and tomatoes. On the top and going all the way through the center of each giant burger was a well-placed butcher knife stabbing through the sandwich to hold it together.

Lester and Jake grinned like monkeys. "My treat, Jake!" Lester said as he attempted to find a place to bite into the behemoth.

"Where's your salad, Lester?" Debi asked.

"I ate salads until I could read. A little deal I made with myself. And I appreciated that you never asked me about it."

"I knew there was a reason and that you would tell me sometime. It was like a game you were playing."

Debi just stared at her giant burger. She finally got out her iPhone, took a picture, and posted it on Facebook.

In a few hours there were more than a hundred likes.

Charles L. (Chap) Harper

Chap Harper is a native Arkansan and retired insurance executive who moved from California to share a cabin on Lake Hamilton in Hot Springs with his wife Susan. Writing was always something he did even in his youth, and in 2012 he published his first novel Once Upon a Reef, which drew heavily on his love of scuba diving. Since then, in 2015, he published Once Upon the Congo (Smoking Gun Publishing.) His latest novel is Beer, Bait, and Ammo by the same publisher is a thriller that is set in the south. A fourth book is in the wings that takes place in French Equatorial Africa in 1933.

Other Books by This Author
Once Upon a Reef - 2012
Once Upon the Congo - 2015